D0122415

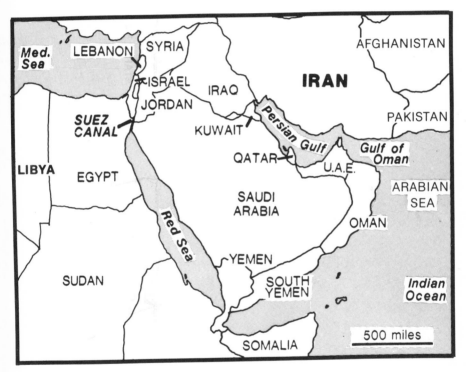

Med.
Sea

LEBANON

SYRIA

AFGHANISTAN

ISRAEL

IRAQ

IRAN

JORDAN

*SUEZ
CANAL*

KUWAIT

Persian Gulf

PAKISTAN

LIBYA

EGYPT

QATAR

*Gulf of
Oman*

U.A.E.

*ARABIAN
SEA*

Red Sea

SAUDI
ARABIA

OMAN

YEMEN

SUDAN

SOUTH
YEMEN

*Indian
Ocean*

SOMALIA

500 miles

SWEETWATER
Gunslinger 201

**A Saga of Carrier Pilots
Who
Live By Chance
Love By Choice**

---

*This is our **first novel** at Aero Publishers.*

Our success in the nonfiction field of aviation and space books has made our firm the largest publisher of such books in the world.

*Ernest J. Gentle
President*

Previous books (listed below) by Robert Lawrence Holt are available from Calif. Financial Publ., P.O. Box 220 Carlsbad, CA 92008

SWEETWATER
Gunslinger 201

A Saga of Carrier Pilots
Who
Live By Chance
Love By Choice

by

Lt. Commander William H. LaBarge, USN
and
Robert Lawrence Holt

First Edition
1984

AERO PUBLISHERS, INC.
Fallbrook, California

Printing

10 9 8 7 6 5 4 3 2

ISBN 0-8168-8515-X

Library of Congress Cataloging in Publication Data

LaBarge, William H.
Sweetwater, Gunslinger 201.

I. Holt, Robert Lawrence. II. Title. III. Title:
Sweetwater, Gunslinger Two Hundred One. IV. Title:
Sweetwater, Gunslinger Two Hundred and One.
PS3562.A18S9 1984 813'.54 83-73237
ISBN 0-8168-8515-X

Published by:

AERO PUBLISHERS, INC.
329 W. Aviation Road
Fallbrook, CA 92028

(see inside last page for ordering information)

This book is published by Aero Publishers, Inc., a private company in no way connected with the Department of Defense or the U.S. Navy. The characters and events portrayed in this novel are of the authors' writing, and are in no way sponsored by the U.S. Navy.

Preface

Few books have touched the subject of what happens on the Flight Decks of aircraft carriers. It has been documented that these decks are the most dangerous places in the world to work. There are thousands of carrier pilots and Flight Deck personnel who will attest to this. They have lost friends on these decks—men who were in the prime of their lives.

Landing on a carrier under the best of circumstances is still a "controlled crash." The concentration necessary to successfully fly aircraft on and off carrier decks builds up a tremendous pressure on carrier pilots, both physically and mentally. For this reason, we make no excuses for the excesses that some carrier pilots engage in while off-duty. Except to note that they pay a price for these excesses.

The characters in this book are composites of many persons whom the authors have known during their military careers. Naturally, names have been changed to protect both the innocent and the guilty. Any resemblance to real persons is strictly coincidental.

Acknowledgments

The authors wish to express their gratitude to the following persons who have helped in the preparation of this book:

Admiral James L. Holloway, III—for his support and encouragement throughout the writing of this story.

Admiral D.C. (Red Dog) Davis—for his initial review of the manuscript.

Rear Admiral Raymond W. Burk—for editing assistance during the preliminary security review of the manuscript and for generating support for the book throughout the U.S. Navy.

Commander Michael T. Sherman—for expediting the final security clearance of the manuscript.

Lt. Commander Randolph B. Brasfield—for personal recollections and essential gathering of research material.

Lt. Commander Hamlin B. Tallent—for providing key technical information on the F-14 Tomcat.

Lt. Commander Carmine L. Petriccione—for providing firsthand information on Flight Deck operations and editing of the manuscript.

Chief Warrant Officer 3 William R. Pincek—for furnishing photographs, research, and editing of the manuscript.

Petty Officer 1st Class Kronberger—for providing photographs from Naval archives in Washington, D.C.

John N. Gros—for providing editing and photographs.

A special thanks is given to Chuck Banks, the vice-president of Aero Publishers, who has given consistent support to this project.

Foreword

This is a story about Naval aviators—carrier pilots. How they fly, how they think, how they live, and how they love. It is a book of drama and excitement, yet without exaggeration and totally uncontrived. It is simply a factual recounting of what it's like flying high performance jets off aircraft carriers.

There is a deeper current below the thrills and escapades. These young men are engaged in their dangerous occupation, not for sport, not for pay, but because they are military men serving on the front lines in the defense of their country. The security of the United States is based on a forward strategy. It embraces the philosophy that if we have to go to war we intend to engage an enemy closer to his borders than ours. It is a strategy that utilizes the oceans as barriers in defense and as avenues for extending our influence abroad. The responsibility for the success of this philosophy—which has been the underlying precept of our national defense since World War II—is the United States Navy. The Navy must control the oceans if the United States is to support allies and to reinforce our own overseas forces in Germany, Japan, and Korea.

But the Russian navy is now the largest in the world, three times the size of the U.S. fleet. The Soviets outnumber us in cruisers and destroyers, have more than twice as many submarines, and enjoy an enormous advantage in patrol craft. However, the United States has fourteen aircraft carriers and the Soviets have only three.

The aircraft carriers of the U.S. Navy are the measure of difference which enables the United States to maintain the balance of maritime power in our favor. It is naval aviation that today enables our Navy to carry out its most important single function—to gain and maintain general maritime supremacy and local naval superiority, to permit our own and allied forces to utilize the oceans as we require to meet an adversary closer to his border than to ours.

This is not a new role for the carrier. In every war since its initial introduction the carrier has played a decisive role in the early stages.

In World War II it was our carriers at the Battles of Coral Sea and Midway that broke the back of the Japanese fleet and led to victory in the Pacific.

In Korea, U.S. Navy carriers were the only source of tactical air support available to the beleaguered U.S. ground forces in the Pusan perimeter, when all of the tactical airfields in South Korea had been over-run by communist ground forces.

In the Lebanon occupation of 1958, U.S. Navy carriers provided the first tactical aviation on the scene, supporting the initial Marine landing and remaining at Lebanon for 52 days until relieved by Air Force units operating out of Turkey.

The first strikes into North Vietnam were flown from the Seventh Fleet carriers and during the Vietnam war more than half of the missions into the North were flown by Navy aircraft.

Carriers played an essential role in the evacuation of Cyprus in 1973, the delivery of replacement aircraft to Israel in the Yom Kippur war, the evacuation of Phonm Penh, the evacuation of Saigon, and the recovery of the Mayaguez crew.

The Iranian hostage rescue operation—although ultimately unsuccessful —could not have been attempted without an aircraft carrier. It was from the U.S.S. Nimitz in the Indian Ocean that the rescue helicopters were staged.

Today as these very words are being written, carriers are deployed to trouble spots around the world in situations where a strong U.S. military presence may mean the difference between resolving a crisis in our favor or not—off Libya, near Nicaragua, in the vicinity of Lebanon, in the approaches to the Persian Gulf, and in the Sea of Japan to cover naval surface forces attempting to salvage the Korean 747 shot down by the Russians.

The effectiveness of our carriers in these critical missions depends on the aircraft they carry and the men who fly them. Without a superiority in planes and people, that thin first line of defense will start to crumble, and our entire forward strategy begins to collapse.

This is an authentic account of carrier pilots operating at the ragged edge of the cold war: why it takes a special kind of intensity to operate high performance aircraft in the confining environment of the carrier deck; why the fighter pilot must combine the finest sense of flying skill with a technical mastery of complex aircraft systems; and how the naval aviator accommodates the privations of sea duty and the long family separations of extended deployments.

These carrier pilots are indeed a special genre. They really have the right stuff. After all, half of the men who walked on the moon were naval aviators.

Admiral James L. Holloway III
★★★★ USN (Ret.)
Chief of Naval Operations (1974–1978)

TABLE OF CONTENTS

LIST OF CHARACTERS

Lt. Francis R. Reilly. . . radar intercept officer.

Lt. Matthew "Sweetwater" Sullivan. . . F-14 pilot.

Captain Dan "Warpaint" Edgars. . . commander of carrier air wing group.

Captain Edward Blackburn. . . Skipper of Kitty Hawk.

Lt. Thomas "Sundance" Karnes. . . F-14 pilot.

Lt. Gerald "Slim" Steiner. . . F-14 pilot.

Lt. Willie "Scoop" Anderson. . . helicopter pilot.

Lt. Freddie Rickfold. . . radar intercept officer.

Lt. Commander Charles "Warbucks" Warrington. . . F-14 pilot.

Admiral Oliver P. Grey. . . battle group commander.

Betty Dodds Blackburn. . . wife of Captain Blackburn

Ensign T.C. Fox. . . bunkmate of Ensign Blackburn.

Carol McIntyre. . . fiancee of Ensign Fox.

Jeff Warrington. . . son of Warbucks.

Commander Barry "Pink Panther" Morris. . . executive officer of F-14 squadron.

Lt. Commander Sandy "M+9" Mapleford. . . Landing Signal Officer.

Angela. . . teacher in Subic Bay, Philippines.

Lucy. . . teacher in Subic Bay, Philippines.

Rabbi Aaron Freeman. . . chaplain on the Kitty Hawk.

Jan "Iron Tits". . . airline office manager, Hong Kong.

Michelle. . . brunette airline stewardess.

Nancy. . . Eurasian airline stewardess.

Captain Blaine "Hook" Putnam. . . CAG of Nimitz.

Ginny. . . airline stewardess with Pan Am.

Phung Nguyen. . . coordinator, International Red Cross.

Johnnie Thompson. . . Texas-Vietnamese boy.

Jessica. . . Johnnie's sister.

Lt. Hambone Tanner. . . radar intercept officer.

Willie Ann Warrington. . . Warbuck's wife.

Dori Robinson. . . telephone operator in Hudson, Texas.

Walter Wood. . . retired police chief of Hudson.

Daisy. . . wife of Walter Wood.

(For those unfamiliar with Naval jargon, a brief glossary has been included on pages 188–190.)

1

BEAR COUNTRY

*(CAMEL STATION in the
Indian Ocean—1980 during
the Iranian crisis)*

"We got a bogey, Sweetwater. Bearing 260, at about 81 miles. He's moving kind of slow and he's on the deck."

"What size is it, Reilly?"

"Can't tell. It doesn't show clearly on the screen. I think it's big."

"Okay, let's go visiting."

The F-14 swung through a tight arc as Sweetwater dove toward an intercept. He was anxious to be the first fighter from the Kitty Hawk to find the intruder. The carrier's Admiral had not been as amused as the other pilots with his wardroom antics the previous evening.

The fighter dropped from 14,000 to 3,000 feet in less than twenty seconds. Visibility was not improved at the lower altitude as the morning haze had not yet cleared.

"They're changing direction, moving directly away from us at three o'clock," said Reilly. "I estimate speed at 340 knots. They're big too——B-52 size."

"We're hunting Bear this morning, Reilly. A big, clumsy Russian Bear."

In the briefing that morning, the pilots had been warned to expect company. A large aircraft had been detected leaving North Vietnam in the middle of the night, heading toward the Kitty Hawk's battle group at Camel Station in the North Arabian Sea.

"Let's give them a run for their money," said Sweetwater as he pushed the throttles to maximum power (military) without afterburner. They experienced exhilaration as the F-14 responded. Within a minute, the fighter was tearing after the intruder at a speed in excess of 600 knots.

Sundance, one of Sweetwater's fellow pilots on the Kitty Hawk, contended the thrust of this acceleration was as sweet as an orgasm, particularly as he let up on the throttle and eased into a cruising speed. Sweetwater wondered if Sundance actually had orgasms in flight. His friend had a reputation for burning more fuel than the squadron's other fighter pilots.

"They're riding the deck," said Reilly. "I show their altitude at no more than 100 feet." It was a common trick of the Russians to attempt to come in under the battle group's radar screen.

"Their speed's slowing," said Reilly. "They're resuming their original course. We should intercept in two minutes."

"They gave up quick," said Sweetwater disappointedly. "In this milk, they might have lasted longer."

As it closed on the intruder, the F-14 Tomcat descended without letting up speed.

"There's the Bear. Dead ahead," said Sweetwater. He intended a dramatic greeting.

Its cover being broken, the Bear had slowly begun to climb. It was the size of a B-52, but a red star on its fuselage indicated it was Russian.

As Sweetwater came screaming in, he passed under the Bear's belly, hit afterburner (Zone 5) power, and climbed straight up in front of the Russian aircraft, making a complete loop of the Bear. As he fronted the Bear, the tips of the F-14's tailfins passed within 30 feet of the Bear's nose.

Sweetwater then veered to the port side of the Bear and did an aileron roll, executing a 360-degree circle around the Bear at close quarters. These would have been dangerous maneuvers for most pilots, but Lt. Matthew "Sweetwater" Sullivan executed them with ease. Completing these movements, he said, "Now, that's reconnaissance, you donkey-drivers."

In the middle of these acrobatics, the Russian pilots leveled off and decreased speed. Their concern for the safety of their aircraft lessened substantially when Sweetwater tucked his fighter just under their starboard tailfin.

The Russian aircraft had a long, sleek, silver fuselage. Its massive wings held four engines, each with two counter-rotating props. Without its electronic gear, it would have been a beautiful aircraft.

Reilly reported to the battle group, "Home Plate. This is

Gunslinger 201. Have intercepted aircraft of interest. Assuming escort duties at this time."

"Roger, continue," was the response.

Sweetwater's face was fifteen feet from that of the Russian manning the gunner's window below the Bear's tail. The Russian wore a leather World War II helmet. He smiled and waved at the Americans.

Reilly said, "That guy's so ugly his mother must have fed him with a sling shot."

Sweetwater backed his aircraft off to 30 feet. Then it appeared that the Russian was giving them the finger. Looking closer, the Americans saw that he was gesturing with more than one finger and tapping his ear. Sweetwater moved back in to 15 feet.

The Russian flashed two fingers, five fingers, eight fingers, and then a closed fist. The Americans tuned their radios to 258.0 and heard the Russian say, "My name is Alex. I live in Moscow with my mother. Who are you?"

Sweetwater immediately responded, "My name is Ivan and I live in Leningrad with your sister."

The Russian laughed, then asked, "Where is the Kitty Hawk?"

"Kitty Hawk is a small town in North Carolina," answered Sweetwater.

With that response, the Russian decided not to ask any more questions.

The Bear climbed to 2,000 feet, where searching for the battle group was more likely to be effective. Crisscrossing the Arabian Sea, the Bear located the Kitty Hawk within forty minutes, being escorted by the F-14 during its search.

As they came in sight of the carrier, Sweetwater was directed to break away, being relieved by another fighter.

Peeling off, Sweetwater saluted and said, "So long, Alex."

The Russian returned his salute.

The Bear made several flybys up and down the battle group. It maintained an altitude of 1,200 feet and kept a distance of half a mile as it passed each vessel.

As Sweetwater climbed out of his cockpit, his brownshirt (plane captain) said, "Congratulations, sir." Word of his special greetings to the Russian Bear had spread quickly through the ship.

By altering the flight path of the Bear unnecessarily, he had exerted a dominance over the Russians which each of the men on the ship savored. To Sweetwater, it had only been a bit of fun. Nevertheless, he enjoyed the attention it brought. At least, momentarily.

As Sweetwater walked off the Flight Deck to his ready room, a blast from the 5-MC intercom blared over the Flight Deck, "Pilot of Aircraft 201, report to Flight Deck Control."

Feet spread and hands on hips, Captain Dan "Warpaint" Edgars faced Sweetwater as the young pilot stepped inside Flight Deck Control. Members of the Kitty Hawk's Air Wing had good reason to call their CAG (commander of the carrier's Air Wing group) Warpaint. Standing six foot three inches, he was built like a boxer. His piercing black eyes wiped the smile off the younger man's face.

"Goddamn it, Sullivan. What the hell do you think you're doing out there? You charged that Russian like a raging bull. You almost hit the sonofabitch!"

Sweetwater stood motionless. Though he had the muscular body of an athlete, at six feet he still felt intimidated before this giant.

Not waiting for a response, the CAG ordered, "Follow

me. The Skipper wants to see you."

As Warpaint and his pilot entered the Bridge, Captain Edward Blackburn immediately saw them. He turned in his Skipper's Chair and stepped down. Blackburn had a kindly face, which had fooled many a junior officer. He said, "Let's go into my sea-cabin." As the three men left the Bridge, the Officer-of-the-Deck announced,

"The Captain's leaving the Bridge."

When they had stepped in the sea cabin just off the Bridge, Captain Blackburn turned to face Sweetwater. The Skipper's deepset blue eyes dominated his face, which no longer held a pleasant countenance.

"We're here to help recover the hostages in Iran, not start World War III. Who the hell do you think you are?" The Skipper stared at Sweetwater for a moment, then continued. "Would you like to know what the Russians reported back to their base? Our monitor told me they reported a near-collision with a 'crazy American pilot.' They thought you were a kamikaze! Goddamn, man. Our radar screen on the ship showed that you not only halted their climb, but you cut their air speed by 125 knots. Where'd you learn to intercept like that?"

Looking into the Skipper's glaring eyes, Sweetwater thought, *don't say anything.*

"We were seriously considering the submission of your name for next year's Blue Angels. You're a better candidate for the Hell's Angels now! You were in trouble before you ever launched this morning. The Admiral chewed my ass out at breakfast. He wasn't amused by your belly-dance last night in the middle of the movie. Did you know he was sitting in back?"

Sweetwater, with Sundance on mandolin, had dressed in a belly-dance costume (a gift for a girlfriend) and given an impromptu performance. From the catcalls and whistles, he thought it had been quite well-received.

"Sullivan, you're restricted to quarters for one week. Now get your ass out of here."

The young pilot smartly turned and rapidly headed for the hatch. As he stepped into the passageway, Warpaint was close behind. When they had reached the deck below, the CAG said,

"Sweetwater, next time save the acrobatics for when we need them. Oh, and go easy on the perfume the next time you perform. You stunk up the entire Wardroom last night."

As Sweetwater headed for his stateroom, his thoughts were not about the restriction to quarters. That had happened before. Instead, he was disappointed over the "perfume" comment. People were always complaining about his wearing too much cologne. Even back in Pensacola. That's where he got his running name.

The most difficult part of being restricted to quarters for Sweetwater was missing the action in Wardroom One during meals. While this daily action was somewhat subdued by Sweetwater's absence, there were still several others who made this location a favored gathering spot for the younger officers of the Air Wing.

One of them was Lieutenant Thomas H. Karnes, better known as Sundance. He was a tall Texas bachelor who wore his mustache in a handlebar. He loved the ladies, and well; but his first love was "Honey." Honey was his F-14. It wasn't unusual to find Sundance down on the hangar deck, observing and sometimes helping in the maintenance of his fighter. He had been asked to leave Wardroom One more than once in a grease-covered flight suit. While Sweetwater might be more daring behind the throttles of a F-14, Sundance was more adept at pushing this aircraft to the limits of its capabilities.

And then there was Lieutenant Gerald M. Steiner. No one on the Kitty Hawk could recall why he was called Slim. This running name didn't fit the 195 pounds that were packed into his five foot nine burly frame. He wore a mustache too—Clark Gable style—and was a superior pilot who could effortlessly match most of the feats of the other two. Slim could also regale the other pilots for hours with his sexual adventures. Instead of one girl, he had a harem in each port. His favorite ladies were big . . . all over. They were the source of his best stories.

It was Slim who intercepted the Bear next. The Russians paid daily visits to Camel Station, no longer trying to initially fly low under the radar. Communications on 258.0 were usually established as soon as the F-14s made formation with the Bear.

This time Slim and Lt. Freddie Rickfold, his RIO (Radar Intercept Officer), were prepared.

"Get dressed," said Slim, as he came in behind the Bear. The F-14 took a position above the tail of the Bear, slowly advanced up the long fuselage to its cockpit, taking a 30 foot stepup slightly forward of the Bear. Freddie had ducked out of sight.

The Russians waved. Slim nodded in response. One of the Russians pointed to the rear of Slim, indicating to his co-pilot that there was no radar officer in the American aircraft. When the co-pilot turned to look, Slim said, "Now!"

Freddie popped his head up, wearing a gorilla mask.

The eyes of both Russians widened, and they laughed. The younger Russian blew a kiss to Freddie and said to Slim, "You have a good-looking girlfriend, American."

Slim replied, "Spasibo. Do you want a date? She likes two at a time."

"No thanks. We have better looking girls at home."

With that, Slim moved in closer and asked, "Can you match this?" Freddie then held up a centerfold spread from *Playboy*. The blonde playmate had been selected for her bountiful, red-tipped breasts.

This time, the eyes of the Russians stayed wide-open as they strained to get a better look. The nearer Russian quickly took up a pair of binoculars. The Bear seemed to drift closer.

"Steady there, Bear," murmured Slim as he eased away to keep a proper interval between the two aircraft. Freddie put the *Playboy* down. The Russians steadied.

Then the nearer Bear pilot reached behind his seat and rolled out a two-foot high Russian pinup. The figure had the overblown body of a Viking warrior goddess. She stood with feet spread, her hands clasped behind her neck. Her waist was non-existent, and one of her pendulous breasts hung significantly lower than the other. While the woman's face was not unpretty, even from thirty feet the Americans were grossed out by the thick hair of her armpits.

The younger Russian said, "I would like to study your magazine. Can we make a cultural exchange?"

"Sure," said Slim. "I'll send you my *Playboy* if you promise to keep your pinup."

The Russians laughed good-naturedly. The younger pilot said, "What would you like?"

After thinking a moment, Slim responded, "Two sable hats. Ten *Playboys* for two sable hats."

With some discussion it was agreed that the "cultural gifts" would be exchanged by mailing the *Playboys* to the Russian air attache in Hanoi and the hats to the American naval attache in Moscow. Slim intended to hold up his end of the bargain. With that, the F-14 drifted 100 feet to the side of the Bear.

A few days later, Russia invaded Afghanistan.

The briefing officer concluded his remarks by saying, "Try to keep the Bear or other foreign aircraft at least 1,000 feet from the Kitty Hawk. The hangar doors will be open most of the day for preparation of the helicopters we picked up at Diego Garcia. Any questions?" There being none, the eight men (four pilots and their RIOs) filed out of the cold, musty-smelling ready room and headed for their planes.

Sundance, Slim, Sweetwater, and "Warbucks" Warrington were the 0400 crew for Alert Five. That meant they were buckled in and ready to launch within five minutes. They would remain in this status for two hours, until relieved by the next air crew.

As the morning started to break, it was obvious that it would not be a good day for Bear-watching. The sky was overcast. The seas were high, causing the deck to pitch 10 to 15 feet.

"Launch the Alert Five. Launch the Alert Five," came over the 5-MC at exactly 0455.

As the pilots gave "thumbs-up" signals to their yellow shirts, the blue shirts broke down their aircraft and pulled the chocks (pulled off the chains and removed the steel blocks).

"Sonofabitch," exclaimed Warbucks. "My right brake is locked." His F-14 blocked Catapults Three and Four, forcing the other fighters to move to Catapult One at the bow. By the time they had moved forward, the remaining pilots had three minutes to get into the air.

As each fighter approached the catapult, their Weight Board was held up. Each pilot in turn rogered with another thumbs-up, to confirm their weights. Sweetwater was in the last F-14 to approach the catapult.

He went up and over the shuttle, ready to go into tension. As the shuttle went into tension, he jammed his throttles to *military*—just like a cocked gun. After "wiping out" the cockpit (checking the stick and rudder to make sure there was free movement), Sweetwater gave the Catapult Officer a sharp salute. The Catapult Officer then touched the deck.

Two seconds later, thirty tons of jet aircraft went hurtling down the Cat-track at 140 miles per hour. The twenty transverse Gs of the shot drove both men back into their ejection seats. Normal vision was reduced to tunnel vision as their eyeballs felt like they were being pushed into the backs of their skulls. The skin on their faces was pulled back and down like saltwater taffy.

"We've got a good shot," said Reilly. "Let's go get 'em, Water." They climbed to 15,000 feet and started a search within their assigned sector.

After twenty-five minutes, Sundance's RIO got a contact on his scope. He relayed an intercept heading to the other F-14s. Sweetwater and Slim pulled their aircraft into the intercept heading and started to descend, increasing their speed to 400 knots.

Within 15 more minutes, Sundance (the flight leader) had the Bear in sight. The Russian aircraft was at 5,000 feet, skimming across the tops of cloud cover. When the Bear spotted Sundance, the Russian aircraft dove into the soup.

As the Bear came through the cloud base, Slim and Sweetwater picked him up at 1,700 feet. Once he knew the other aircraft were in front, Sundance dropped through the clouds and caught up with the formation.

The battle group was 120 miles away. With the overcast weather, it took the Russians a while to locate the Kitty Hawk.

"Don't get too close to that clown, boys," ordered Sundance, as the Bear kept its tail within the clouds. Sundance flew below and to the rear, while Slim took the port and Sweetwater the starboard side of the Russian aircraft. At 280 knots the Bear was aggressive.

"Watch your right, Slim," shouted Sundance as the Russians turned sharply into a low-lying cloud. The Bear also went up into the soup frequently, forcing the fighters to maintain 250-foot intervals below the cloud base.

After 45 minutes, the Russians located the first ship of the battle group and made a photo-run at 1,200 feet. At this point, Sundance broke off and went to tank (an inflight refuel tanker from the carrier).

Peeling off, he directed, "Sweetwater, take over. I'm going for a drink. Be back shortly." As Sundance climbed through the clouds, Sweetwater moved to the rear of the Bear.

A few minutes later, the Bear spotted the Kitty Hawk and

started a flyby of the Plane Guard Ship. This ship was a quarter of a mile behind the carrier.

The Bear rolled into a sharp turn to make a rear approach. This movement forced Slim to momentarily back off to 400 feet to avoid contact. In turn, this enabled the Russians to drop to 800 feet, assuming an approach to the Plane Guard Ship within 500 feet of its port side.

It was at this point Sweetwater decided to tighten it up. "I'm moving into 10 feet on the starboard, Slim."

As they came up on the Plane Guard Ship, the Bear turned abruptly into Sweetwater, crossing diagonally over the ship.

"The mast! The mast!" screamed Slim. Sweetwater yanked his stick, careening by the ship's mast, missing it by less than his plane's width.

"That sonofabitch almost killed us, Reilly!"

Quickly recovering, Sweetwater crossed under the Bear and repositioned his aircraft five feet from the left wingtip of the Russians. If the Bear continued its course, it would pass within 600 feet of the Kitty Hawk's starboard side.

"Get the hell out of here, you sons-a-bitches!" shouted Sweetwater.

The Russian pilots frantically waved them off, but Sweetwater did not budge.

At this point, the Bear moved into the F-14.

Reilly yelled, "Look out," but it was too late. The wingtips of the two aircraft collided. There was no visible damage, but the effect was to push the F-14 away due to the greater weight of the Bear.

Wingtip to wingtip, Sweetwater could do nothing to change the Bear's course. In desperation, Sweetwater dropped just behind the Russian's outer wing.

"I'm going to push the bastards out of here," said Sweetwater. "Hold on!"

The nose of the F-14 approached the aileron of the Bear's wing. Before Sweetwater could push it though, the Russians dipped their wing, hitting the F-14's nose. The blow from the Bear's wing shattered the nosecone of the F-14, forcing the fighter into a 30-degree dive.

"Eject! Eject!" shouted Reilly.

"No. No. I've got it," retorted Sweetwater, as he hit afterburner, pulling the stick sharply. The F-14 curved away from the water, its afterburner creating a 15-foot rooster tail in the sea.

The sharp move by the F-14 exerted tremendous pressure on the bodies of the pilot and RIO. Even the skintight G-suits each wore to prevent the blood from being sucked from their heads could not entirely compensate for these G-forces. As a result, both men were in a state of semi-consciousness as the F-14 struggled upward.

Slim, following the action from the rear, said, "Get out of here and check your controls. I'll take over." Sweetwater climbed to 10,000 feet.

The Bear went into a sharp bank after hitting the F-14. It continued to move away from the carrier in a forward yaw, like a crippled bird. Slim followed it over the horizon at 1,000 feet. The Russians obviously had severe control problems.

"Gunslinger 201. Return to Home Plate," came over the radio.

Sweetwater banked to his port side to approach the Kitty Hawk. Landing without incident, Sweetwater and Reilly walked toward the island. The Air Bos'n joined on and said "Sweetwater, that was a hell of a show. I thought for sure you were gonna buy the farm."

Walking into Flight Deck Control, the Admiral's Flag Lieutenant was waiting for them.

"Follow me," was all he said. Instead of taking the ladders to the Flag Bridge, the aide motioned Reilly and Sweetwater onto the Admiral's elevator.

Sweetwater thought, "This is the royal treatment this time." Entering the Flag Bridge, Sweetwater saw the Admiral seated in his chair, watching the recovery of the other F-14s.

Noticing the new arrivals, Admiral Oliver P. Grey continued to watch the operations below for a minute. He was still debating what to do. As the oldest man on the Kitty Hawk, his thick white hair gave him a grave bearing and craggy appearance. His medium-built body was still trim. Swiveling in his chair, he faced the new arrivals and motioned for the other personnel on the Flag Bridge to leave.

When the bridge was clear, the Admiral said in a quiet tone, "Young man, you have endangered the safety of this ship. You could have killed hundreds of men. In addition, you almost downed a Russian military aircraft, which could precipitate a state of war."

Pausing to catch his breath, Grey stepped down from his chair and walked over to Sweetwater. Standing directly in front of the pilot, he continued, "You have acted in reckless disregard of everything you've been taught to do as a Navy pilot. I have a good mind to put you in the brig and throw away the . . . ."

Reilly interrupted, "Sir, may I say something?"

This interjection surprised the Admiral. And Sweetwater even more. Lt(jg). Francis R. Reilly was basically a quiet, friendly officer who rarely made waves. With this disposition and being only five foot seven, he was seldom noticed in a group.

The Admiral stared at Reilly's innocent face and bellowed, "You're lucky to be alive, young man! If you want to speak, thank God for your deliverance! Don't speak to me. This man almost killed you!"

Not intimidated, Reilly spoke again. "With all due respect, sir. Our plane didn't initiate the contact."

'What the hell do you mean! I saw it with my own eyes."

"Sir, the Bear hit us. He dipped his wing to try to scare us, not realizing we were as close to his wing as we were." Sweetwater mentally thanked Reilly for not including that he had intended to push the Bear's wing.

"Sullivan," growled the Admiral. "Is that correct?"

"Yes, sir."

The Admiral turned away and slowly went to his chair.

Then Reilly added, "We meant to tap the Russian's aileron, in order to discourage a photo-run within one thousand feet, but the Russian made his move first."

The Admiral stared at Sweetwater a long time.

Sweetwater wondered what the brig looked like.

"Well, that makes a difference. But damn little." The Admiral then looked away from the two men and returned to his chair. He studied the movements of the carrier for a few minutes, then turned his head,

"Reilly, you're dismissed."

When the RIO had left the Flag Bridge, the Admiral said, "Sullivan, I don't know whether to court-martial you or commend you. How in the hell do you get yourself in such messes? You almost caused a major international incident today."

Sweetwater's only response was a blank stare. He felt uneasy. A vague dizziness clouded his mind.

Not expecting or even wanting a reply, the Admiral growled, "Get yourself out of here, before I make a mistake."

Sweetwater cautiously backed away a few steps before turning. His legs were stiff as boards. They seemed to be moving him in slow motion. He had the feeling that this was all a bad dream. After turning about, he heard someone call his name, "Sullivan." Then, a second time, "Sullivan." He slowly revolved to again face the Admiral.

"Son, if I were 30 years younger, I would probably have done the same thing. You look like hell. Go get some rest."

Reilly was waiting as Sweetwater stepped off the Flag Bridge in a semi-state of shock. Neither man spoke. A silent throng of hundreds had crowded the passageways of the Kitty Hawk which led from the Flag Bridge to the Flight Deck. Many more men stood patiently on the Flight Deck awaiting Sweetwater's exit from the Flag Bridge.

Reilly steadied his pilot as Sweetwater negotiated the first ladder. It was then that a thousand voices exploded in a crescendo of emotion. Their cheering grew wilder as Reilly and Sweetwater descended.

By the time they reached the Flight Deck, the entire ship vibrated with the roar of 6,000 men. As the Admiral looked out the tinted windows of the Flag Bridge to witness this spectacle, his eyes watered. He was no different than hundreds of other sailors that day in controlling his feelings.

Sweetwater heard nothing. He did not even see the swarm of men who continued to roar as they parted for his passage.

2

DRAGON LADY
ON THE QUARTER-DECK

During dinner that evening, most of the talk in the Wardrooms had been about Sweetwater's latest exploit. Sweetwater didn't appear, but Reilly was available to answer all questions. Reilly had been thoroughly interviewed earlier by Captain Blackburn.

As Blackburn finished his dessert, he received a note from Admiral Grey asking that he stop by Admiral Country after dinner. Blackburn knew the summons concerned Sweetwater. Three weeks earlier, he and the Admiral had discussed the 'special greeting the pilot had given the Bear. Evidently, the mild reprimand and restriction to quarters Blackburn had given Sweetwater at that time had failed to curb the pilot's appetite for danger.

Getting up from the Wardroom table, Blackburn felt somewhat uncomfortable. He wasn't sure whether he'd be catching some of the flak this time.

When the Skipper arrived at the Admiral's quarters, he was called in immediately.

Pointblank, the Admiral asked, "What the hell are we going to report to CINCPAC?"

Unsure of what the Admiral wanted, Blackburn decided to play it safe with his response. "Sir, I would simply report that a Russian TU95/D engaged in aggressive manuevers during a flyby of the Kitty Hawk. Their actions caused the collision between the aircraft. Both aircraft were damaged—the Russian TU95/D more severely."

"Ed, in your opinion, who caused the collision?"

"I interviewed Lt. Reilly, the RIO, sir. He indicated that the Bear caused the contact by dipping its wing."

"Therefore, it's your opinion that the Russian aircraft initiated the contact and caused the collision?" the Admiral again asked.

"Yes, sir," Blackburn answered.

"Captain, do our planes customarily position themselves within two to three feet behind the wings of unfriendly aircraft?"

Blackburn saw his mistake and thought to himself, *how stupid can I be?* To the Admiral, he could only respond, "No, sir."

The Admiral drove his point home by asking, "Did the Bear move in on our F-14? Or did the F-14 move in on the Bear?"

"Well, I suppose I'd have to say our fighter moved in on the Bear, sir."

"Damn right you would," growled the Admiral. "Now, answer my question again. Whose aircraft *initiated* the contact?"

This time, Blackburn simply said, "Ours, sir."

The Admiral didn't appear to take any satisfaction in his answer, though. He continued to glower.

Finally Admiral Grey repeated, "So what do we report to CINCPAC? That we were trying to push a Russian aircraft out of the sky and collided instead? If I report that, my next assignment will be in Antarctica and you'll be the skipper of my dogsled!"

Neither man spoke for a minute. Blackburn didn't want to break the silence.

Eventually Admiral Grey said, "I've read the briefing instructions given to the pilots this morning. They were instructed to keep unfriendly flybys at least 1000 feet from the Kitty Hawk."

"Yes, sir," Blackburn said. "CAG was notified that maintenance of the H-53s required opening the hangar doors this morning. The CAG's briefing orders to the pilots were in accordance with standard operating procedure."

"Goddamn it, Ed. Is it also standard procedure to initiate mid-air collisions in peacetime to keep flybys at 1000 feet?"

Blackburn didn't like being goaded or put on the defensive and responded, "Sir, I think there are two truths to this matter."

The Admiral started to speak, but Blackburn continued, "Admiral, our plane may have initiated the contact technically speaking, but the fact is that the Bear dipped its wing unexpectedly, directly causing the contact. I agree that Sweetwater exercised poor judgement and should be penalized. But this wouldn't have happened if the Russians had not lowered their wing." He prudently added, "Sweetwater only thought of pushing the Bear's aileron. But he didn't. He didn't have the opportunity."

For an instant, Admiral Grey thought of what the effect might have been if the F-14 in fact had pushed the aileron of the Bear. He knew that at their low altitude, the Russians might not have recovered as the F-14 did. He was thankful then that the Bear had dipped its wing.

After a minute, the Admiral calmly stated, "Ed, if we decide our pilot erred and punish him for improper procedure, then we must also assume the responsibility for his actions. His briefing instructions were to prevent close-in flybys."

At that moment they both shared the same thought. It was natural that neither man wished to take such responsibility.

Blackburn broke the silence this time. "Sir, the problem is that our pilot was too aggressive. After the Bear tried to force Sweetwater into the Plane Guard Ship, our F-14 should have backed off."

"I think you're wrong, Ed. I wish all our pilots had the aggressiveness that Sweetwater exhibited. The problem is that during peacetime, it gets them into trouble."

Pausing a moment, the Admiral added, "It gets their superiors into trouble, too."

"I certainly agree with you on that point, sir."

"You know, Ed. I wouldn't trade one Sweetwater for ten conservative pilots. It's the Sweetwaters who win battles, not the milquetoasts. Our dilemma is how to keep a harness on them in peacetime."

The Admiral then moved a notepad to the center of his desk and began to write. After a few minutes, he handed the result to Blackburn and asked, "What do you think of this?"

CINCPAC FLT
Subj: Mid-Air Collision with Russian TU95/D Bear
1. Russian Bear during flyby of USS Kitty Hawk made physical contact at 1320 on 14 Jan with Kitty Hawk F-14. Flyby violated rules of engagement. F-14 did not backoff. Bear aircraft dipped wing, making contact with the F-14 nosecone.

2. The F-14 remained operational, however the Bear's aileron appeared to be damaged. Bear departed with 45° port yaw. USS Kitty Hawk integrity maintained. Full report to follow. FLAG SENDS.

Blackburn handed the report back to Admiral Grey and said, "Very good, sir."

"Thanks for coming by, Ed. I had to sound this all out first before doing anything."

"Yes, sir. May I ask you something also?"

"Go ahead."

"What should be done about Sweetwater?"

"What do you think should be done."

"Well, sir. We can't have all the pilots on the Kitty Hawk trying to push unfriendly aircraft out of the air."

The Admiral smiled before responding. "When the Russians get back to their base, if they get back, you can bet they're going to put all the blame on us. Just as we are on them. Do you realize what effect this will have on the other Russian pilots? I'll tell you right now. They're going to have renewed respect for our fighter pilots. And they're going to respect our airspace a lot more too. I doubt if they'll want to get that close again."

"I hope you're right, sir."

"As a matter of fact, I'm going to recommend to CINC-PAC that they release my full report to the press. That would have a greater deterrent effect on unfriendly aircraft making close flybys than anything else we can do. There's little reason to caution our pilots. Few of them have the competence to match Sweetwater anyway."

"You recommend no action be taken concerning Sweetwater, then?"

"Ed, I don't know whether CINCPAC will agree with my report, but I'm going to protect that pilot to the limit of my authority. Anyone who wants a piece of his ass will have to take a piece of mine first."

The two men stared at each other for a moment. Then Blackburn stood to leave.

"You know, Ed, I remember you in your earlier days. You were a bigger hell-raiser than Sweetwater. Didn't they call you 'Dragon' then?" They both remembered how Blackburn acquired that handle.

Grinning, Blackburn answered, "Yes, sir."

"Get back to your ship, Ed. Leave Sweetwater to me."

Instead of going to his sea cabin, Captain Blackburn went to the Bridge. The Admiral hadn't chewed him out. On the other hand, it hadn't been a pleasant interview either. Even after all these years, Blackburn still felt his gut tighten whenever he was summoned by a superior officer.

Considering Sweetwater's popularity on the Kitty Hawk, Blackburn did not relish administering further discipline to him in the first place. By suggesting the need for disciplining Sweetwater, Blackburn had hoped Admiral Grey would take the opposite tack. It worked, or so he thought.

Stepping onto the Bridge, he automatically walked over to the Skipper's Chair, climbed onto it, and lit up a cigar. Although the sun had gone down hours earlier, the Kitty Hawk was readily visible in the full moon. The ship glided through the water smoothly and quietly.

Sitting in his chair on the Bridge always made Blackburn feel better. He had worked hard and sacrificed much for the privilege of sitting there.

He thought, *the Admiral was right. I raised some hell in my time.* His thoughts drifted back to when he served as a rookie pilot on his first carrier—the Hornet. Admiral Grey well knew about those years. Grey had been Blackburn's first squadron commander on the Hornet.

Twenty-four hours before the Hornet was due to leave San Diego on a seven-month cruise, Ensign Blackburn received a message from the CAG office that he had a phone call from a civilian party. The Ensign had just come aboard a few hours earlier to stay. He was one of the squadron officers in charge of checking off the final supply manifest for his unit, and was also due to become Squadron Duty Officer shortly before the Hornet set sail.

Picking up the phone in the CAG office, he identified himself, "Ensign Blackburn speaking."

"Eddie, I've got something special to tell you," Betty (his wife of three months) said.

"I love you, too, babe," he responded, thinking Betty simply wanted to tell him the same—one last time.

"Is there anyway you can get off the ship for an hour to see me?" she said quietly. "It's important."

They had spent most of the previous night awake—talking

and loving, knowing they would not see each other again for more than half a year.

"Honey, you know I can't do that. I'm on duty now."

"Can't you get off for just an hour, Eddie? What I have to tell you is special."

He thought, *you know better than to ask me this,* but did not say it. Instead, he said, "Betty I love you very much. I wish I could be with you right now. But you know I can't get off the ship now. How 'bout if I call you just before I report at 1800 as SDO? We can talk then. And I'll call you again just before we pull out."

Hearing no response to these suggestions, he asked, "Betty, are you there?"

"Yes, but I have someone with me," she answered.

God, he thought, *this conversation is getting nowhere.* For an instant, he suspected she was trying to make him jealous by suggesting she had another man with her.

"Okay, what's his name?"

"I don't know yet," she responded.

"What do you mean you don't know?"

"I haven't chosen a name yet," she said.

"What are you talking about?" he asked, getting exasperated.

"I don't even know if it's a boy," Betty said.

It occurred to Blackburn that his wife was drunk, but he knew she seldom drank and when she did, it was rarely more than one drink. He thought, *if she has had too much to drink, there's nothing I can do about it now.*

"Honey, I've got to go now. Okay? I'll call you back as soon as I can."

"Eddie, I'm pregnant."

It hit him like a ton of bricks. All he could think to say was, "How do you know that?"

"The doctor just told me."

"That's wonderful, honey," he said, and he meant it. But he thought, *why now? This is all happening at the wrong time.*

Betty again asked, "Can we just see each other one last time? I want you to hold me one last time. I'm not going to see you again for seven whole months."

"Where are you now, Betty?"

"At a doctor's office on Sixth Street."

"What's the telephone number there?"

After she gave him the number, he told her, "Stay there until I call you back."

"Why?" she asked.

"I'm coming."

He said goodbye and rushed down to Wardroom II. It was full of pilots and their guests, mostly wives and girlfriends. Spotting an unoccupied friend, Blackburn pled his case and persuaded the friend to assume his duties checking the squadron manifest list.

Blackburn's next problem was finding his squadron commander and getting permission to go ashore. He found Commander Grey on the hangar deck. Fronting his commander, he asked, "Sir, Ensign Blackburn requests permission to go ashore for two hours."

"For what purpose, Ensign?"

"Sir, my wife is pregnant."

"Congratulations, Blackburn." After a short pause, he added, "Weren't you off the ship last night?"

"Yes, sir," Blackburn admitted.

"Well, I'd say you've done the job quite well already, young man." They both laughed at this comment.

Before more could be said, the 5-MC blared, "Commander Grey, report to the CAG Office." Grey abruptly turned away and headed for the 03 level.

The young pilot stood there, unsure whether he should pursue Commander Grey and the subject. And not totally sure of what he had already been told.

Perplexed and getting desperate, Blackburn headed for his stateroom. He lit up a cigar as he stepped inside, then sat down on his bunk. He could always think better with a cigar.

He had been staring at the black silk bathrobe hanging in his roommate's closet for three minutes before it registered. He quickly tore off his uniform, put on a pair of work shorts, donned the black robe, and looked in the mirror. The robe had a large dragon emblazoned on its back, with smaller dragons on each side of its front.

"You're crazy," he said to himself. He turned to rummage through a drawer until he found a large red bandana. Folding it in half, he wrapped it around his head, tying it under his chin. He looked in the mirror again.

That's when his roommate, Ensign T.C. Fox, walked in with his girlfriend.

"Oh, excuse me," T.C. said, as he stepped back out of the stateroom to check the number above its door.

"It's me," said Blackburn.

T.C.'s girlfriend looked at Blackburn in disbelief. His roommate gave him a hard look, then laughed and introduced his girlfriend.

"Carol, I'd like you to meet my roommate, Dragon Lady. He's the drag queen of our squadron."

Carol smiled at Blackburn, but said nothing, not quite knowing what to say or how serious to take the introduction. Blackburn quickly explained his plight. In a minute Carol was applying strategic makeup to his face. Then T.C. and Carol stepped back to look him over.

Carol said, "There's something not quite right yet."

"You need tits, Dragon Lady," T.C. suggested.

"Where am I going to get tits?" exclaimed Blackburn.

Without removing her short-sleeved blouse, Carol deftly unhooked and removed her brassiere. She handed the warm bra to Blackburn and said, "Here, put this on."

Blackburn blushed as he stared at what his hands held.

"Have you got some string to extend it?" Carol asked. They found a shoelace, filled the bra with a couple pairs of socks, and tied it on a reluctant Blackburn.

"Honey," said T.C., "shake your ass and you just might make it off this ship." T.C. agreed to escort the two "ladies" to the quarter-deck.

As they approached the Officer's Brow (gangplank) on the quarter-deck, Blackburn saw Commander Grey. *Dammit,* he thought, *he's standing right next to the Officer-of-the-Deck.* The Commander was awaiting the arrival of his wife.

Blackburn's last thought before Commander Grey stepped forward was, *well, this is it. My ass is had now.*

Most of the personnel on the quarter-deck were staring at the unusually-attired visitor as Commander Grey looked at Fox and said, "Good afternoon, Ensign Fox. I don't believe I've had the pleasure of meeting your lady friends." As the Commander said this, he looked directly at Blackburn's feet.

The dragon outfit came halfway down the calves of Blackburn's legs and his feet were fitted in thongs. In their haste, they had not thought to shave his legs.

Fox stammered, "Commander Grey, I'd like you to meet my fiancee, Carol McIntyre, and her sister, Dra . . ." He caught himself in mid-word. "Her sister, Drasina," he finally blurted out.

They all looked Drasina up and down. "She" just stood there, wanting to turn tail and run.

Enjoying himself thoroughly, Commander Grey told them, "I hope you've enjoyed your visit on the Hornet." Then, looking directly at Blackburn, he asked, "Drasina, that's a lovely outfit you're wearing. Would you mind if we took a picture of it?"

Grey didn't notice Blackburn frantically shaking his head as he had stepped away to borrow a Polaroid camera from an officer who was taking pictures of his family.

When Grey returned, he said, "Ensign Fox, why don't you put your arms around the girls while I take a picture?"

So they posed, Fox and his fiancee with blank faces, and an expression on Blackburn's face which could only be described as mortified shock.

This photograph would appear in the Cruisebook of the Hornet that year. The reputation Ensign Blackburn acquired thereafter may have been one of the reasons he strove to be an exemplary Navy officer. The nickname, "Dragon," stuck though.

As the camera developed the picture, Fox quickly kissed Carol and the "girls" turned to leave.

"Oh, Ensign Fox," said Commander Grey, "aren't you going to give your future sister-in-law a farewell kiss, too?" Fox stared at his commanding officer, looked at Drasina, and then turned pleadingly to Carol.

She laughed and said, "Go ahead, T.C." Carol was beginning to enjoy the charade almost as much as Commander Grey was. Fox was beginning to enjoy it far less.

There being nothing else he could do, Fox stepped over to Blackburn, grabbed his shoulders, and planted a kiss on his cheek.

Grey was ready. This print was a classic. It would have appeared in the Cruisebook also, if it hadn't been so dog-eared by the end of that day.

Carol and the mortified pilot stepped off the Hornet, and Fox beat a hasty retreat back to the Wardroom.

The Officer-of-the-Deck asked Commander Grey, "How could a good-looking woman like that have such a homely sister? Drasina was so ugly she'd make a freight train take a dirt road!"

Grey chuckled and said, "That was no sister. Drasina is one of my pilots—Ensign Blackburn."

"You're kidding."

"No, I'm not. His wife just called to tell him she's pregnant. It's okay, he'll be back in a few hours. When he does return, I want to be here to greet him. Delay him until you've paged me. Find some way to make him wait on the pier until I arrive."

Blackburn and his bride did get to spend an hour together that afternoon. He had removed his costume by the time Betty picked him up. She thought the bundle under his arm was a gift at first. Betty removed the rest of the makeup on his face as he explained how he had got off the ship.

They drove to Breaker's Point on North Island and parked by the beachhouse. Betty nestled in his arms as they quietly said their goodbyes again. She tried to memorize how his arms felt around her, marveling how his body was always just the right temperature to make her feel good.

She said, "You know what, Eddie? Sometimes, I think God made you special order just for me. We fit together some special way. I don't think we'd ever fit with anyone else. Do you?"

Her husband held her a little closer and touched her eyes with his lips. He nibbled on an ear, then turned her head to kiss her fully on the lips. This was his answer. But he knew that she needed the words, too. So he softly whispered, "I love you."

"Eddie, are you glad I called you? I wasn't sure what to do."

"Sure, honey. This is special. Even if you weren't pregnant, I'd want to see you one more time."

"Do you think it'll be a boy?" she asked.

"I don't know. I guess I kind of hope it'll be a girl."

"I won't look the same when you return. I'll be a blimp, probably with stretch marks too."

He gently told her, "Bet, don't worry about stretch marks. They're the beauty marks of a mother."

The hour passed quickly, seeming like little more than ten minutes. As Betty drove back to the Hornet, she asked, "Can you get us copies of the photos for our baby album? Especially the one with the kiss?" While they tried to joke, neither of them laughed.

"Eddie, you won't get in trouble for seeing me, will you?"

"No, of course not," he assured her, not feeling nearly as confident as he sounded.

When they arrived at the pier, he asked her to mail the Dragon Lady outfit to him, gave her a long kiss, and opened the door of the car. Then he leaned over and nuzzled her ear, saying, "Hang in there, babe. We'll make it." A finger on her chin, he turned her lips to his and they kissed again.

Betty straightened up, put both hands on the steering wheel, and told him what he had always said to her at the end of their first dates, "Okay, get your butt out of here." Facing him, she attempted a smile.

As he started out of the car, Betty reached out to touch him. He took her hand, moving his eyes slowly up the length of her arm until their eyes met. No words were spoken as they drew together for one last kiss. Then he walked onto the pier.

It was almost dark as he strode barechested up the Officer's Brow in work shorts and thongs. Although the OD recognized Blackburn, he was asked for an ID. In his haste to get off the ship, he had forgotten his wallet. The OD told him, "You'll have to wait back on the pier for a few minutes."

Stepping back on the pier, Blackburn heard the Hornet's 5-MC, "Commander Grey, lay to the Officer's Brow."

His first instinct was to get off the pier, out of sight of the Officer's Brow. He started running, but stopped, remembering he had the duty soon. Looking at his watch, he saw that he had exactly 35 minutes to report as Squadron Duty Officer.

Blackburn had run along the pier to a point where he was even with the bow of the Hornet. Now he was considering going back to the Officer's Brow to take his medicine when he saw the rat-line—one of the five-inch thick ropes which secured the carrier to the pier.

The rat-line extended 85 feet from its pier cleat to a porthole just below the catwalk of the Hornet. From the pier level to the catwalk, it also climbed a total of 55 feet. In the dark, it did not appear insurmountable to the young pilot.

Three feet from the edge of the pier, the rat-line passed through the center of a ratguard—a metal, convex-shaped disc four feet in diameter. It was meant to discourage pests and should have discouraged Blackburn, too.

Waiting until there was no one nearby, he slipped off his thongs and carefully placed one foot on the rope. Balancing his body, he lunged for the ratguard with both hands. He was successful in grabbing it, and for a moment he crouched on the rope with the ratguard firmly in his grasp. However, it promptly rotated, dropping him into the water below.

Surprised and spitting water, he swam to a ladder alongside the pier. He had fallen 10 feet to the water and was concerned that the splash might have alerted someone on the ship. When no one came to investigate, he climbed up the ladder and sat on the edge of the pier.

I'm as dumb as a rat, he thought. *That's the same way they try to go up.*

He decided to try a running leap—out to the rope beyond the ratguard. During his AOC School days, he had excelled on the obstacle course. One of the obstacles was an elevated log, to which one leaped from above. The trick was to hit the side of the log with your gut. If you hit too low, you could flip over the log for a rough landing. Or if too high, you could break a few ribs. This log had never been a problem for Blackburn and he wondered why he hadn't thought of this solution earlier.

Backing off from the rat-line a distance of 20 feet, he ran toward the rope and jumped. He easily cleared the disc and caught the rope perfectly in his gut. Gripping a five-inch swinging rope, though, was not as easy as catching his body on a stationary foot-thick log. He hit the water harder this time.

"Sonofa-sonofabitch," he swore as he broke the surface of the water a second time. Again, he hid alongside the ladder until he thought the coast was clear.

Climbing back to the top of the pier, this time he paused long enough to rub his hands dry. Then he again ran toward the rat-line. With this attempt, he decided to hold the palms of his hands facing the line, with his cupped fingers pointing downward.

As his gut hit the rope, he spun around again. But this time, his hands held their grip. When he stopped swinging, he hoisted one leg up and over the rope, and then the other.

Nervous energy helped Blackburn traverse the first 30 feet of the rat-line. At that point, the weight of his body caused the balance of the line to become almost vertical. Gripping the rope more tightly, he felt it begin to chafe the skin of his inner legs.

At the midway point, he began thinking of Commander Grey. With each tug up the rope, he was that much further from being caught in his "trip" off the Hornet.

When he was only 25 feet away from the porthole, these thoughts were replaced by the pain from the raw skin of his legs and hands. He began to doubt if he could make it.

As he paused to rest, Blackburn thought the cool water below would feel good on his chafed skin and he seriously contemplated dropping into it. Then he thought of Betty. *No, this is for you, Betty. This is for you.*

With each pull up the line, he repeated to himself, *this is for you.* He still felt the pain, but now it didn't prevent him from reaching the top of the rat-line.

As Blackburn's head reached the porthole through which the rat-line passed, a long brawny arm reached out and grabbed him under an armpit.

"What the Christ are you doing, mister?" said the arm's owner.

The porthole through which Blackburn hoped to gain entrance led into the fo'c'sle of the Hornet—the working space and office of the Ship's Bos'n.

"In my 29 years in the Navy, you've got to be the biggest goddamn idiot I've ever seen," the Bos'n said as he hoisted the pilot through the porthole.

Blackburn was too exhausted to say anything. The Bos'n eased him into a sitting position on the deck.

"Okay, boy. Tell me who the hell you are, so I'll know who to notify after I throw you in the brig."

Almost inaudibly, the pilot mumbled, "Ensign Blackburn."

"What'd you say?" said the Bos'n.

Blackburn repeated his name.

"I still think you're one helluva idiot, sir. What's going on anyway? What's an officer doing boarding the ship on a rat-line?"

For the third time that day, Ensign Blackburn rapidly explained that he had to see his newly-pregnant wife before the Hornet sailed. And then why he had to come up the rat-line.

When Blackburn finished his story, the Ship's Bos'n looked at his watch and said, "Well, sir, you've got exactly six minutes to report to the ready room. You'd better get up on the Flight Deck if you're going to make it."

Blackburn stood up and headed for a passageway to the Flight Deck.

The Bos'n called after him, "Oh, Ensign. Don't tell any of

your running mates about the new entry you found to the Hornet. I heard you when you hit the water the first time."

"Don't worry," Blackburn said over his shoulder.

Reaching the Flight Deck, he sprinted 600 feet to Catapult One and jumped in the catwalk leading to the 03 level. He didn't stop running until he reached his stateroom. By the time he reached the ready room, he was a minute late. No one said anything or took note of it, though.

Thirty minutes later, Commander Grey strode into the ready room and stopped directly in front of the SDO's desk. Blackburn was standing behind the desk, unable to sit because of the rawness of the skin along his inner legs.

"Where in the hell have you been, Blackburn?" he demanded.

Mustering the most nonchalant expression he could, the Ensign answered, "Jogging, sir. On the Flight Deck."

Grey started to say something, but decided not to. Instead he gave Blackburn a look which the young pilot quickly glanced away from. The Ensign tried to appear busy with the papers on the desk. Grey then marched out as rapidly as he had come in. It would be several more days before Blackburn could sit at a desk again, or even sit in the Wardroom to eat.

Betty gave birth to a girl, which they named Jody. Two years later, a son was born and named Craig.

Five years after the birth of their second child, Blackburn and his wife separated, and two years later Betty obtained a divorce. He had just put in for a third tour of duty off Vietnam. She had warned him that she wanted more than a letter a week during what she considered the best years of her life.

Commander Grey never asked Blackburn how he got back on the Hornet that night. And the young pilot never volunteered the information...to anyone.

As Captain Blackburn sat in the Skipper's Chair of the Kitty Hawk, he debated whether it had all been worth it. He had been divorced for ten years now. Neither he nor Betty had remarried. In fact, they still exchanged cards at Christmas, and occasionally even had dinner together.

He wondered if he would still be the skipper of a carrier if he hadn't put in for that third tour off Vietnam.

3

TAKING THE BARRICADE

It was a night training mission—a simulated raid on a
military target near Tehran. The Alpha Strike called for five
A-6s, seven A-7s, eight F-14s, two E-2s, one EA-6, and two
S-3s.

The Kitty Hawk practiced these missions frequently, as
they knew they might be called upon to do it for real. Of course,
these flights did not enter Iranian air space. The target was
usually at some point in the open sea.

The launches were accomplished without delay or problems. The F-14s that Slim and Warbucks piloted were assigned as TAC CAP; meaning they were to protect the A-6s
and A-7s that carried out the actual attack.

The mission included "topping off" the F-14s with fuel
after they were launched. Topping off the fighters was necessary
to replace the 10 to 15 percent of their fuel expended during
launching and climbing to their rendezvous points. This precau-
tion ensured a maximum fuel supply for the F-14s when they
reached the target area, where the amount of action they could
encounter in a real-life situation might vary greatly.

This night the F-14s rendezvoused for inflight refueling at
15,000 feet above the Kitty Hawk. Warbucks had explained
inflight refueling to his son, Jeff, who had seen the massive
KC-135 tankers which the Air Force used. Jeff couldn't understand how a KC-135 would fit on a carrier deck. Warbucks had
explained that the ship's Air Wing crew could convert an A-6 or
A-7 to a tanker in one hour on its hangar deck.

As Slim approached the A-6 tanker, he stabilized at six-
feet behind the basket, which was at the end of a 50-foot hose
connected to the A-6's fuel supply. The refueling probe of

Slim's aircraft was on the right side of his fuselage. Slim had to keep his eye on the A-6 tanker, while his RIO gave him precise instructions to drive the probe neatly into the A-6's basket. Commander Barry "Pink Panther" Morris was Slim's RIO that night. Morris was the squadron's XO. He had two tours in F-4s in Vietnam, in addition to eight years in F-14s. He knew Slim's aircraft like the back of his hand.

"A little right and up," instructed Morris. "A little more right. Looks good. Looks good. Just a couple of feet."

Inflight refueling requires one-hundred percent concentration, particularly during night operations when it's harder to detect relative motion between aircraft. Even though Slim was considered among the best pilots in the ship's Air Wing, he hated tanking. In addition, a bad head cold was affecting his concentration this night.

"Back out! Back out!" screamed Morris.

Slim thought he had a good latch-up, but his RIO could see he didn't. The iron-mesh basket, weighing close to one-hundred pounds, slammed against the right side of their canopy. Then it almost went down the F-14's intake.

"Back out, you son-of-a-bitch!" Morris shouted, as the basket careened over the canopy and began banging against the left side of the F-14.

Slim slowly retracted the throttles and backed his F-14 away from the tanker. He had tried three times without getting a latchup.

Morris' voice was more calm. "Take a breather, Slim, and give somebody else a shot."

As their plane dropped down and out to starboard, another F-14 was cleared in to tank. Slim then moved back to the port side and got in line, awaiting his turn to plug again. Slim wondered if he had been wrong in not obtaining a down-chit from the Flight Surgeon.

After letting two other F-14s refuel, Slim was cooled down and had no problem hooking up. He and the other fighters then shrieked off like children from an ice cream truck.

The strike over the simulated target went off picture-perfect. On the way home, Slim noticed a vague sluggishness in his controls as he began to descend out of altitude. They were still 80 miles from the Kitty Hawk.

Thirty seconds later he told his XO, "We have a Master Caution Light." This light was level with his eyes and was flickering yellow. It was a signal to check the Telepanel, a rectangular 5 by 14 inch display to the right of Slim's seat.

"What's the problem?" asked Morris.

A quick glance downward told Slim what it was. The hydraulic pressure light was yellow on the Telepanel. Bringing his eyes up to the primary hydraulic gauge, he saw his p.s.i. dropping.

"We're losing pressure from the combined side," said Slim.

A note of concern was evident in Morris' voice. "What do you mean *losing pressure?*"

"Like it's at zero. And the Bi-Di ain't picking it up."

Punching his UHF-2 button, Morris called CAG, who was flight leader for the strike. "Warpaint, this is Gunslinger 202. I've got a bad hydraulic problem. I've got to get on the ship ASAP."

"You going to be okay, Panther?" asked the CAG.

"Yes, sir. But I've got to get this bird on the deck fast."

Captain (Warpaint) Edgars thought for a moment and then keyed his mike, "Gunslinger 206. Escort 202 back to the ship."

"Roger," said Warbucks, as he swung his F-14 around to escort Slim back to the Kitty Hawk. The two F-14s peeled off, separating from the returning Alpha Strike, in order not to endanger the other aircraft.

Warbucks joined on the left wing of the troubled aircraft and reported, "It appears you're losing hydraulic fluid leaking from your left engine bay, forward of the port hydraulic stabilizer actuator."

"Let me know if it gets worse," responded Slim. "Don't get too close. I'm having trouble controlling this hog."

The Pink Panther reached for his *Pocket Rocket* checklist and simultaneously keyed his microphone. "Strike Control, this is Gunslinger 202. I have a hydraulic failure and am returning to the ship."

"Roger, 202," responded the Air Ops Officer on the ship.

A few minutes later, Morris looked up from his *Pocket Rocket*. "Slim, we best dirty-up when we get to twenty miles from the ship."

"Roger that. I'll lower the gear before we drop through the overcast."

As they approached the twenty-mile mark, Morris called

the ship. "Strike, this is Gunslinger 202. I am on your 220 radial at 23 miles, angles 18, squawking 1702. 4.7. 206 is on my wing, squawking 1708."

"Roger, 202. Contact Marshall."

"202, switching."

At this point, Slim slowed his aircraft and lowered its landing gear handle. They both felt the nitrogen charge as the landing gear dropped. Slim then reached over and lowered the tailhook handle.

"Sonofabitch," muttered Slim.

"What's wrong?" asked Morris.

"The indicator for the left wheel mount is barber-poled." The left wheel mount had not locked into position.

Morris keyed his mike. "206, we have got an unsafe left wheel mount. How about flying up and taking a closer look."

"Roger 202." Warbucks positioned his aircraft under 202, looking for the blackstrips near the main mount. If they were visible, it would indicate the landing gear had locked into position. "I cannot see the blackstrips. It's too dark out here. Your hook is down though."

"Roger 206," replied Morris.

Thank God something's gone right," said Slim.

Morris keyed his mike again. "Marshall, Gunslinger 202. On your 220 radial, angles 18, squawking 1702. 4.5. We have lost hydraulics and our left wheel mount is indicating unsafe."

"Roger 202. Stand by," was the response from the Kitty Hawk. Twenty seconds later, the ship told them, "Gunslinger 202. We are launching the Alert Tanker. Can you tank with your gear down?"

"We'll give it our best shot," answered Morris.

"Roger. It will be circling Homeplate at 5,000 feet."

Slim and the XO completed their checklist and descended through the overcast, breaking out at 6,500 feet. As they approached the Hawk, Commander Morris spotted the flashing green lights of the tanker.

"Okay, Slim. Let's stop at the Texaco Station and get a drink." They joined up with the tanker and Slim selected his refueling probe to its external position.

"Well, kiss a fat lady in the ass!" exclaimed Slim. "The damn probe isn't coming out."

"Use the handcrank," suggested his XO.

Slim counted the revolutions as he turned the manual

handcrank. After 120 revolutions, the probe had still not extended. Unable to take on fuel, they would not get more than two looks at the Flight Deck before running out of juice. The XO was beginning to get a bit nervous himself. He knew they would have to either eject or take the Barricade.

"We're in deep kimsche." said Slim.

"I'll report it," said Morris. "Marshall. 202 unable to refuel due to hydraulic failure."

"Roger, 202. We are rigging the Barricade."

Morris then requested that LCdr. Sandy "M+9" Mapleford be the Landing Signal Officer for their trap. M+9 had been in the Navy for 16 years, and that's the rank he would probably be at 20 years, too. His 210 pounds were poorly distributed on a five-foot-nine frame. While he was reasonably respectful to superiors inside the ship, on the Flight Deck he could be ruthless to an officer of any rank who made a poor landing and endangered the lives of the Flight Deck crew. As a result, few pilots made poor landings on the Kitty Hawk. They feared M+9's wrath, and therefore followed his instructions. This was M+9's way of keeping the carnage on the Flight Deck to a minimum. He was the best in the business.

Warbucks' presence not being required anymore, he said, "Slip it in there, Slim," and departed to enter Marshall.

Before the emergency call from Gunslinger 202, the Flight Deck crew was positioning aircraft for the second night launch. This all changed when the 5-MC blared, "Emergency Pull Forward! Emergency Pull Forward!"

This told the men on the Flight Deck that there was a Kitty Hawk plane in trouble somewhere overhead the ship. The speed and efficiency in which the landing area of the Flight Deck was cleared could mean life or death to the men in that plane.

The plane captains for each aircraft in the landing area of the deck immediately jumped into the cockpits of their aircraft. They had to ride the brakes while the yellow shirts hooked up towing tractors to pull their planes forward.

When the Flight Deck was cleared, the Air Boss announced on the 5-MC, "Rig the Barricade. Rig the Barricade. We have a F-14 with unsafe gear and low fuel."

Night procedure on a carrier dictates that the Barricade must be rigged within four minutes after this call. The crew had practiced this procedure many times during the cruise. This time it was for real.

All available Flight Deck personnel helped rig the Barricade. First, the nylon webbing was pulled out and stretched across the landing area, between the No. 3 and No. 4 arresting cables. The webbing was then hooked to metal stanchions, one on each side of the Flight Deck. When the stanchions were raised, they formed a 20-foot high barricade across the Flight Deck. Meanwhile, Slim and his XO were circling overhead and reviewing their ejection and water survival procedures. This was Slim's first major emergency on a cruise during blue-water operations.

"Okay, Slim," said Morris. "Remember, if we have to wave-off on the first pass, make sure we clear the net. If we catch it with the hook, that's going to ruin our whole day. And watch your speed. If we come in too fast, we'll slice right through the Barricade."

Continuing to refer to the *Pocket Rocket*, the XO said, "Is your harness locked?"

"Roger," replied Slim.

"Are your lap belts tight?"

"Yes, sir."

"Good, we're ready to go."

All of Slim's previous training was flashing through his mind—a mile a minute. Before he had time to worry any more, Slim heard these words over his UHF radio,

"Gunslinger 202. You have a Charlie. Bring her home, Slim." The last few words from the Air Ops Officer were meant to pump Slim up. To let the pilot know the deck was ready and they were all standing by.

The crash crew and P-16 fire-fighting equipment were in position. Tilly, the big yellow crane was started and ready if needed. Big John, a forklift with a bucket, was fired up too.

Slim's F-14 broke out of a scud layer at two miles. At a quarter of a mile, Slim called the Ball, "202. Tomcat Ball. 3.2." This meant he now could see the bright yellow ball on the Fresnel lens—a "traffic light" apparatus on the left side of the carrier's deck which indicated the relative position of the F-14 to the Flight Deck. The word *Tomcat* told the Flight Deck the specific type of aircraft which was coming in, so its weight could be properly handled by the arresting cable. The *3.2* meant that the F-14's fuel gauge indicated 3,200 pounds of remaining fuel.

After Slim made his Ball call, his Landing Signal Officer told him, "We have the technology, big fellow. Keep her coming. The deck is moving." As requested, M+9 was waving. "Christ," blurted Slim. "That Ball is moving all over the place." The deck was pitching wildly as the F-14 approached the ramp of the carrier. M+9 didn't like the setup. The deck was moving so much that he doubted Slim's ability to come aboard safely. Although M+9 had various instruments at his disposal to cue him about the F-14's position relative to the deck, this time he relied solely on his visual sight picture . . . and his experience. The F-14 was almost on him when M+9 saw the stern of the ship begin to rise. He had been studying the ship's pitch cycle for fifteen minutes to determine if there was any continuity of movement. As the stern of the ship began moving upward, M+9 knew it would reach its peak in about three to four seconds—just when the F-14 would arrive at the ramp.

M+9 heard Slim reduce power. The pilot, having seen the Ball go high earlier when the deck went down, had reduced power to get the Ball back down on the Fresnel lens. The LSO knew that reducing power would increase the F-14's sink rate, and with the deck coming back up, the consequences could be disastrous.

"Wave it off! Wave it off!" screamed M+9 as he simultaneously made the red wave-off lights flash on the Fresnel lens.

"Sonofabitch," roared Slim as he jammed accelled.

"Watch your attitude and angle of attack!" yelled Morris as their aircraft over-rotated.

The F-14 screamed across the Flight Deck, missing the Barricade by inches.

Sweat began to pour off Slim's brow, stinging his eyes, making it hard to see. "Holy Christ, that was close," said Slim.

Morris said nothing, thinking how close they had just come to making the "Big Muster in the Sky."

The Controller came up and told them, "Climb straight ahead to 1,200 feet. When comfortable, turn downwind."

At this point, Slim saw the low-fuel warning light come on for his left engine. It would flame out within a few minutes. As they rolled in the groove, the starboard engine low-fuel light also illuminated.

"Our go-juice is getting low," said Slim. "We'd better make it this time." His voice lacked its customary jauntiness.

Trying to keep his pilot calm, Morris told him, "Just keep it smooth, Slim. Just like rubbing a virgin's titty."

As the F-14 came in for its second attempt, Slim saw the yellow ball turn red and go off the bottom of the lens, indicating he was dangerously low.

However M+9 calmly said, "Hold what you have. The deck is up." The ship was pitching forward hard. If the stern dropped quickly as he expected, this would correct the alignment of the ship to the approaching aircraft. Slim kept it coming.

The F-14 roared onto the Flight Deck at a speed of 127 knots. Its hook caught the No. 1 arresting wire, but when the left main tire mount hit the deck, it collapsed. The F-14 slammed into the deck. As it scraped along the Flight Deck, a ruptured fuel line ignited and the rear of the F-14 was engulfed with flames.

The plane skidded to the left, hitting the Barricade at an angle.

The Air Boss screamed, "You're on fire! Get out! Get out!"

Within the F-14, Morris yelled to Slim, "Don't eject! We're strapped in by the barricade webbing."

The burning aircraft finally came to a rest just forward of the Fresnel lens, half on the deck and half over the side, at a 45-degree angle. While Slim secured the fuel handles and throttles in an attempt to limit the fire, Morris tried to blow the canopy open.

The canopy jerked upward, but didn't clear the cockpit, the barricade webbing holding it to the aircraft. After unbuckling from their seats, both pilots instinctively pulled their survival knives and began pounding on the canopy with their metal handles.

Watching from the Flag Bridge, Admiral Grey said to his aide, "They'd better get out of that plane before the damn seats cook off." The Admiral had seen enough fires to know the heat could activate the ejection apparatus in the seats which held Slim and Morris. If that happened, the straps of the Barricade would abort the ejection, mangling or killing the men in their seats.

The fire had enveloped the forward section of the F-14 and the cockpit was rapidly filling with smoke. The F-14 had been on the deck of the Kitty Hawk a total of seven seconds.

Two seconds later, the crash crew surrounded the burning plane. Their first act was to hit the F-14 with light water to retard the flames. Then they hit it with foam.

They had to act fast to enable Big John to come up tight to the cockpit. A member of the crash crew in an asbestos suit was crouched in the basket of the forklift as it approached the burning aircraft.

In the smoke the pilots saw the man in the asbestos. They also saw him waving his hand back-and-forth. They didn't understand this message until they saw the K-12 hand-operated saw in his other hand. As the carborundum-tipped blade of the saw sliced into the canopy, the pilots stopped pounding with their knives and moved away from the blade point.

It took the man in asbestos another ten seconds to cut through enough of the canopy to get to his pilots. He helped Slim out of his seat and into the basket of the forklift.

By this time, the rear cockpit was so full of smoke that Morris was no longer visible. Reaching into the cockpit, the man in asbestos found the head of the unconscious pilot and got a handhold on his upper torso harness. In one clean jerk, he yanked Morris from his cockpit and dropped him into the forklift basket. Jumping into the basket himself, the rescuer signalled the driver of Big John to get out of there.

Admiral Grey took a deep breath and unclenched his hands from the railing as he saw the forklift emerge from the smoke. Seeing only two heads though, he muttered, "God damn it. Where's the other pilot?" He stepped toward the Bat Phone to order the Air Boss to move the forklift back into the smoke.

Before Grey reached the Bat Phone, his aide said, "Admiral, they've got him. They're taking a third man out of the basket."

Grey returned to the window and saw the unconscious Morris carried from the basket onto a stretcher. He was rushed into the battle dressing station just off the Flight Deck.

Neither the Admiral nor his aide said anything. Glancing toward Admiral Grey, the aide saw him staring down at the deck in what he supposed was embarrassment. It wasn't. It was in prayer. The Admiral was thanking his God.

Tilly (the crane) pulled out of her spot and headed for the smouldering Tomcat. She hooked the crippled aircraft, lifted it off the deck, and unceremoniously dumped it over the side. The planes overhead were running low on fuel and there was too little time to salvage it.

Other than a few burns on his hands where he had touched the side of his plane when getting out of its cockpit, Slim was uninjured. He had foolishly elected not to wear flight gloves. Commander Morris was revived quickly with a dose of pure oxygen. He walked out of the battle dressing station twenty minutes after being pulled from his plane.

In Wardroom I the next morning, both men sat at their breakfasts quietly. Instead of jocularity, there was a subdued sense of relief among the pilots of the Kitty Hawk.

Sundance came up to his running mate, placed a hand lightly on his shoulder, and quietly asked, "How was the marshmallow roast last night, pal?"

Slim turned his head and calmly said, "Screw you."

Sweetwater looked up from his plate. "Yeah, the big dope tried to use his fingers for skewers."

Glancing at his bandaged hands, Slim looked to Sweetwater. "Screw you, too."

To himself Slim thought, *thanks clowns*. Some of the tension within him had started to fade.

4

LEGSHAVING & SENSITIVITY
SALON

"How high do you fly?" asked Angela.

"Zero to 50,000 feet," replied Sweetwater.

"How do you breathe at 50,000 feet?"

"We use our oxygen masks," he said.

Sweetwater stared into his drink. He and the other pilots on the Kitty Hawk had been invited to attend a "Happy Hour" open house in the teachers' quarters of the Cubi Point BOQ. Cubi Point was the Naval Air Station at the west end of Subic Bay in the Philippines, where the ship had pulled in for re-supply and repairs before returning to Camel Station. Sweetwater and Angela sat on a sofa in the lounge of the second floor of the bachelor officer quarters.

The pilot wondered if it had been a mistake to sit down next to the cute, slightly overweight blonde. So far, he had learned that Angela was a new arrival from the States, she was twenty-five years old, and she asked dumb questions.

"Do you like being a pilot?" she asked.

"Sure."

"Why?"

"It's exciting. Up there, you're all alone. You feel as free as a bird," he responded.

"How long do you stay at sea?"

Sweetwater had been asked these questions a thousand times. Each new woman usually asked them in the same order too.

He answered. "Anywhere from two weeks to a month."

"Do you have a girlfriend?" she asked.

This was the inevitable question. Sweetwater thought, *why do they always ask that? Even if I had a girlfriend, I wouldn't admit it.*

"No," was his answer.

"Does it get lonely on a carrier?"

"Not with 6,000 men aboard." He paused. "Of course, after a month at sea, it's nice to enjoy the smell of perfume and have an intelligent conversation with a woman like you."

"You probably say that to every girl," she responded. Finding no suitable matchups elsewhere, Sundance with a drink in each hand seated himself on the sofa next to Sweetwater. One hand held a whiskey and the other a beer chaser. He leaned forward and told Angela,

"You have some nice real estate."

"I don't understand," she replied.

"You've also got great torpedoes."

"What do you mean?"

Staring at her legs this time, Sundance asked, "If you were going in for a manicure and pedicure, and someone offered to shave your legs, what would you say?"

This time her only response was widened eyes and an open mouth.

Sundance then turned to Sweetwater and asked, "You going to get your ashes hauled tonight?"

Sweetwater didn't reply either, hoping Angela was as naive as she appeared. She was.

"What does that mean?" she asked again.

"Same as getting some mud for your turtle, honey," answered Sundance.

"What does that mean?"

Get laid," said Sundance.

"Come on, Sundance. Go shake the dew off your lily," said Sweetwater.

"What does that mean?" asked Angela, looking to Sundance this time.

"Ask the doctor."

"The doctor?"

Sweetwater and Sundance were doing their usual routine. It normally worked to perfection, but Sweetwater had a few doubts this time.

"Don't you know who you're talking to, honey?" asked Sundance. "This is the world-famous Dr. Sweetwater Sullivan."

Angela turned back to Sweetwater. "You didn't tell me you were a doctor."

"You didn't ask," he responded.

"What kind of doctor are you?"

"I'm a flight surgeon gynecologist."

A willowy brunette standing nearby overheard this comment and ambled over to their sofa. She was twice Angela's age, but her mini-dress also revealed twice the figure. Her dress was light and white, with a strapless top nicely supported by medium-sized breasts. She wore no bra. Suntanned thighs filled the eyes of the seated pilots as she brashly asked,

"Is the Navy so hard up for good men now that they're hiring gynecologists as flight surgeons?"

Sundance was too busy staring to accept this challenge. Sweetwater answered,

"I have a practice here in Subic Bay. This is our home port while overseas. When the Kitty Hawk's at sea, I'm a flight surgeon; and in port, I'm a gynecologist."

"That's a new line, doctor. Tell me more."

Before he could, Angela asked him, "When do you have time to fly if you're the doctor for your ship?"

"These Navy flyboys have been B.S. . . . ing you, dear. You must be new in town," said the brunette.

"Oh, but you're wrong," said Sweetwater. "I really am a physician."

She retorted, "And a gynecologist to boot, right? Okay, sonny. How do real doctors treat polyps on the cervix?"

Answering this was no problem for Sweetwater. His father was the physician in Dexter, Maine. As a boy, he often accompanied his father on night calls. He had even helped his father deliver babies.

"Madam, we . . ."

"Don't call me madam. My name's Lucy."

"Okay, Lucy. If you had a few polyps on your cervix, I would most likely handle them in my office. Are you familiar with cryosurgery?"

"Go on, Doctor."

"I'd use a cryosurgical probe to freeze the tissue of the polyps. This causes the cell membranes of the tissue to rupture and die. You'd experience little or no pain, and you could probably go back to a regular routine the next day."

"Well, you may or may not be a doctor, but don't try to tell me you're a flight surgeon gynecologist," responded Lucy. "My husband works at Clark Air Force Base and I know better.

"Your legs need a shave too," said Sundance, taking an even closer look at Lucy's legs.

"I beg your pardon. Who in the hell are you?"

"Name's Sundance. I'm Doctor Sullivan's QA. Any woman with legs as magnificent as yours should take better care of them."

"The line's getting better," said Lucy. "What makes you think my legs need a shave, Sunshine?"

"Sundance, ma'am. As a graduate of the Sweetwater International Legshaving and Sensitivity Salon, I can clearly see that your legs need a shave."

"And I suppose you want to shave them?" she replied.

"No, ma'am. I'm just a QA. The doctor here takes care of that area."

"What does QA stand for?" Lucy asked. "Queer asses?"

Sweetwater replied, "Sundance is one of my 'quality assurance' specialists."

"Do you shave your pilots' legs, too?" she asked Sweetwater.

"Actually, Sundance shaves his own legs," retorted Sweetwater.

The women laughed. Sundance had no response.

In a more serious tone, Sweetwater said, "I have found that the majority of women hate to shave their legs. Most of the time, you cut yourselves—either around the ankle, kneecap, Achilles' tendon, or shinbones. How many times did you cut yourself, Lucy, the last time you shaved?"

"You have a point. I still think you're a couple of lechers though," replied Lucy.

Sweetwater continued, "I've perfected the proper stroke to shave a woman's legs. Having shaved more than one thousand pairs, I've never drawn blood yet. And I've graduated more than three hundred from my Sensitivity Salon."

"Three hundred what?" asked Lucy.

"Quality assurance specialists," said Sundance.

"I still think QA stands for queer asses," snapped Lucy.

"I always carry my kit to parties. Would you like a demonstration?" Sweetwater asked Lucy.

"I shaved my legs last night, thank you."

"You did a lousy job," said Sundance, leaning forward and peering at her calves. "A man could get whisker burns down there."

"Are you his nurse, Sunshine?" Lucy asked.

"No ma'am. Like the doctor says, I'm his quality assurance specialist."

"So what does that mean, Sunshine?"

"I handle the hot towels, apply the shaving cream and lotion, and check the quality of the doctor's work."

"You guys are quite a team," replied Lucy. "You should charge for your services."

"We do," said Sweetwater. "Do you want our summer or winter rates?"

"What's the difference?" asked Lucy.

Sweetwater told her, "The winter rate is for removing the hair up to your kneecap, and the summer rate is for as far up as necessary to make your swimsuit appealing."

"How long does the summer job take?" Lucy asked.

"That depends on how hairy you are," answered Sundance.

"You guys sound like real Boy Scouts," rejoined Lucy.

Pretending to give up on the older woman, Sweetwater said, "Angela, can I demonstrate with one of your legs?"

"I don't know," she responded slowly.

Sundance leaned around Sweetwater on the sofa, again peered at Angela's legs, and asked,

"What do you shave your legs with, honey? A butter knife?"

Lucy then drew the attention of the two pilots back to herself. Though the pilots' eyes were only a few feet away, they saw no more than a flash of her upper thighs as she suddenly hitched the sides of her skirt up and swiftly drew her pantyhose down the magnificent suntanned thighs.

"Let's see how good you boys are," said Lucy. "I'll try your winter rates on one leg. Can we use your bathroom, Angela?"

Before Angela could say anything, Sweetwater told Sundance, "Go out to the car and get my kit."

Then looking to Angela, he asked, "Do you want your legs done too?"

Angela hesitantly answered, "Can I wait to see how you do with Lucy first?"

"Sure," said Sweetwater. "Watch us. Lucy's leg will feel like a newborn baby's bottom when we're finished."

When Sundance returned (he had knocked on the doors of the first floor until he found the necessary equipment), they all walked down the hall to Angela's room. It was the size of a large living room and shared a bathroom with the room next door. Lucy sat on the edge of the vanity and placed her left leg in the sink, modestly covering her thighs with a towel.

"Sundance, prepare the leg," ordered Sweetwater.

"Okay, Lucy," said Sundance. "First, we heat the hair on your leg with a towel." He warmed a towel and then wrapped it around her entire lower leg, gently massaging her calves and ankles for a few minutes.

"What I'm doing now is bringing the hairs on your leg up off your skin," said Sundance.

"Sunshine, that's what you *think* you're doing."

He returned the compliment by saying, "You've got nice wheels."

"What are wheels?" asked Angela.

Sweetwater, Lucy, and Sundance exchanged glances.

"You're looking at them," Lucy finally said.

"Okay, Wheels. Now we apply the Noxema shaving cream," said Sundance, as he generously covered her lower leg with lather and gently smoothed it over her skin. With a satisfied smile, he then said, "She's all yours, Doctor."

Sweetwater commenced shaving her ankle. Feigning professionalism, he formally explained, "As you can see, Lucy, I'm holding the razor shaft as close as possible to the blade. By holding the shaft high, I can maintain maximum control."

"Is this what they teach in flight school now?" she asked.

He added, "Another benefit you're now receiving is that the blade can be applied at the proper angle to the hair, as I don't have to bend over awkwardly to reach the back of your leg. Also notice how I rinse the blade after every two strokes. That permits it to smoothly slide over the skin during the stroke."

When Sweetwater had shaved half the leg, he told Angela "Go ahead and feel where I've shaved."

She did and said, "That's pretty smooth."

Sundance didn't disguise his enthusiasm as he asked Sweetwater, "Would you like me to finish shaving her leg, Doctor?"

"You haven't been in the business long enough, Sundance."

Lucy said, "Why don't you give him a try? Where's he going to get his experience?"

"Not on you, my dear," replied Sweetwater.

Angela surprised them by saying, "Sundance, I wouldn't mind if you practiced on me."

"Fine," said Sundance, although with less fervor than his earlier interest in Lucy.

In a minute Sweetwater said, "Okay, Sundance. The cool towel."

As Sundance again gently massaged her lower leg, he explained, "This towel is to remove the residue of hair and cream. When you do this yourself, don't place a hot towel on your legs after shaving. That aggravates the skin."

"Angela, do you have a hair dryer?" asked Sweetwater.

"What do you need a hairdryer for?" said Lucy.

"Relax, Wheels." said Sundance. "You're in the hands of professionals."

As Sundance again warmed and then dried her leg, Lucy closed her eyes and leaned back on the wall.

Sweetwater asked her, "Do you want another drink?"

Without opening her eyes, Lucy said, "Angela, would you get me another glass of punch?"

After Angela had left, Lucy asked, "Do you guys always work as a team?"

Sweetwater answered, "We fly, steam, and fight together."

"Stay on the same leg, doctor. I want the summer treatment too," Lucy murmured, as she undraped her left thigh.

"Fine," said Sweetwater. "But we have to finish your lower leg first. Sundance, the lotion."

"Wheels," said Sundance softly, "it's time for the coup de grace." He proceeded to massage Vaseline Intensive Care Lotion over the shaved areas of her leg. The pringling sensation this caused came within a minute.

Sundance quietly asked, "How does it feel, Wheels?"

Lucy was slow in answering. "Beautiful, just beautiful," she finally said. She rested her head on the wall, feeling warm all over—soothed and sleepy.

Nothing more was said, even after Angela returned.

Kneeling first, Sundance rested Lucy's left leg on his left shoulder. After wrapping her thigh in a hot towel, he massaged the thigh with both hands thoroughly. Then he applied the shaving cream, continuing to support her leg as Sweetwater shaved her thigh.

Lucy's modesty had surrendered to the pleasure she was experiencing. When Sweetwater realized that she had worn nothing under her hose, he delicately adjusted her skirt—for his sake. There were few matters on which he concentrated as much attention as he did when shaving a woman's legs.

When Sweetwater finished, Sundance pointed to a towel and motioned for Angela to rinse it in cool water; which she did before handing it to him. A minute later, she also handed the hair dryer to Sundance.

After the lotion had caused the pringling sensation again, Lucy appeared to be in a deep trance.

A few minutes later, she was the first to speak, "Doctor, do you do armpits too?"

"Only in the shower," Sweetwater replied.

Sweetwater then said to Sundance, "Why don't you bring us some more drinks?"

Sundance asked Angela, "Where'd you get the punch?"

"I'll show you," she replied.

As Angela stood up, Sundance told her, "You're next."

When Angela and Sundance had left, Lucy reached over to the door, turned its latch, kicked the door shut, and turned on the shower.

"You're next, Doc."

5

RUSSIAN FISH FRY

"Wave it off! Wave it off!" roared the Air Boss over the UHF radio.

Slim was on short final when the wave-off lights flashed red on the Fresnel lens, along with the blast from the Air Boss.

"Damn it," Slim exclaimed as he pushed his throttles to *military* power. "What the hell is wrong now? We had a good start going."

His RIO said, "Looks like the Russkies are playing games again. Sundance got waved off ahead of us, too."

Then the word came from the Air Boss. "99 Aircraft. Signal Delta. Flight operations are being disrupted by converging traffic. Expect Charlie in fifteen minutes." This instructed the planes preparing to land to go into a circling pattern at different altitudes over the ship.

The Kitty Hawk's battle group had been in the northern part of the Arabian Sea for two weeks, and the Russian ships which followed the battle group were becoming increasingly inquisitive. They had been crossing back and forth in front of the Hawk, causing the ship to alter course. This particular morning, the course changes were causing the wind across the deck to be "out of limits," thereby necessitating the wave-offs.

"Sundance," said Slim, "go tactical."

"Roger," responded Sundance.

"Want to have some fun?" asked Slim.

"What do you have in mind?"

"Let's see if we can talk the Boss into letting us do a couple of flybys on the Russkies?" said Slim.

"Why not," answered Sundance.

"Boss, Gunslinger 202," Slim called.

"202, go ahead."

"Request permission for a couple of low flybys with Playmate 209 on that Russian trawler," said Slim.

"Stand by, 202," replied the Air Boss.

Inside Primary Flight Control, the Air Boss picked up the Bat Phone—a direct line to the captain's bridge.

"Captain, Boss here. 202 and 209 would like a couple of low passes on that Russian off to our left."

Captain Blackburn told him, "I'll get back to you."

The CAG was already on the Bridge with the Captain discussing the problem. When Blackburn told him of the Air Boss's request, Warpaint said, "Those Russian bastards have almost put two of my aircraft in the water already. Yesterday, two A-7s were running low on fuel and got waved off twice before they could come in. I'm getting tired of this bull hockey."

Captain Blackburn then called Flag Operations and asked to speak to the Admiral. The Admiral came on the line.

"Admiral, Captain Blackburn here, sir."

"Go ahead, Ed. What's on your mind?"

"CAG is on the Bridge and we're discussing the problem these Russian trawlers are causing to our flight operations. The Russians are ignoring the international flag codes I've been sending them on the yardarm. We just changed course for the second time this morning to avoid a collision. Two of our pilots who just got waved off have requested permission to make a few low flybys of the Russians. I recommend approval of their request."

"Sounds good, Ed. Permission granted."

The Admiral put the phone down, then picked it back up and buzzed the Bridge, "Wait a minute. Sweetwater isn't in one of the aircraft requesting permission for the flybys, is he?"

"No Sir," said Blackburn. "It's Slim and Sundance."

"Shoot," exclaimed the Admiral, "that's not much better!" After a short pause, he said, "Go ahead."

"Thank you, sir."

Blackburn called the Air Boss and said, "Make it happen."

The Boss keyed his mike, "Gunslinger 202 and Playmate. Permission granted for a couple of flybys."

"Roger that, Boss," said Slim, as he felt his juices flowing. "Did you hear that, Sundance? We've got our flat-hatting license!"

He told Sundance, "Follow in trail about a quarter-mile. On the first pass, step it up to 700 knots plus."

"Roger," said Sundance. "I'll be on your Six."

While this convention was going on above the ship, the Admiral called the Air Boss.

"Have your cameraman track both our aircraft, so the crew can watch the show on our closed circuit TV," said Grey.

Admiral Grey then relayed his instructions to Blackburn, who made an announcement over the 1-MC.

"There will be some low flybys on the Russian trawler off our port beam. If anyone wants to watch, they'll be on the PLAT Channel. That is all."

At this point, Slim and Sundance had pushed over at 12K (12,000 feet) and were accelerating to 650 knots. As they approached supersonic speed, they were 100 feet off the deck within an eighth of a mile behind the trawler.

"Okay, let's give them a show," said Slim.

As Slim went screaming by the Russian ship, his shock wave hit just as Sundance approached its fantail. Slim yanked his stick in his lap and pulled 5 Gs as he pulled his aircraft into a vertical climb, doing victory rolls as he bled off some of his speed. Sundance was less than 60 feet from the Bridge of the trawler when he smoked by. After passing the Russians, he popped his aircraft a couple hundred feet and did an aileron roll, then pulled into a 5 G left climbing turn.

"Did you see that clown standing on the fantail?" said Slim.

"Sure did," answered Sundance.

"Remember what happened to the plane captain who got behind that A-7 last week?" asked Slim.

"Wasn't that Scoop Anderson's sixteenth rescue?" said Sundance.

"That's right," said Slim. "I'm going to give him his seventeenth."

"Hey, Slim. Didn't that laundry hanging on the fantail need some starch?"

"Probably does," replied Slim.

The two young pilots were having more fun than a gopher in soft dirt as they swung around for another pass at the Russian ship.

The Russian sailor below was hanging out his ship's laundry on crisscrossing lines which were strung haphazardly across the fantail. This was not an uncommon sight on the Russian ships which followed the battle group.

As the fighters passed the trawler overhead, Slim snapped his Tomcat inverted and started to descend. Sundance followed suit five seconds later.

Slim made a wide turn so he'd have a nice long straight-in on the fantail. As he came up on the trawler, he saw the Russian sailor waving his arms.

"Watch this," Slim told his RIO. "I'm going to give that sucker something to wave about!"

At 275 knots, 60 feet off the deck, Slim approached the trawler's fantail. As the nose of his aircraft reached what he projected as a good turning point, he wrapped the F-14 into a 90-degree angle of bank and hit his afterburner, pulling sharply.

"Sonofabitch," shouted Sundance. "You blew the bastard

overboard? And half the laundry's airborne."

Sundance was smoking in at 300 knots a few seconds behind, also 60 feet off the deck. Timing it perfectly, he yanked his stick back just as he approached the fantail, and hit Zone 5 afterburner.

As Sundance climbed overhead, Slim was yelling, "Helluva show! Helluva show!"

The fireball created by Sundance's afterburner not only cleared the rest of the laundry off the Russian's fantail, it also ignited it.

"That looked like the Fourth of July," shouted Slim.

"Just doing my patriotic duty," responded Sundance.

The Russian ship continued steaming ahead.

"It doesn't look like they know they've lost a man," said Slim.

"You're right," said Sundance. "We'd better go fishing."

"Boss, Gunslinger 202," called Slim.

"202, go ahead."

"There is a Russian fish in the water. We are commencing search and rescue operations."

"Roger. Sending helo," said the Air Boss. "You guys may be in trouble," he added.

When the Air Boss relayed the news of the Russian in the water to the Skipper of the Kitty Hawk, Blackburn immediately informed the Admiral.

"Sir, it seems we've got a problem. A Russian sailor fell off the fantail of the trawler during one of the flybys. We have already sent a helicopter to search for him."

"Ed, that's not a problem. That's a solution. Get that Russian out of the water quick. Send in another helicopter if he's not spotted immediately."

"Yes, sir," said Blackburn.

Circling at 3,000 feet, the two hotdogs quickly found the wet Russian. He was still waving, but more frantically than before.

When Sundance flew over the Russian, dipping his wings, the waving stopped. They reported the Russian's position and the helicopter was on the scene in less than three minutes.

Once the helicopter got on station, the SAR swimmer dropped in the water. He was a big 6'3" 210 pounder, and the Russian didn't protest as the American pulled him into the horse collar. The collar in place under the Russian's arms, the swimmer signalled a thumbs-up. Scoop held it at a steady 40 feet off the deck as the winch operator hoisted them up and into the helicopter's side cargo door.

The Kitty Hawk was five miles away by this time, with the Russian trawler still playing tag. Scoop received orders to cross the bow of the trawler on the way back to the Kitty Hawk. This was an international signal for the Russian ship to follow the helicopter back to the Kitty Hawk.

The first time Scoop crossed the Russian's bow, it failed to respond. Scoop was then ordered to hover opposite the Bridge of the trawler and hold his Russian passenger securely at the cargo door of the helicopter. When the helicopter's guest was finally noticed by the Russians, there was some excited movement on the trawler's Bridge.

When Scoop again crossed the Russian's bow, they quickly swung around to follow the helicopter.

Scoop landed his helo on Spot 5, where his passenger was met by two Marine guards, Captain Blackburn, and Rabbi Freeman. Seeing the soaked and frightened man, the Captain ordered him taken to the ship's dispensary.

The Air Boss then gave the overhead aircraft a Charlie, and all planes landed without incident. As Slim and Sundance came into Flight Deck Control, they were the center of quite a celebration. Sweetwater was waiting for his two friends. After congratulating his running mates, he added, "Your butts are in a sling, now." There was even talk of painting a small Russian man on the side of Slim's aircraft. Slim also temporarily acquired another nickname—Deuce. His shipmates couldn't call him an "ace" for downing a Russian sailor, so "Deuce" was the next best term they could award him.

Being of Russian parentage, Rabbi Freeman was able to adequately communicate with the frightened sailor. Once he had changed into dry clothes and been checked out by a doctor, the Russian was taken to the Admiral.

After a cursory interview, the Admiral directed the Kitty Hawk to tell the Russian trawler to come up on a common radio frequency. With Rabbi Freeman doing the interpreting, Admiral Grey inquired how badly the Russian skipper wanted his sailor back.

Of course, the Russian skipper was anxious to get his man

back. He had not yet reported it to his superiors, and definitely preferred not having to do so.

It was not difficult for the Admiral to convince the Russian skipper to promise to maintain a 5-mile interval during the carrier's future flight operations and to never again cross the ship's bow.

Admiral Grey was unsure whether the Russian skipper would keep these promises, but there was nothing to lose. The Admiral wanted to get the Russian sailor off the Kitty Hawk as soon as possible. He didn't relish reporting a Russian sailor aboard the Kitty Hawk any more than the skipper of the trawler.

That evening, Slim and Sundance were invited to take dinner with the Admiral, who good-naturedly cautioned them about future flybys. He also awarded Slim the Russian Navy issue, turtleneck sweater which the Kitty Hawk's guest had left on the ship earlier that day.

During dinner, the message came back from CINCPAC in response to the report which the Admiral had sent concerning the day's incident. It included the phrase:

"ADMIRE YOUR INITIATIVE. WE'LL NOTIFY YOU WHEN WE NEED ANOTHER RUSSIAN FISH."

6

HOLLYWOOD SHOWERS

"If they don't get this friggin' ship cooled down soon, I'm going overboard," muttered Slim.

"I'm going with you," said Sweetwater. It was the second time in three days that the air conditioning on the Kitty Hawk had gone on the blink.

It was 1900 hours (seven o'clock in the evening) and operations for the day had ceased. The three pilots sat in their ready room watching the television. Their staterooms were too hot and muggy and the Flight Deck was still baking from the subtropical sun.

On the screen appeared a curvacious blonde in a red bathrobe. She hitched her shoulder to partially drop one side of it and said,

"Good evening, men." Then she dropped the robe off her other shoulder. "It's time to conserve our water again."

The blonde then dropped the robe to the floor and stepped into an open shower stall. She turned the water on, twirled completely around to wet her body, turned the water off, and proceeded to lather herself down.

The men ignored her.

They had good reason to. While she had a beauty contestant figure, it was well-concealed beneath a conservative two-piece swim suit. And this was the second time she'd appeared that evening. After lathering down, she turned the shower on again, twirled twice to rinse off, and stepped out of the shower stall.

Wrapping the bathrobe around her still wet body, she

said, "Good night, men. Remember, let's take Navy Showers."

It never occurred to the personnel who filmed this short scenario that it would encourage the exact opposite of what it recommended. The tease angered the men of the Hawk more than it motivated them.

When the regular movie resumed, Sweetwater said, "We should go down and lose that Navy Shower tape. It's worse than commercials!" This attitude was shared by the others in the room.

"I got a better idea," said Slim.

"Oh, oh. Another brain fart," snickered Sundance.

"Listen to me. Why don't we make another one?" suggested Slim.

"Sure, and Sweetwater can be your model," said Sundance. "Hey, Water. Where's the belly-dance outfit that the Admiral liked so much?"

"Your turn this time, buddy."

"No, that's not what I'm talking about," said Slim. "I mean get a real woman, and do it right."

"What do you mean, right?" asked Sundance.

Slim explained, "Well, we get some gal to do a slick strip, and take a real shower, too."

"Forget it," said Sundance. "They'd never put that on the air."

"Who says they'd put it on the air?" answered Slim. "We'd do it for them."

The three pilots discussed their new project a while longer, then settled back to watch the movie again.

Five weeks later, the Kitty Hawk steamed into Hong Kong for some badly needed R&R. The ship had been at sea for more than a month, and Sundance summarized the feelings of the men when he said, "I'm so horny that the crack of dawn could turn me on!"

Hong Kong was Slim's favorite port. He had numerous friends in the Crown Colony—all of the female variety. Knowing this, Sweetwater and Sundance decided to tag along with their friend. The three pilots were among the first men off the Hawk. They wore their finest suits, as directed by Slim.

"Where to?" asked the cab driver, as they piled into the tiny Datsun.

"Annie's," said Slim.

"Okay, boss," said the driver, as he jerked the Datsun out

of its space. The taxi careened around people and other cars as it literally roared down the middle of the street toward downtown Hong Kong.

"Hey sucker," yelled Sundance sitting in the suicide seat, "what do you think this is? The Indianapolis 500?"

The driver ignored the jibe. He was in a hurry to deliver his load and get back to the fleet landing for another.

On one boulevard with a set of trolley tracks running down its middle, the driver simply took over the trolley's tracks to avoid other traffic. This was fine with the pilots, as they were anxious to get to Annie's too. Until they had company.

Sundance's legs stiffened as he braced his arms on the dash. Bearing down on them from the opposite direction was a trolley car. At 100 yards, the taxi driver did not even appear to notice his competition. At 50 yards, he was still traveling an even 45 miles an hour, and Sundance was leaning so far back, he was almost in the rear seat with the amused Slim and Sweetwater.

"Now I know why you bastards got in the back seat," yelled Sundance.

At 30 yards, the driver attempted to get his tires out of the trolley tracks. The car started to sway back and forth. At 20 yards, Sundance wished he'd had the presence of mind to jump out of the taxi earlier. The trolley missed the left rear of the Datsun by one-half second as the driver finally managed to jerk out of the tracks.

Still stiff in his seat, Sundance turned his head to see the driver grinning from ear to ear.

"Where'd you learn to drive, you sonofabitch?" shouted Sundance. Slim and Sweetwater were roaring with laughter. The driver continued to break every traffic law on the book in order to swiftly deliver his charges.

Pulling up in front of Annie's Cleaners, as the sign said over its door, the taxi came to a smooth halt. Thankful for being delivered from the jaws of death, the pilots tipped the driver generously. . .just as the driver knew they would. The taxi then burned rubber as it negotiated a mid-street U-turn and sped away.

Entering the lounge of Annie's, Sweetwater said, "This place always reminds me of a Baskins & Robbins." Sundance followed the other two pilots to a desk at the far end of the lounge, where each of them took a plastic, numbered card off a hook. Then they sat down among four or five rows of chairs in front of a television set playing a rerun of MASH.

"Now, when your number comes up, Sundance, I want you to behave yourself. Do whatever the girl tells you to," ordered Slim.

"What do you mean?" asked Sundance.

"You'll find out," answered Slim, getting up from his chair and walking over to the desk. After speaking a few words to the matron at the desk, Slim returned to his chair.

Within a quarter of an hour, all of the pilots' numbers had been called. Sundance was called last.

"Dirty grape," said the matron, looking directly at Sundance. When Sundance didn't budge from his chair, she asked, "You dirty grape?"

Sundance looked at his plastic card which displayed the numbers *38* and realized he must be "dirty grape." He walked over to the desk and offered the plastic card to the matron. She shook her head and pointed to a short, squat woman standing in the hallway behind the desk. Sundance guessed he should give the card to the squat woman.

He did, and without a word the woman turned and headed down the hall. She looked back once to see that he was following. He was. . . at a distance. The woman wore a white halter which seemed two sizes too large and a baggy pair of white shorts.

What a pumpkin! Sundance thought. *She looks like she just walked in off the farm.* The woman's face was puffy like the rest of her. Sundance wondered what Slim had said to the matron at the desk.

Pumpkin opened a door and motioned for Sundance to enter. The pilot walked into the center of a two-room suite. There was a massage table to his left and a dresser with a mirror on his right. The second room held a low wooden enclosure and a large, tiled sunken tub.

Sundance stood there checking out his surroundings, not noticing the woman had knelt in front of him. Feeling his trousers being loosened, he looked down and realized she had already unbuckled his belt and was unzipping his trousers.

It suddenly occurred to him, *I'm going to be standing here naked from the waist down if I don't do something quick.* He hurriedly removed his jacket and vest as he stepped out of his pants. Pumpkin then stood and took his jacket and vest. These were neatly placed on a hanger and hung in the small closet. As he unbuttoned his shirt, she untied his shoes and removed them along with his socks. These were also placed in the closet. Sundance stood there in the middle of the room with his shorts still on. Pumpkin stood there with her hands on her hips, waiting. When he made no move, she smiled, walked over, and unceremoniously pulled his shorts down. He stepped out of them gingerly, wondering, *now what?*

Turning her back on him, she deposited the shorts with the rest of his clothes.

It was about this time he realized the woman spoke no English; and she in turn, realized he had never been to an Oriental massage parlor. As a matter of fact, Sundance had never been to a massage parlor at all.

Pumpkin stepped over to the naked Sundance and took his hand, leading him to the wooden enclosure. She raised its top, opened a side door, and motioned him inside. He entered and sat down, immediately developing a trapped feeling as she lowered the top and snapped the side door shut. Only his head protruded from the top of the enclosure.

Pumpkin bent over, turned a valve, and Sundance felt warm steam entering the enclosure. He leaned back and closed his eyes. Within five minutes, his body was perspiring freely and he felt thoroughly relaxed. After another five minutes, the pleasure had begun to ebb.

A few minutes later, Pumpkin got up from the bench in front of her dresser and walked over to him. She spoke, but he couldn't understand a word. Thinking she was asking if he wanted out, he shook his head up and down. Getting this response, Pumpkin walked back to her dresser and continued to apply makeup to her round face.

Sundance thought, *this is getting hot now! When's she going to let me out of here?* Having no idea how long he was supposed to stay, he assumed she'd let him out at the proper time.

After what seemed like 20 minutes (actually it was only another five minutes), Pumpkin came back and asked what appeared to be the same question.

This time he nodded his head sideways back and forth, hoping this response would release him. Pumpkin turned around again and went back to her dresser.

Sonofabitch, he thought, *she must have asked the question differently that time!* So Sundance boiled a little longer, swearing he'd never get in this predicament again. There was no way he could let himself out.

When Pumpkin came back, Sundance just gave her what he hoped was a pleading look. It worked. Pumpkin opened the doors and he slowly emerged from the boiling steam. He felt like a prune.

She then brought a low stool, set it directly in front of him, and motioned for him to sit down. Seeming like a harmless move this time, he sat down. Pumpkin placed a small bucket of soapy water beside him and began washing his neck and shoulders. Her hands moved smoothly over his still-steaming body, covering it with a thick lather. It felt mighty good.

As she moved lower with the soap, he wondered, *how much of me is she going to wash?* Crouching first on his left, her hand slid gently back and forth across his belly, then his right buttock, and then around his thigh. As Pumpkin washed his inner thigh, she answered his question. Sundance was beginning to forgive her for leaving him too long in the steambath when she stood up and moved to his other side.

His right buttock, thigh, and other extremity again received due attention. Just as he was beginning to react to this lavation, she moved down his legs to complete the bath. Sundance would remember this experience the rest of his life, yet nothing happened that he could brag about to Slim and Sweetwater.

After he was thoroughly covered with lather, Pumpkin brought a fresh bucket of water over and rinsed most of the soap from his body. She then led him to the sunken tub. Sundance stepped into the water and eased himself into heaven.

Sundance would have stayed in this pool of hot water the rest of the afternoon if Pumpkin hadn't motioned him out after one short minute. As he stood dripping wet, she brought a large towel over and proceeded to use it as he expected. Closing his eyes, he dreamt he was on a South Seas island as she gently rubbed him dry.

Pumpkin again took his hand and led him to the massage table. After some awkwardness, she managed to position him on his back. A small towel was placed across his middle. Applying a small amount of oil to her fingertips, she placed her thumbs in the center of his forehead and repeatedly moved them smoothly down the sides of his head, making small circles at the corner of his eyes. Then she applied light pressure along his eyebrows with her index fingers, once more ending at the corners of his eyes with circular motions. Next, she placed two fingers under each cheek bone, kneaded for a moment, then glided her fingers up the cheek bones to again circle the corners of his eyes. Finally, grasping his chin with two fingers of each hand, she firmly brought them up his jawbone until she reached the eyes again. Every time she reached this spot, he wished she'd stay longer.

The coup de grace came next. Ever so lightly, she brushed the tip of an index finger over his closed eyelids.

Pumpkin then climbed onto the table, kneeling above his head. She moved her oiled hands down the center of his chest, pulling firmly on the sides of his rib cage as she returned to a position under his neck. Each time she returned to his neck, she moved her fingers under his neck muscles as if she were playing a piano.

Hopping off the table, Pumpkin stood to the side and raised his left arm high. Wrapping her hands around the wrist, she moved her hands down the muscles of his arm several times. Then she did the same to his raised leg. *God, this is luxury,* mused Sundance.

After giving his right arm and leg similar treatment, Pumpkin lifted the towel off his midriff. This interrupted his state of relaxation, as he wondered what she was going to do next.

Pumpkin reached one arm under his back, and with the other gently rolled him over—replacing the towel across his buttocks.

Climbing on the table again, she straddled his buttocks, and began to move her thumbs up each side of his backbone, returning her hands firmly down the sides of his ribcage. This she continued to do for five minutes. For years afterwards, Sundance would insist that his girlfriends massage his back in this manner prior to lovemaking.

Then Pumpkin stood atop the table and slowly placed one foot on the small of his back. Initially, her weight seemed a bit uncomfortable; but when she distributed it by placing her other foot higher along his backbone, it felt fine. As she gently paced up and down his backbone, Sundance felt the joints of his backbone snap into place.

Jumping down from the massage table, Pumpkin moved her hands firmly over his back muscles for another minute.

She moved to his hands now, and lightly cracked each joint of each finger. After doing the same to his toes, she placed a large towel over his entire body. Pumpkin returned to her dresser as Sundance fell asleep.

His partners were anxiously awaiting him when he finally returned to the lounge of the massage parlor. Slim and Sweetwater regaled him with the unbelievable sexual acts they had experienced with their attendants. Sundance just listened. It was not until several days later that he began to doubt the tales he'd been told.

"Come on, you jokers. We're late," implored Slim. "My ladies are waiting."

They caught another cab. Sundance shouldered his way ahead of Slim into its backseat. It wasn't necessary though, as the driver this time drove with only a normal disregard for safety.

"Hey, Slim! What'd you say to the gal at the desk before we went into the steam rooms?" asked Sundance.

Thinking for a moment, Slim answered, "I told her to tell your attendant to leave you alone. That we were saving you for something special later." Slim refused to explain any further. Actually, Slim had asked the matron to assign her number one masseuse to Sundance.

Their destination was the Imperial Hotel, the home away from home for stewardesses from the United States. Slim had called the ticket office of Trans Pacific earlier. His favorite Hong Kong girl was their office manager. Her name was Jan.

Even though they had never met, Sundance and Sweetwater felt they knew Jan like the back of their hands. So did every other pilot in Slim's squadron.

Jan was a redhead and five foot ten, the perfect height for a high fashion model—which she was until a passion for sweets pushed her out of that profession. Jan packed 165 pounds into "the most glorious figure in the world," as Slim often extolled. She had a 32-inch waist, but the balance of her body made this waist look small. Her hips almost matched her 44-inch bust. In addition to other talents, she was a body builder. Her thighs were firm, as was the rest of her body.

One of Slim's favorite pastimes was to oil her well-toned figure at the beach. On one occasion while doing this, a wealthy Chinese walked up and offered to buy Jan for $100,000. When Slim graciously turned him down, the ante was raised to

$200,000. There were few women in the world who could fill out a bikini like Jan could.

"Wait till you meet Jan," said Slim as they exited the taxi at the foyer of the Imperial. Having heard these words a hundred times, the other two pilots thought Slim a bit weird but didn't want to say so.

Jan met them at the door of the Trans Pacific suite.

"Slim...," she shrieked, throwing her arms wide open.

The pilot stepped forward, wrapped his arms around Jan, placed one foot behind her, bent her body over backwards in the best Valentino style, and kissed her.

Sundance thought, *Christ, I hope he doesn't drop her.*

Bringing Jan upright again, Slim turned around to face his friends.

"Sweetwater, Sundance, I'd like you to meet Jan."

"Glad to see you're keeping good-looking company, honey," she said, stepping up to Sweetwater, again with her arms spread wide.

A bit surprised to be hugged the first time he met a woman, Sweetwater awkwardly raised his arms as she pressed into him.

"What's the matter, honey?" she asked. "Cat got your tongue?"

Actually, Sweetwater had lost his breath for a moment while being squeezed.

Jan turned to Sundance, who by this time was looking forward to the coming embrace. With a broadening smile on his face, he said, "Pleased to finally meet you, Jan. I've heard quite a bit about you."

"All good, I'll bet," she said as she bearhugged Sundance.

Sundance felt the breasts of this Amazon bore into his lower chest and thought, *she must be wearing an iron bra!* He returned her embrace, holding it as long as he dared.

"Ummmmm..., you must be a lover," she purred as they released each other. Stepping back, she gave him a playful pinch on his cheek.

"Come on in, fellows."

As the pilots filed past her, Sundance gave closer scrutiny to Jan's outfit. It included high heels, bright red slacks, and a layered, filmy white blouse which was loose at the waist. And cut low. Sundance was surprised to note that she didn't appear to be wearing a bra...but he wasn't sure.

Before they could sit down, Jan asked, "Didn't you guys bring anything with you? No luggage?" Without waiting for an answer, she turned and walked into one of the adjoining bedrooms. Returning quickly, she handed Sundance and Sweetwater each a swimming suit and said, "Go down to the pool till my girlfriends get here. Slim and I have some matters to work out."

Taking the hint, the two pilots changed, grabbed towels, and headed for the hotel pool. On the way, Sundance asked, "Was she wearing a bra?"

"Nope," Sweetwater replied, "Slim told me she never does. Doesn't have to. She keeps 'em up weightlifting."

"Wow!" said Sundance. "When she hugged me, I thought she'd break my ribs. She's got a pair of iron tits." From that moment on, the two pilots referred to Jan as "Iron Tits." The name stuck. Slim liked it, and when he told Jan, she liked it too.

"Hey, this is the life," exclaimed Sweetwater, lounging in a chair with a daiquiri in each hand. He was admiring a trio of Chinese beauties in silk skirts slit up their thighs who were serving drinks.

It was more than an hour before Slim and Jan joined them at the pool. Jan was wearing heels and a pink crocheted bikini. As she walked along the edge of the pool, the eyes of all the males feasted on the sight.

"My girlfriends just came in. They'll be down in a minute," she told them.

She was right. A brunette and a black-haired Eurasian arrived at their table in little more than a minute. The brunette was five foot five, with a lithe body and lovely legs. The Eurasian had almond-colored eyes and an unusually well-muscled body on a five foot nine frame.

"Meet Michelle," said Jan, referring to the brunette. "And this is Nancy. She lifts weights with me."

After playing water polo in the pool for an hour, they were all quite familiar with each other. Resting in the sun for another hour, they decided to have an early dinner. After debating several choices, they selected the dining room of the Imperial, since it was one of the few places in Hong Kong that didn't require reservations for Peking duck. More important to the men, it was nearby.

Following dinner, they discussed several possibilities for

entertainment. After relatively little debate, the girls agreed to stay at the Imperial for dancing. By the seventh dance and third round of drinks, each couple had disappeared, not to be seen again until the following morning.

The Kitty Hawk was in Hong Kong for three days and the three pilots saw the sights of the city from the windows of their Imperial Hotel suite. During the day while the girls worked, the men sat by the pool, soaking up the warm sun and more than their share of daiquiries.

The morning of the third day as the three couples shared breakfast in the living room of the suite, Slim realized he'd almost forgotten why he had called Jan this time he made Hong Kong.

"Hot damn!" he exclaimed. "We gotta hustle."

"What's the matter?" said Jan, thinking the men had to leave.

Turning to look Jan straight in the eye, he told her, "You've got to make a movie for us." After he explained what he'd planned, Jan said, "Where's the camera?"

So the men hustled up the video camera and other equipment for their tape and that morning became Hollywood producers. The final night ashore was a marathon for all concerned, and the men's appearance as they staggered up to the Officer's Brow was a far cry from that when they came down it 72 hours earlier. But they had accomplished their mission.

A week later, back in the Indian Ocean, Slim and his cohorts waited patiently for the air conditioning to go out again. They had done their reconnaissance and found that the television room technician took a coffee break each evening at 2030 hours. The round trip for the cup of coffee took slightly more than six minutes, which was perfect. The new Navy Showers show was just over five minutes in length.

On the ninth day at sea, the air conditioning broke down, and the three pilots prepared for action. After the technician stepped out of the television studio at 2030, Slim slipped in.

As the standard Navy Shower girl appeared on Channel Four, Slim turned its transmitter off, replaced the ship's cassette with the new one, turned the camera back on, glanced at the monitor to see that Jan's face was now on the screen, and quickly stepped out of the studio. He and his lookouts beat a hasty retreat back to their ready room to watch the show.

In Admiral Country, Captain Blackburn was playing

bridge with Admiral Grey and two other officers. As the Admiral had drawn the dummy hand, he was sitting back, casually watching the television screen.

When the screen expanded from Jan's face, she was in the same frontal pose with which the ship's version started. She also held a large white towel in front of her body by tucking its ends under her arms.

"Ed, I see you've got a new Navy Shower video," commented the Admiral.

Blackburn looked up a moment from his cards. "Yes, sir."

The television was turned down low, so they didn't hear the music or the words which Jan was saying. Her initial words were essentially the same as the original, but the music was not. Jan's entire performance was accompanied by the bump-and-grind of a striptease record.

After giving her introduction, Jan turned to enter the shower stall, dropping the towel to her waist, revealing that she wore no bikini top. And she was in no hurry to enter the stall, as she meticulously unwrapped a bar of soap, standing with her side to the camera, still moving to the music. The sight of her gorgeous, elongated breasts with their nicely-pointed, dark-red nipples was more than the Admiral could take sitting down.

"Hot damn," he exclaimed, standing up. This stopped the card game, as all eyes followed the direction of the Admiral's stare. None of them said a word as he walked over to the set and turned up the sound. He remained standing by the screen and was soon joined by the other officers.

That's when Jan let the towel slide off her hips, as she bent over and slowly removed each of her heels. This time there was no bikini bottom above her long shapely legs. Then she stepped into the shower. Just as the original girl, Jan turned on the shower, twirled her body in the stream of water, turned the water off, and commenced the application of soap.

At this point the camera panned to her shoulders where she started sudsing herself. As she leisurely worked her way down, the camera followed the soap. Leaning over slightly, she washed the sides of each breast, causing the suds to drip generously off her nipples. By this time, there wasn't an able-bodied seaman on the Kitty Hawk whose eyes were not riveted to Channel Four.

Straightening up, Jan sucked in her stomach and heaved her bosom into the air. Then she crisscrossed her arms around her waist and washed her midriff, undulating to the music. At this point another unclothed woman entered the shower stall and placed a short stool directly under the shower head. This was Nancy, who stepped back out of the picture as quickly as she had appeared.

Jan raised one of her supple legs and set its foot on the stool. She proceeded to wash its length with deliberate speed, not missing an inch. Bending over to reach her lower leg, she smiled at the camera and said,

"I don't like showering alone. Do you?" Blackburn and the Admiral thought they heard a muffled roar in the ship at this juncture in the tape.

Smiling broadly, the Admiral asked, "Ed, where'd you get this tape?"

"I don't know... I mean I haven't seen it before, sir."

"I don't think it came through Navy Procurement," said Grey.

Jan had washed her other leg and now turned her ample derriere to her audience. Arching her back, she circled each buttock with a hand a few times. Then she grasped a buttock in each hand and to the beat of the music moved them sideways back-and-forth, up-and-down, and round-and-round. Another muffled roar resounded through the Kitty Hawk.

Her body was thoroughly hidden by soap suds now. Jan turned to face her audience and said, "Now, watch this!"

That's when Michelle came into the picture, also wearing her birthday suit, and turned the shower on again. As Michelle moved out of the picture, Jan said, "No, dummies. I meant, watch *me*."

The Admiral chuckled.

Jan, ever so slowly, moved her body in a circle in front of the stream of water. Coming around to a frontal view, her hands modestly crossed in front of her lower body. The eyes of the men didn't mind that though, as Jan was also squeezing her bountiful breasts together with her arms. She said,

"Now, that's a Navy Shower, men."

Jan was then handed a large white towel which was again tucked into the corners of her armpits. Turning to face the camera, she said,

"Good night, men. This is Iron Tits signing off." The camera began to back away from Jan, who then raised her hand and motioned for the camera to return. When it had, she said,

"Good night to you, too, Captain Blackburn." In a whisper, she added, "Rumor has it you've been taking Hollywood Showers." Shaking her finger, Jan said, "Naughty, naughty."

The screen then returned to the regular movie. In the Admiral's quarters, everyone looked to Captain Blackburn for an explanation. In the ready rooms and elsewhere, the men were in an uproar. They couldn't believe what they'd seen.

Later that night, Blackburn decided there was only one pilot on the ship with both the nerve and type of girlfriend to make such a video tape. And then air it. Before he could take action the next day, the Ship's Engineer reported to him that 22 percent less water had been consumed the previous evening. That, combined with the fact that the Admiral had complimented him on the more realistic video message, made the Skipper decide to replace the original with Iron Tits. At least until they reached Hawaii.

Of course, the special "goodnight" to the Captain of the Kitty Hawk was omitted. Water use on the ship during the evenings continued at a lower level. Blackburn was unsure whether this was due to a change in the men's showering habits or to the greater number of men watching the new Navy Showers tape three times every night.

7

ANYTIME, KHADAFY BABY

The pilots of the ship's Air Wing snapped to attention as Captain Dan "Warpaint" Edgars strode into the fo'c'sle of the Kitty Hawk. His sharp-featured face held a serious expression — which was normal for the CAG.

"Be seated," were his first words. When the CAG had something to say to the pilots of the Hawk, it was usually over the television screens in their ready rooms, so there was considerable speculation over what his message would be.

"Gentlemen, most of you know that the Midway and her battle group will be taking over our assignment in the Indian Ocean tomorrow. When we're relieved, we're heading west instead of east."

A few ears perked up, as the Hawk was scheduled to head east toward its home port of San Diego after relief by the Midway. Concerned looks came over several of the pilots who were expecting to see their families soon. Seeing the alarm on these faces, the CAG said,

"Don't worry. We'll be headed home as soon as we complete our assignment . . . which is to fly CAP for the Nimitz as she comes through the Suez Canal. The Nimitz has been temporarily attached to the Pacific Fleet for the duration of the Iranian hostage crisis. Her nuclear power plant will enable us to keep maximum firepower on station at all times."

In the back of the fo'c'sle, Slim nudged Sweetwater in the ribs and said, "Wake up, Water. We're going sightseeing." The other pilot had nodded off, having been a duty officer the previous night.

After the chattering among the pilots subsided, the CAG continued, "Those of you who stay current on the news know Colonel Khadafy of Libya held a press conference yesterday and announced that his air force would attack the Nimitz if she entered the Canal. We were told this morning our State Department informed Libya that any Libyan aircraft which comes within 50 miles of the Nimitz will be considered hostile." You could have heard a pin drop. The CAG paused to let this sink in. Everyone in the room knew what "hostile" meant, and each of the pilots wondered if anyone would get lucky. Only a few of them had seen action over Vietnam.

"We'll be entering the Gulf of Aden in 72 hours, and from there we'll steam into the Red Sea. It will be another 2 days before we take our position at the northern end of the Red Sea. You'll be flying CAP for the Nimitz in pairs, and the standard rules of engagement will apply...with these modifications. You already know to engage any aircraft which fires upon you. You will also be directed to fire if you receive the proper code words from the Admiral. In addition, you are to destroy any unfriendly aircraft which enters within a 50-mile radius of the Nimitz. All aircraft in a formation should be considered hostile if one of its members fires. For our purposes, a formation will consist of all aircraft which are within your visual radius."

The CAG paused and asked, "Are there any questions?"

A rookie pilot raised his hand. "Will the Nimitz be putting their fighters in the air, too?"

"That's unlikely," answered the CAG. "The speed of the Nimitz as it traverses the Ditch and the likelihood of unfavorable wind conditions will probably preclude their launching of aircraft."

There were no other questions. Captain Edgars had saved the best news for last.

"CINCPAC has directed the Kitty Hawk to take up our station in the Red Sea two days prior to the Nimitz entering the Ditch. If you're lucky, you're all going to have the opportunity to engage in simulated dogfights with the Libyans. For the last ten days, the pilots of the Nimitz have been intercepting Libyan fighters consistently. While there has been no hostile action, they've been getting plenty of practice with the

Libyans. The reason we're getting on station two days early is so we can get some practice too. . . before the Nimitz enters the Ditch.''

Sweetwater was wide awake by this time.

"If you've been wondering who the stranger is sitting behind me, it's Captain Blaine 'Hook' Putnam, CAG of the Nimitz. He's joined us this morning to give you the lowdown on the tactics of the Libyan fighter pilots. Captain Putnam.''

"Good morning, gentlemen. We've been playing with these cookies since we came on station in the Med four months ago. We call the Libyan pilots the 'Colonel's Cookies' because we've eaten them up everytime they come at us.''

"First of all, the Libyans rarely fly in formations of more than two aircraft. They usually break at one-half mile when we run a head-on intercept with them. They are generally aggressive and will try to maneuver for offensive positions whenever possible. Most of them are good enough that you'll have a tough time taking pictures. The Libyan pilots have been giving the F-4s on our sister ship, the Forrestal, a run for their money. The F-4 pilots can eventually take whatever the Libyans throw up, it just takes them a bit longer to do it than it does in an F-14. You've got F-14s on the Kitty Hawk, so you've got an automatic advantage already. You may see either the MiG-21 Fishbed, MiG-23 Flogger, MiG-25 Foxbat, Su-22 Fitter, or maybe the French Mirage V. Their most competent pilots seem to be in the Foxbats and Mirage Vs.''

After answering questions for 30 minutes, Captain Putman announced he'd be available in Wardroom I for the balance of the day to discuss tactics.

As the Kitty Hawk steamed toward the Gulf of Aden, its pilots received intensive briefings on both the rules of engagement and the terrain over which they'd be flying. Around-the-clock coverage of the Nimitz was arranged by assigning the Kitty Hawk pilots into two-plane sections. Each section would fly one-and-a-half hour missions, in order to cover all sectors.

When the ship reached its station at the northern end of the Red Sea, the tension on the Kitty Hawk was matched by a high degree of anticipation that the ship would see action.

At dawn the first day the Kitty Hawk was on station,

Sundance and Slim were at 20,000 feet in clear skies, patrolling their 80-mile sector. The Pink Panther was Sundance's RIO. Both F-14s were cruising at 300 knots.

The Pink Panther's eyes widened. "I've got 2 bogies inbound."

"Where?" asked Sundance.

"Two-thirty. 35 miles. Angels 18. In excess of 450 knots."

"I'm turning into a head-on intercept," said Sundance, stepping his aircraft up to 500 knots and nosing down toward 18,000 feet.

"202. Have target at two-thirty position, coming at us at 450 + ."

"Roger." replied Slim.

"Get into your loose deuce," said Sundance.

"Wilco," said Slim. He moved his F-14 out one mile to Sundance's starboard side, climbing 4000 feet as he did so. He also moved one mile aft of Sundance, who now became his "eyeball."

Ninety seconds later, Slim heard Sundance say, "I've got a visual at twelve o'clock at 8 miles."

"Tally ho," replied Slim.

In twenty more seconds, Sundance told Slim, "It looks like two Foxbats."

Even before the MiG-25s had closed to a mile, the lead plane broke to the left and climbed fast in the vertical. The other MiG rolled right, inverted, and headed in the opposite direction.

The tail chase was on.

"Fight's on," said Sundance. "Let's go get 'em!"

Within fifteen seconds, each F-14 was at a Foxbat's six o'clock position (directly behind), at less than three-quarters of a mile.

"Christ," said Slim, "These guys must have got their wings from Dumbo the Elephant!"

Sundance's Foxbat then put his aircraft into a thirty-degree dive, accelerating to 650 knots. Eight seconds later, the Libyan pulled out of his dive, climbing straight up to the vertical.

As Sundance started to pull his nose up through the horizon, the Pink Panther behind him groaned like he was trying to lift a 500-pound rock. The G-forces compressed both men into their seats. Their helmets pressed down on their skulls. Neither man tried to talk, as anything they tried to say would have sounded like an unintelligible grunt.

Sundance's Foxbat reached the top half of his loop in an inverted position, then rolled one-hundred-eighty degrees to an upright position. The Foxbat was then headed in the opposite direction, the same as his partner.

"Nice Immelman," said Sundance, complimenting the Libyan's maneuver.

"For Christ's sake, Sundance," said the Pink Panther. "You almost blacked me out!"

"Well, we've got to show these ragheads what we're made of," replied Sundance. His F-14 was now only one-half mile behind the Foxbat.

Slim had no problem staying behind his Foxbat. It turned sharply to the left, but Slim easily stayed inside.

"Hey, Sundance," yelled Slim. "How many times have you smoked your bogey?"

"Half a dozen or so. How 'bout you?"

"Shoot, this duckhead acts like he's flying blindfolded!"

Tired of being pole-whacked, the Foxbats headed west for their home bases after another 10 minutes of acrobatics.

"Sundance, what's you posit?"

"On Mother's zero-one-zero, at 18 K."

Slim rendezvoused with Sundance and they both headed back to the ship.

The tail chase that Slim and Sundance enjoyed was one of the few with the Libyans that day.

Sweetwater and Warbucks were only sightseers the first day. In the wardroom that evening, the pilots of the Kitty Hawk who hadn't seen action hung onto the words of those who had. And most of the sightseers silently itched to be among the chosen few the next day.

It was generally agreed among the pilots who had flown intercepts with the Libyans that Khadafy's cookies weren't half of what the Nimitz CAG had beefed them up to be. A few even suspected that they had been too easy.

After the second day on station in the Red Sea, the CAG of the Kitty Hawk reported to Admiral Grey. "The sandbox was empty today, sir. No one wanted to come and play. Our E-2s reported no contacts and our fighters had no intercepts."

When Admiral Grey conferred with his counterpart on the Nimitz, he learned this was quite unusual. Even before it was announced the Nimitz would traverse the Suez Canal, the Nimitz planes had had daily contacts with Libyan fighters. These contacts were welcomed by both countries, as they sharpened the abilities of their fighter pilots.

The Nimitz was scheduled to enter the Ditch at 0600 hours the following morning, approximately one hour after dawn.

As the sun rose above the horizon, Warbucks was on the Cat and Sweetwater was positioned next behind the jet blast deflector.

Going into tension, Warbucks told his RIO, "We have. Ignition. Standby to launch."

The catapult fried as their plane accelerated down the Cat Track at 140 knots. Sweetwater followed approximately 2 minutes later. The morning was crisp and they were at their assigned sector to the west of the Nimitz within 30 minutes.

Sundance and Slim were already in their sector, to the north of the Nimitz.

At 0545 hours, Sweetwater received a message from one of the E-2s flying reconnaisance off the Kitty Hawk.

"Gunslinger 201. This is Blackhawk. Have a contact at 030, heading toward your sector."

"Roger. Looking," answered Sweetwater.

Directing his attention to the indicated radius, Reilly quickly said, "Tally ho. Got them on our scope. Looks like three bogies inbound at 20,000 feet. Let me confirm with Blackhawk."

"Blackhawk, Gunslinger 201. I have a tally on the bogies. Confirm number of aircraft."

"201. Looks like three."

"Roger. Concur," said Reilly.

"Hey Sweetwater," said Warbucks. "Let's get into a combat spread."

"Roger. Moving out," responded Sweetwater. He backed off and pushed out a mile aft and to Warbucks' starboard, with a 4,000 foot stepup. When he was in position, he called back,

"201 in position. Looks like they brought a babysitter along this time."

Yeah," said Warbucks, "they're going to need one to

change their diapers when we finish with them."

After speculating over who would end up two-on-one, their thoughts turned to a more important matter — were the Libyan pilots for real this time? The men in both F-14s knew fear, but they were also anxious to exercise the skill they'd acquired through thousands of hours of tortuous training on both the ground and in the air.

"201, I'm turning to a head-on intercept," said Warbucks. Step it up to 425."

Both F-14s were at 22,000 feet when Reilly told Sweetwater, "They appear to be climbing toward us."

"Good," said Sweetwater. "Let the bastards come."

At first Warbucks thought it was a bug on his windscreen. When he looked at the spot on the windscreen a moment later, it had expanded to a tiny cluster. "There they are. Dead ahead," he told Sweetwater.

Twelve seconds later, Warbucks added, "One's larger than the others." In a few more seconds, he said, "Looks like we have a Mirage and two Foxbats."

Sweetwater could see the Libyan formation now too. "What the hell's the Mirage doing?" The Mirage had peeled away from the Foxbats, headed in the direction of the Nimitz.

"Christ," thundered Warbucks. "He's headed for the Bird Farm!"

As Sweetwater and Warbucks riveted their attention on the departing Mirage, Reilly shouted, "Did you see those flashes under the Foxbats?"

"Those bastards have shot at us!" said Warbucks. "Let's get out of here!"

The Foxbats had each released a missile at three miles. Within 8 to 10 seconds, the missiles would close on the F-14s.

Warbucks hit Zone 5 afterburner, made a hard left turn away from his missile, pulling 6 to 7 Gs. He then dove for the deck, twisting to the right.

Sweetwater also hit Zone 5 and made a sharp turn to his right.

As Warbucks twisted to the right, his RIO announced, "The missile's clear."

Sucking in a deep breath, Warbucks said, "Sweetwater, I'm going after the babysitter."

Sweetwater got the message, but didn't reply. He was busy. Like many unseasoned pilots in a combat situation, he had reacted too soon.

Watching their missile on his radar scope, Reilly yelled, "It's tracking us!" The missile had turned with them. Being a heat-seeking missile, it had locked onto their exhaust. "Do something!" Reilly shouted.

Still in Zone 5 afterburner, Sweetwater yanked left, rolled inverted, and dove for the deck, pulling 8 Gs. Sweetwater saw a vision of a tall, beautiful woman. Then both men blacked out.

When Sweetwater came to, he wasn't sure whether he had made the "Big Muster in the Sky" or evaded the missile. The noise of his F-14 engine told him that he was still in this world. Then a bright flash blinded Sweetwater and Reilly as the missile exploded.

Oh, goddam . . . goddam, thought Sweetwater. *I've been hit.*

Reilly's voice snapped him back to reality. "That was the Foxbat!" There was debris all over the place.

The Libyan pilot was as unseasoned as Sweetwater and had made the mistake of following his shot. Sweetwater's evasive move had turned the missile toward the oncoming MiG.

The Libyan pilot never knew what hit him.

Realizing what had happened, Sweetwater pulled up to his left. This manuever had the effect of placing him two miles behind the remaining Foxbat. He didn't realize this though until Reilly looked on his scope.

"I can't believe it!" shouted Reilly. "We're right on the other Foxbat's tail."

Getting the cobwebs cleared out of his head and the circulation back to his limbs, Sweetwater's adrenalin started pumping again.

By the time Warbucks had evaded his missile, the Mirage was seven miles away. After closing half this distance, the American pilot got on the Libyan fighter's Six and squeezed his trigger.

The Sidewinder was only five inches in diameter, but it measured nine-and-a-half feet in length. Weighing in at 150 pounds, the missile ignited and dropped off the 1A station of Warbucks' left wing. For a moment it was suspended in the air beneath the F-14's wing. A split second later, the Sidewinder shot out ahead, making the F-14 appear to be standing still.

As Warbucks saw the missile shoot towards the Mirage, he snarled, "Eat it sucker."

The pilot in the Mirage must have picked up the missile on his scope, because he banked into a hard right after the Sidewinder had closed three-quarters of the distance to the Libyan aircraft.

"That's pure poetry," said Warbucks as his missile gracefully curved with the Mirage and neatly slipped up its exhaust. Even from two miles, the explosion was spectacular. When the Mirage came out of the orange fireball, it was minus its entire tail section and twisting grotesquely through the sky.

Ten seconds later Warbucks asked his RIO, "Did you see an ejection?" The answer was negative.

The remaining Foxbat had turned tail for home, with Sweetwater in hot pursuit. When the Libyan pilot saw that he couldn't outrun the F-14, he took evasive measures. At the conclusion of each of these moves, he found the American pilot even closer. Within five minutes, Sweetwater had closed to one-quarter mile.

Reilly cautioned his pilot, "Hey, Water. Don't smoke that bird from this distance. His debris will be all over us."

That's not what Sweetwater had in mind. He wanted the Libyan pilot to sit in the hot seat, just as he had a few minutes earlier. The Libyan knew his plane could neither outrun nor out-manuever the American's aircraft, and it was just a matter of time before he'd lose his ticket home.

Sweetwater stayed on the Libyan's tail for another 15 seconds before the pilot in the Foxbat outwitted him.

Both Reilly and Sweetwater saw the canopy go first, then a flash along the top of the Foxbat's fuselage as the pilot ejected from his aircraft.

"That sonofabitch!" exclaimed Sweetwater. His first thought was that now he wouldn't get credit for shooting down the Libyan. The empty Foxbat was still at 16,000 as it slowly veered toward the south. Below, the American pilot could see the heavily-populated coast of Egypt. That's when he decided to destroy the still-armed Foxbat. Backing off a mile, he reluctantly fired a missile at the abandoned fighter and rolled to his right.

When the plane exploded, Sweetwater again muttered, "That sonofabitch." He was responsible for downing two Foxbats and probably wouldn't get credit for either one.

"Want me to call it in?" asked Reilly.

"Yeah, go ahead," said Sweetwater despondently.

"Homeplate, this is Gunslinger 201."

"We have you, 201," said the Kitty Hawk.

"Have engaged two MiG-25 Foxbats. Both aircraft destroyed."

"Roger. Rendezvous with 206 and come home. Your relief is inbound. Great show."

"Roger," said Reilly. He then called Warbucks to get his position for a rendezvous. After joining with Warbucks six minutes later, they headed for home. It took a while to explain to Warbucks exactly what had happened between Sweetwater and the Foxbats.

"You get yourself into the damnest situations, Sweetwater," was all Warbucks could say.

By the time they landed their planes safely on the Hawk, the word had spread throughout the ship. Whether Sweetwater would get credit for either of the Foxbats did not matter to the crew and other pilots of the Kitty Hawk. As far as they were concerned, they had two bonafide dogfighters aboard the ship.

While Warbucks was as happy as a clam at high tide, Sweetwater took the congratulations with far less joy.

The Admiral requested their presence soon after they came aboard. After changing out of their flight suits, the pilots and their RIOs made their way to Admiral Country. They were ushered into the Admiral's wardroom as soon as they arrived. The Admiral was ecstatic — his battle group had downed three Libyan fighters. In great detail, the pilots explained how the Libyans went down. Admiral Grey then told each man, "You're each going to get a case of your favorite whisky when we get back to San Diego." He was duly thanked for his generosity. When Admiral Grey stood up, indicating the men could leave, Warbucks said,

"Sir, I'd like to say something."

"Go ahead," replied the Admiral.

"Nailing the Mirage was as easy as a turkey shoot, but I doubt if I would have had the ability to manage what my partner, Sweetwater, did. I just want you to know that, sir."

"What are you trying to tell me?" demanded the Admiral.

Sweetwater wished Warbucks had kept his mouth shut. The younger pilot wanted to forget the whole thing. Having a chance to shoot down a hostile aircraft, in his opinion, he had blown it. Twice.

Warbucks answered the Admiral hesitantly. "Well, sir. If I get credit for downing a Libyan aircraft, I don't see why Sweetwater shouldn't, too."

"In the opinion of the world," said the Admiral, turning to Sweetwater, "you downed two Libyan fighters who deserved everything they got. That happens to be my opinion too. However, I do not wish to be countermanded by higher authority. Based on what you've both told me, I'm going to send a report to CINCPAC with my recommendations."

"Thank you, sir," said Warbucks.

The Admiral shook everyone's hands, and the four men slowly made their way through the crowded passageways back to their ready rooms. Warbucks and Sweetwater shook so many hands in the next few hours that their hands became sore. As had happened before, Reilly did most of the explaining to the members of the crew concerning the exploits of his pilot.

Sweetwater didn't perk up until he, Warbucks, and their RIOs were again summoned to the Admiral's stateroom.

When they had assembled, the four of them were taken before the Admiral who immediately gave them the news.

"We've just received instructions to have the four of you in Naples tomorrow morning. You're going to appear at a press conference to explain to the world what happened today. I'm also giving you 48 hours liberty after the press conference. You leave in three hours. Carry on."

Just before sunset, the four men were helicoptered off the Kitty Hawk and flown to an airbase in Egypt, from where they were flown directly to the U.S. Naval base in Naples, Italy.

At ten o'clock the next morning, the four Naval officers were led into a large auditorium. It was packed, not only with members of the press from more than 60 nations, but with a standing-room-only crowd of Naval personnel. No one wanted to miss this show.

Most of the questions were directed to the pilots of the F-14s. These men looked resplendent in their dress whites. Sweetwater's mood had improved noticeably.

After both pilots gave a short review of their dogfights, they began fielding questions. Some of the questions from the Third World press members were almost as hostile as the Libyan fighters had been. A Syrian newspaperman asked,

"Why did none of the brave pilots from Libya survive the encounter with you Americans? Did you kill them as they parachuted to safety?"

Warbucks fielded this question. "I would remind you that we did not attack the Libyan fighter aircraft first. Two MiGs fired on us initially hoping to sneak the Mirage through our sector to attack the USS Nimitz. The Libyan pilots would be alive and well today if they had not attacked us." There was scattered applause to his answer.

While Warbucks had been answering this question, a State Department officer had been whispering something into Sweetwater's ear. When the applause ended, Sweetwater added,

"We've just been authorized to reveal that the USS Forrestal did recover one of the Libyan pilots yesterday. He will be returned to Libya within 30 days."

This time there was applause even among members of the Third World Press. The next question was asked by an Associated Press reporter,

"Lieutenant Sullivan, there's been some discussion we understand in Navy circles whether you will be given credit for downing either of the Foxbats. How do you feel about this?"

"As Casey Stengel would have said, 'I was robbed.' " When the laughter died down, he continued, "While it's a fact that the first Foxbat went down due to its pilot's stupidity, the second Foxbat bit the dust due to superior American firepower, and I'd like to think manpower too." He couldn't say these words without igniting the Americans in the audience into enthusiastic applause, particularly from the hundreds of Naval personnel in back.

Sweetwater had more to say when it quieted down. "To tell you the truth, when I had the second Foxbat in my sights, I hesitated to pull the trigger because the fight was essentially over. Even though the Libyan pilot had just tried to kill my wingman and his RIO, he never had a chance at succeeding. His was a suicide mission. Actually, I'm glad now that he chose to eject before I destroyed his aircraft. I'd rather not receive credit for downing a hostile aircraft than take the life of a defenseless man."

After this statement, the crowd began applauding, with some restraint at first. Then a few persons stood, continuing to applaud. They were joined by others, until every man and woman in the auditorium was standing and expressing their approval of the American for sparing the life of the Libyan pilot.

This was somewhat embarrassing to the young American particularly in view of what he had to say next. As the audience was seating itself, he told them,

"Fortunately for me, it has turned out that I didn't make that choice. Just before this press conference began, I was notified that I would receive credit for downing one of the Libyan fighters." This time the applause was wild as all the Navy people in the auditorium jumped to their feet again to share in Sweetwater's good news.

There were scattered questions after that. These were fielded easily and when the State Department officer announced the press conference was over, Warbucks stood and asked,

"May I make a short statement?"

"Of course," said the man from the State Department.

Warbucks slowly scanned the audience, looking for the Syrian newspaperman. When he had locked his eyes on this hostile questioner, he said,

"The four of us up here have a special message. We hope it gets to where it can do the most good:
ANYTIME, KHADAFY BABY."
The audience exploded again.

8

SWEETWATER'S DREAM

After the tumult of the press conference, Warbucks and Sweetwater headed for Rome. They were to be center attractions at a reception at the American embassy. Warbucks was particularly anxious to reach Rome, as the Navy had flown his wife to Rome to share in her husband's triumph. Actually, she had been added as a nice afterthought to the passenger list of a VIP Navy aircraft carrying several high-ranking officers to Naples for the celebration/press conference and embassy reception.

Warbucks wasn't saying much and neither was Sweetwater as their limousine entered the outskirts of Rome. The older man had not seen his wife in four months. He planned to go through the receiving line and then out the first open door with Willie Ann.

"Hey, Sweet," he said, "I'm not going to stay long at the embassy. Think you can hold our end up?"

"Where you going?" Sweetwater asked.

"To the first hotel I can find, dumbbell."

"Oh, yeah," said Sweetwater, remembering Willie Ann. "You're a lucky sonofabitch."

"I keep telling you—find yourself a good woman. Get your family started. If you don't have kids soon, you're going to be over 50 when your kids are teenagers."

Sweetwater had heard this lecture many times from Warbucks. It made more sense this time. Before Warbucks spoke, the younger pilot had been thinking about the dogfight with the Foxbats. It had occurred to him the dogfight might have ended other than it did.

"Good women are few and far between," said Sweetwater.

"Maybe so, but you're not even looking."

"Who has to look? I let women do the looking," said Sweetwater lightly.

"Yeah, and look what you get. When you only take what comes looking, all you're getting are the ones looking for a meal ticket."

"Well, they haven't suckered me yet," said Sweetwater.

"That's right," said Warbucks, "and all the good women are going to someone else."

That ended their conversation. Warbucks returned to thoughts of Willie Ann, and Sweetwater thought about what the other pilot had said. *Maybe Warbucks is right,* thought Sweetwater. *I'm getting a few gray hairs and the booze seems to take longer to wear off.*

The Naval Attache, Captain Livingston, met them at the door of the Embassy. He offered Warbucks the vehicle to pick up his wife at her hotel and suggested that Sweetwater take a rest before the reception started in two hours. Warbucks left for his wife and Sweetwater was guided to a private suite in the Embassy.

Later at the reception, Sweetwater mixed with the guests and didn't notice when Warbucks and Willie Ann slipped out. The ballroom of the Embassy was full of Navy officers who were all senior to Sweetwater and formally-dressed diplomats with their over-dressed wives.

After relating the shootout with the Libyans for the tenth time, Sweetwater was considering the same route Warbucks had taken. Most of those interested in his story were the women, and Sweetwater had begun to change the story for his own entertainment.

One of the women asked how far away he was from the Libyan fighter when he shot it down. To this he answered, "I put my nose about 30 feet behind his tail and fired. You can't miss when you're that close."

Off his left shoulder, he heard, "Are you one of the pilots that shot the Libyans down or did the Navy send a substitute?"

The question unsettled him for a moment, and Sweetwater wished he'd made his exit earlier. Turning to see his antagonist, he was surprised to see someone his own age.

She said, "You couldn't have fired that close. The explosion when your rocket hit the Libyan aircraft would have engulfed yours, too."

Sweetwater felt like he'd been caught with his pants down.

And he had. All he could think to say was, "What makes you say that?"

"You haven't answered my question yet, Lieutenant. Are you for real or just a substitute?"

Sweetwater debated saying that he was just a "substitute" as she suggested. In enough trouble already, he said, "Okay, you nailed me. What are you? A pilot?" After admitting he had lied, the crowd around him drifted away. The two of them stood there, staring at each other.

"No," she said, smiling, "just a stewardess."

"You may not believe this either, but thanks for helping me get rid of the audience."

"You're welcome."

"How'd you get in here?" Before she could answer, he asked another question. "What's your name?"

"Which question do you want answered first?"

"I didn't mean to ask you the first one. It's just that everyone else in this room is double my age and it surprised me to see someone my own age."

"How old do you think I *am*?" she asked. She thought he looked at least three or four years older than she.

Cornered again, Sweetwater guessed several years younger than he knew she was, "You look maybe 22, possibly 23."

"Thanks, Lieutenant. I'm 28. How old are you?"

"Thirty-two."

While not beautiful, she was pretty—a distinction that women are more apt to discern than men. To Sweetwater she was lovely, and therefore a challenge. So far he was losing in the verbal exchange, which only made him more determined.

"Have you told me your name yet?" he asked, somewhat confused.

"No. It's Ginny. What's your name?"

"Sweetwater," he said.

"I mean your *real* name."

Realizing what she meant, he said, "Matt."

Sweetwater couldn't remember when he had such difficulty simply learning what a girl's name was. Usually, they gushed their name out when he asked. And women usually acted a bit uncomfortable when first introduced to him. Now, he felt like the nervous one.

They stood there, neither knowing what to say next. Ginny decided to wait for him to speak. She was amusing herself and enjoyed watching him fidgit.

"You haven't told me how you got in here yet, either." he finally said.

"My father's the vice-consul in Naples. He suggested that I might not be bored with the reception."

"Are you?" he asked.

"Yes, as a matter of fact."

"So am I. Let's get out of here," said Sweetwater.

"You can't leave. You're the star of the show."

"You just shot my star down, Ginny."

"Who says I *want* to go with you?"

"I do," he answered, taking her hand and pulling her out of the ballroom.

Not willing to cause a scene in the ballroom, Ginny waited until they reached the door of the Embassy before saying, "Wait a minute, buster!" As she said this, she jerked him to a halt.

For a moment they both leaned in opposite directions. He looked at her with feigned disappointment.

She said, "I want to say goodbye to someone."

"Who?" he asked.

"My father."

He relaxed his grip on her hand and followed a few paces behind until she again entered the ballroom. He saw her approach a tall, dark-haired man who bore some resemblance to the tall, black-haired Ginny. She spoke a few words in her father's ear, bussed his cheek, and walked back in Sweetwater's direction. Her father glanced at Sweetwater without smiling.

The couple stepped out of the Embassy. Sweetwater searched a few minutes before finding the Navy sedan that had brought him to Rome. As the driver pulled out of the compound, Sweetwater asked Ginny, "Where do you want to go?"

"Have you been to Rome before?" she countered.

"No."

"Take us to the Spanish Steps," she directed the driver.

"What are the Spanish Steps?" asked Sweetwater.

After hearing a brief description, Sweetwater said, "Let's go somewhere else."

"Well, how about the Catacombs?" asked Ginny.

"What's that?"

Again she described this attraction, and again Sweetwater asked for another choice. Tiring of this game, Ginny asked, "Okay, where'd you like to go?"

"I'm thirsty," he said quickly. "How about a bar?"

"I don't go in *bars*," she told him.

Thinking for a moment, Sweetwater said, "Fine. How about a restaurant then."

They stopped at the next restaurant they came to. Releasing the driver, they sat at a sidewalk table. After he ordered a scotch and water, she asked, "Aren't you going to have anything to eat?"

"No. Go ahead and order some food, though...if you're hungry," said Sweetwater. Ginny ordered a glass of chianti.

"Who do you fly with?" he asked.

"Pan Am."

"How long?"

"Three years," she answered.

"Do you like it?"

"The benefits are nice."

"What benefits?" Sweetwater asked.

"I like to travel. I like to see new places."

This time it was Sweetwater who was asking the dumb questions. Ginny insisted on ordering some food before having another drink, so Sweetwater let her order their meal. While she ate heartily, he spent most of the time asking more questions.

By the time Ginny finished her dinner, Sweetwater knew where she'd graduated—*UCLA*, her major—*political science*, where her hometown was—*Malibu*, what her hobbies were—*tennis and mountain hiking,* and whether she enjoyed cooking —*sometimes*. His last question was, "Do you have a boyfriend?"

"That's none of your business," she responded.

He assumed she had no boyfriend and simply didn't want to admit it. Actually Ginny had several boyfriends, one with whom she was quite serious.

"Hey, I'm just trying to be friendly. Don't get mad about a question like that," Sweetwater said. He swiftly changed the subject. "Do you like to dance?"

"Sometimes," she answered.

The streetlights of Rome had come on by now and Sweetwater wanted to 'warm his woman up.'

"Okay, let's go dancing," he said.

"What if I'm already engaged tonight?" she asked.

"Get unengaged."

"You don't have a lot of class, do you?" Ginny said.

"Got all I need," he said with a big grin.

Ginny thought about commenting on that, but decided not to.

"You're fortunate, Lieutenant. I don't happen to have a previous engagement tonight."

"Matt, baby, Matt," he said.

"I prefer Ginny, if you don't mind," she responded.

"Where do you dance in this town?"

"What kind of dancing do you like?" she asked.

He began to say quiet dancing to slow music, but thought better. He was beginning to realize Ginny was a smart cookie and would easily see through a comment like that. So he said, "All kinds. What kind do you like?"

Mildly surprised to be consulted, she also said, "All kinds."

"Okay. Let's find some American music," he said.

They found a place to dance. Italian words to American music, and Sweetwater learned that Ginny was an excellent dancer. He didn't talk much anymore, and he also didn't let go of her hand. They danced the slow dances and the first time he tried to pull her body into his, she smiled and rested her left elbow on his chest.

He got the point, but wasn't discouraged. He thought, *she's tough, but I've seen tougher.*

As they continued to dance and drink, Ginny did warm up a bit. During one of the slow dances, she finally rested her head on his shoulder.

When Ginny placed her head on his shoulder a second time, he thought, *she loves me.* He considered pressing her body again to his, but decided to let the music do this naturally. Her breasts were small for a woman of five foot eight, however he noted their firmness as the music occasionally brought the two dancers together.

When they sat down, he asked, "Are you getting tired?"

Ginny thought, *so now you want to go to bed, do you?* She told him, "No, I'm not tired. Are you?"

"Yeah. It's been a long day."

"Okay," she said, "let's go."

"Where?"

"Back to my hotel."

Sweetwater couldn't believe his luck.

They walked 12 blocks before finding a taxi, and arrived at her hotel shortly before 11 p.m. Sweetwater said relatively little on the way to her room.

Arriving at her door, she handed him the key. He took it, unlocked the door, and prepared to enter.

Ginny stood outside her door, with her hand out, palm up. Sweetwater handed her the key.

She took a step toward Sweetwater, placed a hand on his shoulder, tapped his lips with hers, and said, "Thanks, Matt. I had a nice time." Then she stepped into her room and closed the door.

For a second Sweetwater stood there, thinking, *hey, what the hell's going on?* He rapped on her door and called out her name.

She opened the door almost immediately. With a blank expression on her face, she asked, "What do you want?"

"Aren't you even going to offer me a drink?"

"Wait a minute," she responded. The door closed again. After waiting less than a minute, Sweetwater heard her call out, "Be right with you."

"That's more like it," he said to himself, thinking she must be changing into a nightgown.

When the door opened, Ginny handed him a glass of water, said "Goodnight," and closed her door.

He stared at the glass in his hand. *This is a drink?* Then he shouted through the door, "Hey, what is this?"

There was no answer this time. So he stood there, feeling like a fool. Finally, he knocked lightly on her door.

After a minute, Ginny opened the door. This time she had changed into a robe, which was drawn tightly across her neck.

"Can I see you tomorrow?" he pleaded.

"I'm leaving tomorrow."

"What time?" he asked.

The expression on his face resembled that of a small boy whose feelings had been hurt, though Ginny was unsure whether to believe what she saw.

"In the evening," she answered.

"Have breakfast with me," he blurted out.

She stared at him for a moment, trying to understand the motive of this new man in her life. To Ginny, he had simply been an amusing afternoon and evening. From the look in his eyes, she sensed his feelings toward her were not as casual.

"Okay. What time?" she said.

"How about six o'clock?"

"You've got to be kidding," she said.

"Okay, seven."

"You're crazy, Lieutenant."

"All carrier pilots are crazy."

"Okay, call me at seven. You can wake me up then, and we'll talk about breakfast," Ginny said.

"That's a deal," said Sweetwater. Her hand held the side of the door. Cupping her hand in his, he said, "Goodnight, Ginny. I love you."

Saying this, he turned abruptly and headed for the elevtor. He knew that she would be less likely to believe his words if he remained standing by her door.

It did surprise Ginny, and her perplexed look followed him down the hall. This had never happened before. Men usually professed their affection in hopes of an immediate return.

She murmured, "Good night." He didn't hear her. Sweetwater was already planning Ginny's breakfast. As he entered the elevator, he realized Ginny was the woman he had seen in his vision during the dogfight.

At precisely seven a.m., her phone rang. She said, "Hello."

"Good morning, beautiful!" Sweetwater half-shouted. "Are you hungry this morning?"

"A little bit," was her answer.

"Fine," he said and hung up.

"What the...?" exclaimed Ginny. Rising from her bed, she splashed some water on her face. As she finished brushing her hair, there was a sharp knock on her door.

Throwing a robe around her shoulders, Ginny thought, *I'm not ready yet. He can just cool his heels in the lobby for a half-hour until I am.*

Opening the door, she stepped back in surprise. Before she could say anything, three colorfully-dressed musicians began singing. One played a violin and the other two strummed guitars. They sang a short love song, the words of which neither she nor Sweetwater understood. But they sang it so tenderly that Ginny forgot her anger. As the musicians finished, they bowed low and stepped aside to reveal four food carts.

Behind each cart stood an elegantly-dressed steward. Having previous orders, the first steward wheeled his cart into her room. Ginny half-stepped aside as he carefully manuevered his cart around the surprised woman. On its tray was a giant array of flowers. Tall, yellow daffodils dominated the center and were ringed by white and lavender irises, which in turn were surrounded by red carnations. The flowers had been a last-minute idea the previous night, after Sweetwater had arranged a lavish breakfast through the hotel's dining room. The only flowers available at that hour were those off the dining room tables. With some fast-talking, he had bought them all.

The second steward then wheeled his cart in. It contained every conceivable fruit that the country of Italy could offer. The fruit was stacked two feet high and impressively arranged.

The third steward winked at the open-eyed Ginny and asked, "Where would Madam take breakfast this morning?" She stared at him blankly, still clutching her robe.

Sweetwater, nattily dressed in white trousers and a white silk shirt, stood at the side of the door and said, "Over there on the balcony."

As the fourth steward prepared to enter, Sweetwater asked, "May I have breakfast with you, or would you like me to eat out here in the hall?"

She gazed at him, turned to look again at the three trays now in her room, and turned back to Sweetwater.

Throwing her arms around him, she cried out, "You super jerk!" and kissed him.

The four stewards all cheered and clapped their hands. After they filed out, Sweetwater slowly removed Ginny's arms from around his shoulders, took her hand, and led her onto the balcony.

Seating her, he sat opposite and said, "Ginny, you're just as lovely without makeup."

"You told me you were crazy last night," she said. "Now I believe you."

"Eat your food," he told her. "We've got a big day ahead of us."

As she ate, she thought, *maybe this guy does love me. Either that or he's rich.* After they finished their breakfasts, Ginny sent him down to the lobby while she dressed. She kept him waiting less than twenty minutes, which is all he required to hire a car and driver.

They spent the morning visiting the Trevi Fountain, the Spanish Steps, the Forum and the Colosseum. As Ginny explained the backgrounds of these sights, Sweetwater asked more questions of her background. Finally realizing he had little interest in the sights of Rome, she asked, "Matt, would you like to stop at a restaurant?"

"Sure," he said. "Are you hungry again?"

"No, but you're not listening to me and I've seen these places already. Why don't we get off our feet and have a cool drink?"

Ginny directed the driver to a restaurant which overlooked St. Peters and the rest of Rome. Tiring of answering so many questions, Ginny began asking questions of Sweetwater's past. She learned that his father was an obstetrician and moved from New York City to Dexter, Maine shortly after Matt was born. Matt's childhood in Dexter, whose population was less then 3,000, was full of the rich experiences only a small town can offer. Matt related the time he hitched a train ride at the age of ten. Another boy had encouraged him, then failed to hop on, too. His father had learned of his train ride from the local stationmaster. When Matt arrived home three hours after supper, his father grabbed him by the collar, and on the way upstairs the boy missed all 13 steps. Ginny also learned how the father and son had trapped black bears which preyed on the local cattle and sheep.

When Ginny told him she had to get back to the Metropole, both were reluctant to enter their car. They were only a block from her hotel when Sweetwater yelled to the driver, "Stop the car!" He jumped out, pulling Ginny with him.

"What are you up to now?" Ginny asked.

Still pulling her, he said, "I saw a store I want to go into." They entered a jewelry store and Sweetwater immediately told a clerk, "Show me your diamond rings." Sweetwater swiftly selected the largest diamond he could afford.

Ginny asked, knowing the answer, "Who are you buying the ring for?"

"For you," he said.

"Why are you buying *me* a ring?"

"I want you to marry me." To Sweetwater this was an adequate explanation. To Ginny it was preposterous. She told him, "You haven't even asked me *if I want to marry you.*"

By this time the clerk who had sold the ring was developing a worried look on his face. Other customers in the jewelry store were also turning to watch the two Americans.

"Okay, will you marry me?" he asked.

She thought, *I've had more romantic invitations to go to a movie!* She responded, "How can I marry you? I hardly know you."

Sweetwater had never before asked a woman to marry him and couldn't understand Ginny's reticence. It never occurred to him that any woman he asked to marry would not automatically accept. And gratefully at that.

"Ginny, I told you last night that I love you. And I meant it. Now, will you marry me?"

"Do you think *I love you?*" Ginny asked.

He couldn't answer this question. Sweetwater stood there in the middle of the store, holding the diamond ring, until she said, "I've got to get back to the hotel. I'm going to miss the pickup bus." With that she hurried out of the store, with the dumbfounded pilot following.

"Do you like me, Ginny?"

"Sure I like you," she said.

"That's great! Then you'll learn to love me. I'm one helluva guy!"

Getting exasperated, he said, "Just take the ring then. We'll iron out the details later."

"Do you do this to all the girls you meet?" she asked, immediately regretting her words.

Grabbing her arm, he swung her around. Ginny lost her balance and would have fallen if he hadn't grabbed her with his other arm, too.

"Ginny, I've never asked another woman in the world to marry me. I've never loved another woman. I love you. Can't you understand?"

"You're hurting my arm."

He released her. She remained standing where he had stopped her. The sadness in her eyes immediately softened the impulsive man.

"I need some time," she said. "Time to think about all this."

"I'm sorry, Ginny. This is all new to me, too. I don't know what to do."

"I've still got to get to my plane," Ginny said.

"Don't worry. I'll get you there."

They ran to her hotel, but the Pan American pick-up bus had just left. "Get a taxi," she said. "I'll be down in five minutes."

He called a taxi to the curb and anxiously awaited her. When five minutes were up, he started to worry that she might be trying to skip out on him. After another three minutes he was sure she had and began to curse himself for being too forceful.

Having turned his back to the foyer of the hotel, he didn't notice Ginny until she rushed by his side.

"Let's go, Matt." After they'd jumped into the cab, she explained, "I had to call Pan Am to tell them I'd be late." She traveled light, having only a clothing bag and a large shoulder bag. Ginny said nothing, hoping that Sweetwater had finally calmed down.

"Where are you flying to?" he asked.

"New York."

"Then where?"

"Back here."

"How long are you flying that route?"

"I just started it. Probably another two weeks."

"Great. Can you meet me in Singapore in three weeks?"

She looked at him questioningly.

"My ship comes into Singapore for a port call in three weeks. We'll be there for three days. You can get to know me then."

Thinking she was making a mistake, but not wishing to encourage another confrontation, she said, "I'll try. No promises though. If I can get a trip trade, I'll meet you."

He gave her a hug with one arm. He wanted to kiss her, too, but something told him not to...yet. They spent the balance of the ride working out details of their meeting. He suggested the Raffles Hotel in Singapore, this being where the younger pilots of the Kitty Hawk usually stayed.

"You'll have a chance to meet some of my friends, too," he told her.

"Are they all like you?" she asked.

"Sure, they're all great guys. They're real characters."

"That's what I was afraid of," Ginny said, smiling.

Hesitant to broach the subject of the ring again, Sweetwater looked for a place to stash it on her clothing or in her luggage. The shoulder bag was on the seat between them. As Ginny looked out her window, he tucked the ring box in a pocket of the shoulder bag.

Pulling up at the Pan American terminal, Ginny looked at her watch and said, "I'm six minutes late to report already. Can you take care of the taxi?"

Sweetwater pulled out a wad of lira and threw half of it over the front seat, as he followed Ginny out of the taxi.

As they ran through the terminal, he said, "Ginny if you just give me a chance, you'll see that I'm not so bad."

"I don't think you're bad, Matt. I don't even know whether you're good or bad."

When they reached the immigration barrier, she turned to him. "You're something else, you know. At least, you never bore me."

"Now you're talking, Ginny. I promise never to bore you."

With that, he enveloped her with his arms and kissed her brusquely on the lips. She returned the kiss, then remembered she was late, and pushed away.

"I'm sorry. I have to go."

"I love you, Ginny. Don't forget that."

As she ran up the ramp, Sweetwater called out, "The ring's in your shoulder bag."

She turned a distressed face for a moment, glanced back at him, then continued to her plane.

9

SINGAPORE FLING

The Kitty Hawk turned east, on her way home to San Diego. Leaving the Indian Ocean, she entered the strategic Strait of Malacca. The eastern end of the Strait of Malacca opens to the South China Sea and is commanded by a diamond-shaped island, 27 miles from east to west and 14 miles from north to south.

The city which dominates this island is called "Lion City" by the Malays...or in their own language, Singapore. Within the confines of this city live three million people, in one of the cleanest ports of the Orient. The Kitty Hawk would stay in Singapore for three days, to replenish her supplies and rejuvenate her men.

As the Kitty Hawk entered its harbor shortly after dawn, every man aboard was looking forward to the pleasures of this city-state. Most of them would head for the kaleidoscope of colors and amusements offered by its Chinatown.

The younger pilots of the carrier headed for the legendary Raffles Hotel, where they usually reserved a block of rooms. Sweetwater was anxious to see Ginny, of course. He always thought it would take an intelligent woman to get him married; and now that he'd found one, he wanted to show off his prize.

Ginny had arrived the day before and, as requested, had booked a room at the Raffles. When Sweetwater and his friends arrived she was sunning herself at the Palm Court alongside its pool. She had left a note at the desk directing Sweetwater to the pool.

When Sweetwater received the note, he insisted that Slim

and Sundance immediately accompany him to meet Ginny. Entering the Palm Court, they were not disappointed.

When Sweetwater picked Ginny out of the crowd of sunglassed beauties sunning on lounge chairs, he called her name out, "Hey, Ginny!"

The slightly embarrassed Ginny was half-standing by the time the three pilots reached her. Sundance let out a wolf whistle, elevating Ginny to a fully-embarrassed state.

Sweetwater swept her into his arms, bearhugging her, and kissed her boldly. The surprised woman wondered for a moment how Sweetwater assumed such familiarity, then realized it was a show for his pilot friends.

Damn, she looks good, thought Sweetwater. Ginny wore a one-piece, skin-colored bathing suit—which was mostly string. This was the first time Sweetwater had an opportunity to view her figure, and he was proud. Her model-thin waist nicely accented the slim hips and long tanned legs of her five foot eight frame.

Her well-oiled skin glistened in the sun. The pert breasts were dominated by prominent nipples, and her long black hair was pulled back in a ponytail.

Releasing Ginny, but keeping an arm around her waist, he announced, "Sundance, Slim, I'd like you to meet the California Goddess."

"Do you have any sisters?" said Sundance.

Even Slim, who preferred his women solid, was surprised at Sweetwater's classy find. He said, "Sweetwater, she's too good for you. Why don't you let me take over from here?"

Sweetwater was a bit embarrassed too, expecting his running mates to exhibit better manners.

"Pleased to meet you both," said Ginny. "You're just like Matt described."

Both the pilots looked to Sweetwater, who said, "I told her you were both a couple of jerks."

Noting the sharp edge to this comment, Ginny said, "No, he didn't. He told me you were great guys...that you were real characters. Why don't you join Sweetwater and me here at the pool? The water's just right."

"Good idea," said Slim. "We'll be right back." With that, the two pilots left. When they had gone, Ginny noticed Sweetwater staring at her left hand.

"Why are you staring at my hand?"

Looking her straight in the eye, he asked, "Where's your ring?"

"Do we have to start on that again?" she asked, frowning.

"I...I was just hoping...oh, forget it."

"Matt, we've got a lot of talking to do. I do like you. But for heaven's sake, we've both got to know each other better before making any commitments. Why don't you get changed? We'll have lunch here at the pool, and then we'll decide what to do the rest of the day. What room are you in?"

He was hesitant to reveal he didn't have a room yet. Sundance and Slim thought he was staying with Ginny. Sweetwater thought this too, but he was beginning to have a few doubts.

"I haven't checked in yet," he finally told her.

He went to the hotel's desk and booked a room just in case.

By the time he arrived back at the pool in his swimming trunks, Sundance and Slim were already getting better acquainted with Ginny. As Sweetwater pulled a lounge chair up, Ginny suggested, "Let's have lunch. I'm famished."

Lunch was ordered by all and the men ordered their first drinks. Their second round of drinks was ordered before lunch was served. Midway through his meal, Sundance suddenly decided to take a swim—about 15 seconds after a Malayasian beauty began swimming laps. Sundance had managed an introduction within a minute and did not rejoin the group to finish his lunch.

After eating, Slim decided to take a nap and pulled his chair into the shade.

Having spent half the day in the sun, Ginny asked Sweetwater, "Why don't we take in some of the sights this afternoon? I'd like to see the House of Jade. What would you like to see?"

Sweetwater responded, "I'd just like to sit here and look at you."

"Thank you, but you've been doing that for the last two hours."

"You're getting lovelier by the minute," he said.

"If you want to keep me in the sun longer, I'm going to have to put on more sunscreen."

Reaching for the sunscreen container, he said, "Allow me. Why don't you stretch out on your towel and I'll give you a Sweetwater Special."

Ginny cocked her head to one side. "What's your Special?"

"It's a surprise," he replied. "Lay down and find out."

She surprised him by laying down.

"Face up first," he ordered.

After placing a rolled towel under her head, he told her, "Close your eyes and start dreaming."

Sweetwater tried to remember what the masseuse had done at Annie's Cleaners in Hong Kong. And he did a creditable job. After finishing her face, he began moving the fingertips of both hands down the center of her chest, spreading them to her hips when he reached the waist, then pulling back along the sides of her body.

When he paused to straighten his back, Ginny murmured, "Don't stop."

Encouraged for the first time since he met Ginny, he began caressing her body longer in those areas he felt she would enjoy. When his back began to ache again, he moved to her side, enveloped her upright arm at the wrist and moved his hands down to her shoulder. After doing this a minute, he laid her arm on his leg and began making light circles on her belly with one hand. This brought a smile to her lips.

Moving himself down to Ginny's knees, he raised her right leg, resting its foot on his shoulder. Oiling his hands well, he clasped her ankle and moved his hands slowly down the leg to her mid-thigh. He had never felt such lovely legs before in his life. He would have offered to shave them, but they were already satin smooth.

He paused at her feet to massage each toe and her soles, before moving around her body to the other leg and arm. When he had finished them, he said, "Okay, roll over."

Ginny didn't respond. Her eyes were still closed.

Bending over, he gently kissed her and whispered, "Roll over, Sleeping Beauty."

She opened her eyes, puckered her lips, and closed her eyes again. He leaned over to kiss Ginny again and was gratified when her arm enveloped his head to hold the kiss longer.

Ginny was thanking him for the massage; but as most men would, Sweetwater took it to mean far more than it did. Ginny rolled over, and he untied the strings of her suit.

When her back was bare, he kneeled on both legs, straddling her just below the hips. Placing a thumb along each side of her backbone, he pushed firmly along this ridge to the top of her neck, spread his hands to her shoulders, then pulled down along her ribcage. The third time he did this, she said, "You can stop that in a year."

After ten more minutes of this, Sweetwater laid down next to Ginny and asked, "Are you ready to see the sights of Singapore now?" He didn't get the response he hoped for.

"Sure. Twenty laps in the pool and you're on," said Ginny, pulling herself up to a sitting position. Seeing the disappointment on Sweetwater's face, she briefly debated the other alternative up in her room. She thought, *not yet.*

As they strolled to the pool, she said, "That felt fabulous, Matt. You're the first man to ever do that to me."

"You're the first woman I've ever done that to," he responded.

"Come on. As expert as you are, do you expect me to believe that?"

"Believe it or not. You're the first," he repeated. He was telling the truth, but she didn't believe him.

"Can you walk on water, too?" Ginny said as she pushed him into the pool. She dove in before he surfaced.

When Sweetwater's head popped out of the water, he thought Ginny had disappeared until she surfaced at the far end of the pool. He swam to her and they did laps until she was tired.

Returning to their chairs, Sweetwater awoke Slim by flicking cold water over his prone body.

"Better get up, Slim," said Sweetwater. "The girls will all be taken soon."

Slim grunted, turned over on his back, placed the edge of his towel over his eyes, and went back to sleep. Sundance was nowhere in sight.

"Let's get dressed and sightsee a bit," asked Ginny.

Wanting to make a favorable impression this time, Sweetwater didn't protest. After dressing in separate rooms, they caught a cab and Ginny directed its driver to the House of Jade. Walking through its halls of priceless treasure, Sweetwater tried to act enthusiastic.

The balance of the afternoon was spent visiting the island's Botanical Gardens. Strolling through the open rows of flowers and manicured bushes, Ginny took his hand for the first time. He squeezed her hand a moment, but didn't receive a return signal.

Their talk was mostly of her interests, which were myriad. When Ginny asked the pilot what his hobbies were, Sweetwater repeated a few of his childhood interests. It occurred to him that he didn't have any hobbies, at least none which he could admit to her.

After dinner, the desk at the Raffles recommended the lounge of the Sheraton for American music, which was where they headed.

This time he carefully held her half an arm's length away as the combo played slow dances. When she placed her head on his shoulder, he didn't try to press her body closer. She drank Perrier water, while he ordered one scotch and water after another.

They stayed at the lounge until it closed. Ginny suggested they share a MaiTai, then call it a night. He agreed.

When they entered the elevator of Raffles, he punched the button for his floor. She noticed this and said nothing as they passed her floor. Walking down the hall to his room, he placed an arm around her. She placed her arm around his waist, too.

Entering his room, Ginny said, "Why don't you lay down and I'll massage you."

Without a word, he did as she suggested. Ginny unbuttoned his shirt and raised his shoulders to remove it. Then she said, "Excuse me," and went into his bathroom. They had left the lights off in the room.

When Ginny returned, she held a glass of water in her hand. Sitting on the bed above his head, she began to massage his forehead and temples. She followed the same sequence that he had earlier by the pool, except she was slower and more gentle.

As she moved her hands down his chest and pulled back along his ribs, she debated where she would sleep that night. She thought, *if Matt is worthwhile, how am I going to find out if we spend all the next two days in his room?* She knew once they started, there'd be no stopping.

After massaging his arms, she decided to turn him over.

She whispered, "Matt, turn over."

He didn't move.

When he didn't respond, she placed his arms at his sides and turned him over herself. Getting astride his upper thighs, she massaged his back. Tiring of this soon, she lay down on top of his sleeping body. Within a few minutes, she was asleep too.

It was past nine the next morning when Ginny was startled by loud pounding on the door. Still in her dress, she straightened her hair and opened the door.

There stood Sundance in his shorts, holding a bottle of bourbon, with a surprised look on his face. He looked the fully-clothed Ginny up and down.

"Oh, excuse me. Hope I'm not interrupting anything," he mumbled.

"Come on in. You're not interrupting anything."

They both walked over to the still-sleeping Sweetwater.

"How long's he been sleeping?" asked Sundance.

"What time is it?"

Looking at his watch, Sundance said, "Nine twenty-five."

"He's been in bed about seven hours then," said Ginny.

"That's long enough," Sundance said. He picked up the glass on the bedside table and poured the remainder of its contents over Sweetwater's blissful face.

The blissful face jerked away from the falling water, and a pillow went flying in its general direction.

The pillow caught Ginny square in the face and bowled her over backwards. Landing on her behind, she got back up, grabbed the pillow and threw it just as hard back at her assailant.

Not noticing Sundance through his wet eyes, the drenched pilot said, "What the hell?"

Ginny laughed.

When Sundance started laughing too, Sweetwater turned and saw the empty glass in Sundance's hand. Realizing what had happened, he tackled Sundance and tried to drag him into the bathroom for a real drenching.

"You know where your head's going?" he threatened Sundance.

"After you, sucker!" Sundance shouted. They wrestled and tossed each other around the room, knocking over chairs and tables in the process. Sundance finally pulled a curtain down and wrapped it around his opponent's head. When they had both tired, each lay exhausted on the floor.

"I came in to see if you wanted to rent a boat and go waterskiing, Water," said the other pilot.

"Hey, Ginny. You want to go waterskiing?" asked Sweetwater.

"Sure."

"Slim and I are going to have breakfast down on the Terrace. Why don't you join us?" asked Sundance.

"How soon?" said Ginny.

"Right now."

"If you can make right now about 20 minutes, I'll join you," she said. Not waiting for Sundance to respond, she left the room, leaving the two men still laying on the floor.

"How was she?" asked Sundance.

"Great. Great, I think."

"What do you mean, think?" asked Sundance.

Looking at the floor, Sweetwater repeated without enthusiasm, "She was great."

"You sound nuts, pal. She must be getting to you."

Sweetwater turned his head to look Sundance straight in the eye, but didn't say anything.

Jumping up, Sundance said, "Get your butt in gear, Water! We got a big day going. How many cases of beer should we bring?"

"Who's coming?" asked Sweetwater.

"You, Slim, and me, plus our girls."

"Two cases of San Miguel should do it."

"Okay, I'll order them while you shave. Let's go," said Sundance, pulling his friend to his feet.

At breakfast Ginny met the girls the two other pilots had picked up the previous day. While nice, they were typical of the women who lounged around the pools of the more expensive hotels in Singapore, and the rest of the Orient for that matter. They were looking for "means of support," and while waiting, they weren't adverse to having some fun. Ginny began to regret agreeing to accompany Sweetwater's friends for the day.

Once on the boat, however, she enjoyed herself. The beer went fast, although the girls drank little of it. The pilots had a contest to see who could stay up the longest, under the tightest turns. Ginny entered the contest and did well, until the strings of her suit began to yield.

After her third spill, in an effort to keep at least part of her suit on, she tied its top around her waist. When the boat pulled her out of the water topless, the men let out a wild cheer. The other two girls promptly dropped their tops, too. With her suit secure, Ginny had no trouble outlasting the men on the skis.

By the middle of the afternoon, the San Miguel was nearly gone. They decided to tie up to a floating restaurant for something to eat. Ginny was astonished that the pilots continued drinking heavily, switching to scotch and bourbon now.

Returning to the speedboat, they spent the balance of the afternoon touring the harbor. As they pulled up to the Kitty Hawk, which was moored in the middle of the harbor, Ginny was surprised at its size. The men debated whether to show their girls the ship. After reviewing their conditions, they decided not to. The last of the San Miguel had substantially mellowed the three men by the time they tied up the speedboat.

Everyone headed for the Raffles and agreed to meet again in the dining room after an hour nap. This time Ginny suggested, "Why don't we nap in my room?" She was still undecided on what she would permit to happen.

As it turned out, she needn't have been concerned. Sweetwater collapsed on her bed and was out in a minute. Ginny showered, changed into a terrycloth jumpsuit and lay down beside him. She thought, *with all they drank, I'm surprised he didn't pass out sooner.*

It was dark when she awoke. Checking his watch, Ginny was amazed to see they had slept for three hours. She decided not to immediately awaken her pilot. Bringing a chair to her balcony, she sat and looked at the sleeping Sweetwater. In addition to being good-looking, she had learned he was reasonably bright, a first-rate dancer, charming, and fun to be with... most of the time. She began to seriously consider his proposal made back in Rome.

It wasn't the first time an eligible man had asked for her hand. Sweetwater was tempting, but she wondered whether he would make a permanent husband.

Becoming hungry, she decided to awaken him. She cautiously shook the bed to do so. He sat up, bleary-eyed, and asked what time it was. She told him, and they decided to find a quiet place to eat.

Sweetwater went to his own room, quickly showered, and changed into evening clothes. They sat through a candlelight dinner of Indian curry and roasted lamb, saying little, listening to the plaintive notes of a sitar.

After dinner, they wandered slowly along the boulevard which held the major hotels of Singapore, stopping occasionally at interesting store windows, exchanging their tastes in the articles they viewed.

Coming to a window displaying jewelry, Sweetwater decided to bring up the ring. Hesitantly, he asked, "Ginny, can I ask you something?"

"You're going to anyway, aren't you?"

"Whether you say 'yes' or 'no,' I don't want it to make any difference in how we feel about each other right now. Okay?"

She was feeling too mellow to protest. She knew the window of jewelry had reminded him of the ring.

"Ask your question."

"Would you mind wearing the ring I gave you as a sign of our friendship?"

She thought, *that's clever. How do I say 'no' to that?* They walked in silence for a few minutes as Ginny considered her answer. She knew what it was, but didn't want to say it. It was rare when she was unable to control the men in her life— few of them had the intelligence to out-think her. Now, he had trapped her into wearing his engagement ring.

"Yes, I'll wear it in friendship."

Facing Ginny, he kissed her lightly. They continued walking. It was nearing ten p.m. as they entered the lobby of the Sheraton and found a table in the lounge where they had danced the night before. They waited until the combo played a slow number before getting on the dance floor.

Their bodies melded together and they moved as one. When the music ended, they remained on the floor, waiting for the next number. This time they *both* thought they were falling in love.

As they danced later, Ginny slowly moved away. Her body shimmered to the beat of the music the way a field of tall grass sways in a gusting breeze. With her eyes closed, her face had a dreamlike quality.

Sweetwater fought opposing impulses as he watched this goddess before him. She was the most beautiful woman in the world to him that night. To possess her, he knew would require far more than he had ever given a woman before. Yet he was unsure what to give.

When the combo finished playing at two a.m., Ginny and her pilot were not tired and chose to walk back to the Raffles. On the way, they decided they both liked the same foods, the same music, and walking on quiet streets at night. Both also carefully avoided any differences which came to mind.

Arriving at the Raffles, Ginny asked if they could sit beside the pool. And they did.

"From the way you were dancing, I thought you were going to ask to be taken somewhere else," said Sweetwater cautiously.

"What do you mean?" she asked.

Speaking bluntly, he told her, "Your body moved as if it wanted a man."

Thinking for a moment, Ginny said, "You're right. It did. Doesn't dancing do the same for you?"

"I don't understand."

This time she spoke bluntly. "When you dance with a woman, doesn't it make you want to make love with her?"

Giving her question some thought, he realized she was right. Before he could respond, she added, "Don't you want to make love to almost every woman you dance with?"

He knew this was true also, but didn't want to admit it. This night he wanted to believe his desire for Ginny was unique.

"What were you telling me then tonight...when you moved away from me and began swinging your hips?"

"Matt, I wasn't telling you any more than the music was telling me. If you stop to consider the mating rites of primitive societies, most of them precede mating with dancing. This is especially true in the South Pacific."

"You make dancing sound like it's bad," he said.

"No, it's not bad. It's beautiful. It's just that I think it sometimes encourages two bodies to move faster than their minds have."

"Is this why you asked to sit by the pool?" he said.

"Matt, I'm not sure about you...about us, I mean. I don't want you to think that I think of you casually." She added, "And I don't want to be considered casually by you."

"I don't think casually of you," he said. "You know that."

"Would you hold me tonight, Matt? Right now?"

"Here?"

"If we go upstairs, I'm not sure what will happen."

This was one of the most unusual requests he had ever received from a woman. For a moment he was tempted to stand up and tell her good night.

He did stand up, at the same time remembering this was the first woman to whom he had seriously said 'I love you.' Instead of walking away, he told her, "Okay, on one condition."

"What's that?" Ginny said, hesitantly.

"You go for a moonlight swim with me."

They stripped to their underwear and quietly slipped into the water. It was slightly cooler than the warm night air. As she sidestroked, he moved beside her. When she tired, he wrapped her in his arms. In a corner of the pool, they nuzzled and caressed each other. After a while, Ginny asked, "Can we get out now?"

Climbing out of the water, Sweetwater arranged some lounge chair mats along the edge of the pool. Finding a few stray towels, he dried her partially-clad body.

As they reclined, Ginny said, "You lay next to the pool's edge."

"Why?"

"If I accidentally cause you any problems, I want to be able to cool you off quickly," she playfully told him.

"I think I got a problem already," he kidded her.

"In you go," Ginny said, as she pushed his hips. He went into the water like a rolling log.

When his head reappeared at the edge of the pool, she asked, "Any better?" She received a stream of water from Sweetwater's mouth in answer.

"That's to cool you off, too," he said, rolling back beside her.

They joked about sex.

"Speaking of sex, how many kids do you want, Ginny?"

"At least one, maybe two," she replied. "How about you?"

He thought the ideal family would include three children, and told her so. He had grown up with two brothers, one older and one younger.

"Do you like to cook?" he then asked.

"I cook for a living, remember? Sometimes, I serve more than 200 meals a day. On some flights, I never get a chance to sit down. One meal seems to follow another."

He didn't pursue the subject, other than to briefly tell her what his favorite meals were. After he finished describing six of these, she asked him, "Do you like to cook?"

"I don't cook."

She was tempted to tell him that he'd better learn. Ginny resented his automatically assuming that she would do the cooking if they married.

They quietly chatted until he began having trouble keeping his eyes open. She rolled over on her side, with her back to him, then pulled his arm around her body, holding his hand in both of hers. He freed his hand for a moment to pull a few towels over their bodies. That's the way the cleaning attendant found them when the sun came up.

Pulling his trousers on, Sweetwater asked, "How do you feel?"

Smiling, she replied, "Like a sleepy virgin."

Sweetwater wondered for a moment if she was.

"How do you feel?" she asked.

"Like a sleepy virgin's boyfriend." They both laughed as she tried to push him in the pool again.

Except for an hour of tennis in the late morning, they spent the day around the pool at the Raffles. Sweetwater explained that this being the last day before he had to go aboard the ship, he just wanted to relax.

Ginny felt intimidated by the raucous behavior of the other pilots, who by the middle of the day had built an impressive tower with their empty beer cans. She played in a spirited game of keep-away with a ball in the pool until it became a contest of who could keep their bathing suit on at the same time.

Sweetwater again massaged her body and she fell asleep, after which he sheltered her from the sun with a large umbrella.

"I'm going for another swim," he said. "Then I'm going to take a nap." When he came out of the water, the combination of beer, the sun, and the previous night told immediately. He was completely out in three minutes. Ginny went to her room to wash her hair.

He was still sleeping when she returned two hours later.

Slim came over and laid a cold beer can on his belly, which woke Sweetwater with a start. He threw the can at Slim, who expertly caught it.

"Come on, Water. Singapore awaits us," said Slim.

Slim explained to Ginny, "The last night in port, we usually take a grand tour."

Ginny arched an eyebrow and looked at Sweetwater.

Sweetwater told her, "That means we tour the clubs all night."

When he saw the less-than-thrilled expression on her face, he said, "Don't worry. You'll love it."

This wasn't how Ginny would have preferred spending their last night in Singapore, but it solved the problem of where to sleep. So she agreed to come.

After a sumptious dinner at one of the finest restaurants in Chinatown, they headed for Boogie Street. Ginny had heard of Finnocio's in San Francisco and was amazed what Singapore had to offer. She couldn't believe how beautiful the men were, or their voices as they performed on stage. She didn't even realize they were men until one-third the way through the show.

Their next destination was a club which specialized in magicians, in addition to live contests between snakes and a mongoose. The magic act was not unusual, but Ginny was terrified when a man dropped an irritated cobra into a cage with the mongoose. A strap restraining the mongoose was released just as the cobra reared to strike. Ginny had difficulty following the lightning fast movements within the cage and didn't realize what had happened until the crowd broke into loud booing. The mongoose held the snake firmly in its teeth, just behind the snake's head. Ginny turned away, not seeing the neatly-severed snake head drop to the bottom of the cage.

The next destination was a strip-tease club, where they received a ring-side table due to their women. The dance floor was elevated two feet above the level of the surrounding tables. Numerous sailors from the Kitty Hawk were also in the crowd. Each performer did a slightly different act.

Without using her hands, one of the dancers began removing her apparel by twisting prone on the dance floor. By the time she was down to a flimsy bra and G-string, she was writhing on the floor next to Sweetwater. The stripper started to make progress with these items too, but Sweetwater decided to ease them back into place. His efforts were followed by good-natured booing from the crowd. It became a lively contest between the stripper and the pilot.

Ginny was not as amused as the others. Sweetwater eventually let the dancer win, and their table received a free round of drinks in consolation.

After leaving the strippers, they decided to go somewhere they could dance. The pilots unanimously selected The Sling.

It was three in the morning when they arrived at one of the most exceptional nightclubs in the world. Even at that hour, they had to wait 20 minutes to get in. Once inside, Ginny understood why they had come to this club.

At street level they walked into a large dance floor with a small revolving stage in the center, on which five men were performing an excellent imitation of the Rolling Stones. They even looked like the Rolling Stones.

Instead of stairs, a circular ramp along the entire room's perimeter led to the second level. Reaching the second floor, Ginny was astonished to see a band in country-and-western regalia belting out, "You Picked A Fine Time To Leave Me, Lucille." Continuing along the outer ramp, the men picked up San Miguels and the women selected Mai-Tais from the narrow bars located between the ramp and the dance floors. There were no chairs or tables in The Sling. Alongside the bars were also small grills where exotic dishes steamed.

The third level was quieter than the others, but still crowded. On its center stage, a short bespectacled Malayasian started to sing, "Rocky Mountain High." Ginny wanted to stop here, but Sweetwater asked her to check out all five floors of the club first.

As they came around to the fourth level, four musicians were singing "Hard Day's Night" in the best Beatles style, and the dance floor was solid with gyrating bodies. The singers bore a striking resemblance to the original artists.

"Guess who's on the fifth floor, Ginny," said Sweetwater.

"Who?"

"Probably the King," answered Sweetwater.

"Who's that?" she asked. "I can't believe all this!"

They heard the song before they came entirely around to the top floor.

Ginny said, "That's 'Heartbreak Hotel.'"

Barely in the room due to the packed crowd, they stood together and watched the tall singer finish his song. The dance floor was a mass of people. After listening to a moving version of 'In The Ghetto,' they threaded their way back down the ramp.

The three couples spent most of their time on the dance floors, resting occasionally at the bar rails. They did spend half an hour listening to the John Denver impersonator, after the women asked for a time-out to take their heels off.

Tiring, Ginny asked, "What time is it?"

"It doesn't matter in here," said Sweetwater. "The Sling swings all night."

"Do you know how many beers you've had today?" she asked.

"Have you been counting, Mother?" Like most drinkers, he didn't like being asked this question.

Ginny didn't like his response either.

"Hey, you jokers," said Slim, looking at his watch, "the Hawk leaves in two hours!"

The men finished their drinks as the women put their shoes on. When they reached the ramp, Sweetwater put his arm around Ginny and began shouldering his way through the throng. As they stepped out of the club, Ginny was surprised to see it was broad daylight. The streets were beginning to fill with people on their way to work. They piled into a cab. Ginny sat on Sweetwater's lap, but the two didn't speak until the cab pulled up to the Raffles.

"Why do you do it, Matt?" she asked.

"Do what?"

"Drink so much."

"It helps keep the malaria away," he answered.

Ginny did not respond.

The men decided to grab a quick breakfast with the women before dashing to the ship. The women went into the dining room to order the breakfasts while the men checked out of their rooms.

When Sweetwater returned, he sat next to Ginny. He had shaved, but his appearance was still marred by bloodshot eyes and the beginning of a hangover. They didn't talk as the men wolfed down their food.

The girlfriends of Slim and Sundance decided to say goodbye at the Raffles, so the three men and Ginny climbed into a cab. They arrived at the pier, where several boats were shuttling men of the Kitty Hawk back to their ship.

Sweetwater stood on the pier with Ginny in his arms.

"I always have drank too much, I guess. Ever since I got out of Pensacola. We all do. I don't know if you could understand why."

"Try me," said Ginny.

"When we get off the ship, we're wound tighter than a..." He couldn't finish the phrase without offending her, so he tried another explanation. "Ginny, do you have any idea how much pressure the captain of a 747 feels when he brings his plane in for a landing with 300 people aboard? I don't care how

many times he's done it already, for that short space in time
before the wheels touch down, his blood runs cold. He stops
breathing. His senses are frozen in concentration.''

"I get some of that same feeling whenever I land, too,''
admitted Ginny.

"Well, multiply that intensity by 100 times and you know
how a carrier pilot feels each time he comes aboard. A carrier
deck is not like the runways your 747s have. Our landing area is
measured in a few hundred feet, while a 747 has several thousand feet. A carrier deck pitches and rolls, and tries to bounce
you off—it's not stationary like yours.'' He thought he saw a
glimmer of understanding in her eyes.

He continued, "The concentration required to safely land
on a carrier deck is so total it pushes everything else out of your
mind. Afterwards, it's like there's a void within you, mentally
and physically. You feel hollow inside. Instinctively, you know
that you must rid yourself of this tension. Or it'll eat you up.
It'll harm your concentration the next time. It's hard to explain,
Ginny.''

"Is that really why you drink so heavily?'' she asked.

He considered his words carefully. "I don't know...may-
be. When I raise a beer can, it's also to celebrate I'm still alive.
On last year's cruise, I lost three friends in an accident. Two of
them were younger than I.''

"Hey, Lieutenant,'' shouted a uniformed man on the
pier. "This is the last liberty boat back to the ship.''

"Ginny, I love you. When I see you in San Diego, I'll be
different. At the end of a cruise, we all change.''

She continued to stare at him, seeking more explanation.

"Give me a chance,'' he pleaded.

She raised on her toes as they kissed and embraced one
last time. Their lips hurt as they parted.

Sweetwater sat numbly in the boat, thinking only of Ginny
and what had gone wrong. Camel Station was a million miles
away. And San Diego seemed a hundred light years in the
future.

10

JOHNNIE ADRIFT IN THE SOUTH CHINA SEA

The morning air was heavy with mist as Sweetwater climbed up the ladder to the Officer's Brow. He missed Ginny already, but he felt a sense of relief, too—he had survived another in-port period.

While the Ship's Company prepared to get the Kitty Hawk underway, most of the Air Wing personnel were checking their aircraft and preparing themselves for flight operations the next day.

As the carrier glided out of the channel, dodging smaller vessels, the anchor was only a couple feet above the waterline. In case the ship had to make an emergency stop, the anchor could be dropped in seconds.

Singapore was the next to last port call before returning home. The last stop would be the Philippines in order to pick up the necessary supplies for the trip home. Transitting the South China Sea would take only two days, and then the Hawk would be on the last leg of its 60,000 mile journey.

The second day out of Singapore was scheduled to be a light day for flying—basically a refresher so each pilot could make a couple of arrested landings during the day and one night landing. Sundance and Sweetwater were scheduled to go in the afternoon.

As Sweetwater rolled up to CAT 1, Sundance was right behind him.

Even as he went into tension, Sweetwater was still daydreaming about Ginny.

"Everything looks good, Water," said Reilly. "Let's go."

Sweetwater snapped back to reality at Reilly's comment. He looked to the Cat Officer who would touch the deck to signal that their plane would be whipped off the Flight Deck. Instead of touching the deck with his hand though, the Cat Officer crossed his arms over his head. The Cat shot was suspended.

"Everything looks okay to me," said Sweetwater. "What happened?"

"There must be something wrong with the Catapult," offered Reilly.

The Cat Officer walked out in front of them and gave the "throttle back" signal. Sweetwater reduced power to idle, awaiting further instructions.

The Cat Officer pointed out in front of the ship, as the Hawk started to heel port. Looking through the canopy, Sweetwater saw what appeared to be a small raft.

"Hey, Reilly. Do you see that?" Both pilots strained to pick out the cause of their delay.

"Looks like a man on a raft," said Reilly. "Huckleberry Finn in the middle of the ocean." The raft was no more than 10 feet square, with a wooden mast from which hung a dilapidated make-shift sail.

"There goes the helo," observed Reilly.

Once the helicopter was hovering over the raft, the pilots heard the word passed back to the Air Boss on UHF 1.

"There's one man laying face down on the raft. I see no movement."

By the time the raft was passing alongside the ship, they could see the man. The lower half of his body was hanging in the water. His arms were tied around the short wooden pole which served as a mast.

The smaller ships of the battle group had been directed to pick up all *boat people* while passing through the South China Sea. Since the other ships were already overcrowded with refugees, the Kitty Hawk was now stopping to pick them up.

"Looks like that guy is one of the 50 percent who didn't make it," said Reilly.

"Yeah," replied Sweetwater. "The poor son-of-a-bitch. Here we sit in a 30-million-dollar aircraft and that guy dies on a miserable raft."

They heard the Air Boss' message to the helicopter. "Pick him up and bring him aboard the ship." At the same time, Sweetwater received notice that flight operations were being resumed. After Sweetwater and Sundance were airborne, several S-3As were launched too. The S-3A's mission today was to locate more of the boat people.

Sweetwater and Sundance hadn't been airborne more than ten minutes when they heard the Stallion, plane commander of one of the S-3As, call back to the ship, "Homeplate, this is Eagle 404. We have a sighting on a boat on your 240 radial, at 35 miles. We can see approximately 20 people. The boat is listing badly."

"Roger, 404. Stay on station until the helo arrives."

Scoop Anderson was then sent to standby the refugee boat until the Kitty Hawk could get close enough to launch its whaleboat.

"99 Aircraft. Return to Homeplate."

All the aircraft were recovered within 20 minutes.

Sweetwater and Sundance met Slim in their ready room. "You should have seen the body on the raft," said Slim. "The doctor thought he'd been dead for at least ten days."

"Glad I didn't see it, then," replied Sundance.

"They put him in a body bag and returned him to the sea," added Slim. "He was just a young man."

The pilots didn't say any more, but they didn't stop thinking about it. Instead of escaping to freedom, the refugee had found a lonely death in the middle of the South China Sea. The pilots often had nightmares of being lost at sea in their own rafts. This was a little too close to home for them.

The excitement was high on the Kitty Hawk when the word was passed that they would be picking up the refugees on the boat spotted by the S-3A.

"Let's go out on the bow and watch them come in," suggested Slim. When they arrived at the bow, it was crowded already.

The medical personnel of the ship's dispensary were waiting at the top of the ladder. Reports from the other ships with boat people had not been good. Dehydration, malnutrition, and disease were commonplace among the refugees. The senior medical officer had set up an area in the hospital wards where the refugees would be given medical care, food, clothes, and other necessary items.

The refugee junk was now one-half mile away, and the Ship's Bos'n was lowering a whaleboat into the water. It held five men: the Bos'n, two seamen and two Marines. Once in the water, they moved out to the junk, threw it a line, and towed it alongside the ship.

The junk was about the same length as the ship's whaleboat—twenty feet.

Captain Blackburn stood at the Conning Station on the 09 level where he could view the operation. The Conning Station jutted out over the side of the ship, offering the Skipper a view directly down to the water.

"What's the head count, Bos'n?" asked Blackburn on his walkie-talkie.

After pausing to count, the Bos'n replied, "I count 34, sir."

"Okay, have the Marines check each one as you take them off the junk."

"Aye, aye, sir."

The Bos'n faced the refugees. "Do any of you speak English?"

The men on the junk had all crowded to the edge nearest the whaleboat. One of them half-raised his hand. "I speak English."

"Okay, I want you to come aboard my boat one at a time. Women and children first. Understand?"

The man nodded his head up and down. Then he started to climb over the side of the junk into the whaleboat.

"Wait a minute," said the Bos'n. "I said the women and children first!"

As their two cultures clashed, the man gave the Bos'n a blank stare. Motioning behind him, he told the Bos'n, "They can come after the men."

With that, the Bos'n extended his arm out and pushed the man back into the junk. None of the women or children made a move to get off.

"Harris," the Bos'n said to one of his seamen, "get in the junk and start passing the children over."

"Yes, sir," responded the seaman, jumping into the junk. As Harris passed the younger children into the whaleboat, each was searched by the two Marines. They were inspected for food, weapons, and other items which could not be taken aboard the Kitty Hawk. Before he was finished, Harris had handed over 16 children.

"Now the mothers and their babies," ordered the Bos'n. As the first mother was assisted into the whaleboat, he told the Marines, "Check the babies, too."

The last mother to come aboard had a frightened look and would not release her child to the Marines. Seeing this, the Bos'n turned to the man who spoke English and said, "Tell her to release the child."

The man spoke harshly to the woman, who reluctantly permitted the Marines to hold her child.

"Bos'n," said one of the Marines, "you'd better look at this baby."

The Bos'n stepped over. His face flinched as he looked down at the child. Picking up his walkie-talkie, he said, "Skipper, it looks like one of the babies is dead. What do you want me to do?"

Blackburn hesitated a moment, then ordered, "Get them all aboard. We'll let the doctors take care of that."

The whaleboat being full, the Bos'n ordered it to pull alongside the ladder of the ship leading up to the quarter-deck. As each child and mother reached the quarter-deck, they were met by a ship's doctor. After a short inspection, each refugee was led down to the ship's hospital wards, where they would be kept in quarantine until the Kitty Hawk reached the Philippines.

Then the whaleboat returned to the junk and took the men aboard. Several knives and one gun were confiscated. As the last man boarded the whaleboat, the Bos'n asked the one who spoke English, "Is that all of you?"

The man said, "Yes."

"Okay," said the Bos'n, turning to the Marines, "go aboard and decide how you want to sink it." Whenever boat people were picked up by the battle group, their vessels were sunk to eliminate possible hazards to other ships.

The Marines jumped into the junk and began poking around to determine where to fire their rifle grenades once the Kitty Hawk pulled away. Reaching the stern of the junk, one of the Marines raised a tarp which had been thrown over some empty barrels. Between two of the barrels was a large pile of rags. Poking among the rags with the muzzle of his rifle, the Marine jumped back.

"Hey, Bos'n," he shouted. "There's someone back here." He had uncovered a slender, lifeless arm.

The other Marine came back to the stern. As the first Marine pulled the rags off the body, he saw it was a young girl. She looked to be about eight years old. The Marine knelt down to feel her arm. It was cold, but he felt a faint pulse. That's when he noticed a second body. It was larger and curled around the young girl. Removing all the rags, they saw it was a boy of about 11 or 12. He too was alive, but barely.

Each of the Marines shouldered their rifles and gently picked up a child. As the first child was handed over to a seaman in the whaleboat, the Bos'n turned to the Vietnamese men and growled, "Why didn't you tell us they were aboard?"

The English-speaking man said, "They don't matter. Their mother died two days ago."

The Bos'n started to say, "You son-of-a...," but he just shook his head. Picking up his walkie-talkie again, he reported, "Skipper, we've just found two children in the stern of the junk. Both are in bad shape. They're going to need medical attention quick."

"Okay, Bos'n. They'll get it. Get them aboard as fast as you can," said Blackburn.

The Marines quickly searched the junk one more time. When the whaleboat returned to the ladder alongside the Kitty Hawk, one of the Vietnamese men tried to step onto the ladder in front of the two Marines holding the limp children. The Bos'n grabbed the man and slammed him back into the whaleboat.

Once the two children were on the quarter-deck, the doctors told the men carrying them, "Get them down to the operating room, quick!" One of the doctors followed.

The fact that two abandoned children had been found at the last minute on the junk passed quickly through the ship. The crew's interest in their welfare was so high that periodic announcements were made on the ship's closed circuit TV concerning their progress.

The boy recovered before the girl did. Sundance decided to pick up a few items at the Ship's Store for the boy and take them down to the hospital ward.

Finding the boy, Sundance offered him a baseball cap with Kitty Hawk insignia on it, plus some pogey bait.

"Thank you, sir," said the boy, in perfect English.

Sundance was staring at the boy's eyes. Until now, the color of the boy's eyes had always been a source of discrimination. They were blue.

"You speak good English," said Sundance. He wanted to ask about the blue eyes. Sundance couldn't help but continue to stare at them.

The boy knew what the man was staring at. He asked, "You like blue eyes, mister?"

"Well, sure...I like...." Sundance stammered.

"My father had blue eyes," the boy told him.

When the pilot did not say anything, the boy added, "My father was American."

Sundance saw that the boy did have characteristics different from the other Vietnamese children. Now that he was getting some food down, the boy had filled out. His face was larger than those of the other refugee children of the same age. He was also stockier. His hair was a medium brown, much lighter than that of the other Vietnamese.

"What's your name?" asked Sundance.

"Johnnie. My mother named me after my father."

"Where's your father?"

"He's dead." It was beginning to make sense to Sundance now. Was this why the Vietnamese on the boat had abandoned the boy? Sundance didn't want to ask about his mother. He could guess what happened. There was no food left on the junk when the Kitty Hawk recovered its occupants.

"My father was killed near DaNang in 1975," the boy volunteered.

Sundance knew the refugees would be dropped off at the next port at which the Kitty Hawk called. This would be in the Philippines. From there, the refugees would wait until some country was willing to take them in. The pilot thought, *but this kid's not Vietnamese. He's American, goddamn it!*

A great well of anger arose in Sundance. Grinding his teeth together, Sundance continued to look down at the blue-eyed boy in the hospital ward bed. *This can't be. This just can't be.*

"Johnnie," said Sundance. "Where was your father from?" The pilot thought he would contact the parents of the boy's father. He had to do something.

"Texas," was the reply.

"Where in Texas?"

"I don't know," said Johnnie.

"What was your father's last name?"

"Thompson."

"Wait a minute, Johnnie," said Sundance. "I'll be right back."

Finding one of the doctors, Sundance asked if he could speak with him. After they had stepped outside the ward, Sundance said, "Doctor, that boy back there is American!"

"What boy?"

"The one back there, laying in the bed by the door. He speaks English. His name's Johnnie."

"Lieutenant, most of the kids we take off these junks do speak English. Did he tell you he was American? He's probably just trying to get your sympathy."

Frustrated, Sundance said, "No, he didn't tell me he was an American. I can tell it! Didn't you look at his eyes. They're *blue*, Doctor."

The doctor sighed and looked down at the deck. When he returned his gaze to the pilot's face, he reluctantly told him, "Lieutenant, there are thousands of kids like that one. Maybe tens of thousands. You weren't in Vietnam, were you?"

"No," said the pilot.

"The kids with American fathers have it pretty tough. From what I've heard, most of them live on the streets. The new regime won't let them attend schools. He's lucky to get out."

These words didn't make Sundance feel any better.

"Doc, he speaks English just like you and me. We've got to do something. He's just as American as we are."

"Lieutenant, he's half Vietnamese," replied the doctor. "I don't like it any more than you, but as far as our government's concerned, that makes him all Vietnamese."

"Bull crap," said Sundance.

"Look, don't get mad at me. I don't make the rules."

"Yeah. I'm sorry, Doc," muttered Sundance. "It's just that it's wrong."

"Lieutenant, I don't think there's much we can do about it."

Returning to Johnnie's bedside, the pilot pulled himself together. "Johnnie, don't you worry about anything. The doctor and I are going to work something out." After talking to the boy a few more minutes, Sundance excused himself.

Johnnie had heard similar words many times from his real father. Nothing had ever come of those words though, and he didn't expect this American would be any different. As a matter of fact, he didn't even expect to see Sundance again. He had seen the guilt in the pilot's eyes.

Sundance felt more than guilt as he headed for his stateroom and laid down in his bunk. In his opinion, anything that was part Texan was all Texan. He didn't know how to explain this to anyone though. *And if Johnnie was Texan, then wasn't he American, too?* The thought kept repeating in his mind.

Sweetwater popped his head in the door. "Hey, we're getting a friendly game of poker going. You want to play?"
Sundance raised his sullen face. Seeing his expression, Sweetwater asked, "What's the matter? You broke?"
"No, I'm pissed."
"Well, get unpissed and let's play some poker."
The disgruntled pilot covered his face with a hand and shook his head. "You know that boy they took off the junk yesterday?" asked Sundance.
"What about him?"
"He's American."
"What do you mean, American?"
"He's got blue eyes, and his father's from Texas," answered Sundance.
Sweetwater stood at the door, not fully comprehending the gist of the conversation.
"We've got to do something about it," demanded Sundance. "We can't just dump him in a refugee camp."
"You want to stow him someplace?" offered Sweetwater.
Looking up, Sundance thought for a moment. "If I have to, goddamn it."
"Hey, if the kid's really American," said Sweetwater, "why don't you go see the Skipper?"
"You want to come with me?"
Sweetwater hesitated. "I've got to get back to the game. Let me know what happens."
Sundance first went to the CAG, to request permission to talk with Captain Blackburn. After Sundance explained his problem, Warpaint eyeballed the pilot for a few seconds.
"Let's go see the kid," he ordered Sundance.
After meeting Johnnie and assuring himself that everything Sundance said was accurate, Warpaint told his pilot, "I'm going with you to the Bridge."
Warpaint led the way. Sundance was surprised the CAG took an interest in the matter. He knew that Warpaint had a family, but he didn't know it included four sons. Sundance was also unaware the CAG had been born in El Paso.
Stepping on the Bridge, Warpaint immediately aproached the Skipper and asked to speak in private. Thinking the CAG had a problem of a serious nature with his young pilot, the Skipper led them to his sea cabin just off the Bridge.
When they were all in the cabin, Blackburn asked, "What's the problem?"

"Sundance here has found himself a son," said the CAG.

Both of the older men looked to Sundance.

"He's not my son, sir," Sundance paused. "But, damn it, he could have been. He could have been the son of anyone on this ship!"

"Now, wait a minute," said Blackburn. "What are you talking about?"

Again, Sundance explained about the blue-eyed boy named Johnnie down in the hospital ward.

The Skipper told everyone to sit down. "Is that the same boy the Marines found abandoned in the junk yesterday?"

"Yes, sir," answered Sundance.

"Well, what do you want me to do about it, Lieutenant?"

Looking at his Skipper, Sundance didn't know what to say now. He blurted out, "The kid's a Texan, sir. He may not be an American, but he's a Texan. We can't just leave him to rot in some stinking refugee camp."

"I still don't know what you expect me to do, Lieutenant."

At this point, Warpaint spoke up. "Skipper, I've seen the refugee resettlement center outside of Olongapo. It's a cesspool. Some people have been there since '75 when the war in 'Nam ended." Olongapo was the Filipino city adjacent to the Naval base in Subic Bay. When the Kitty Hawk's battle group picked up refugees in the South China Sea, they were normally dropped off at this refugee center.

"What do you suggest, Warpaint?" asked Blackburn.

"We'll be coming into Subic Bay in about 36 hours. Why don't we fly Sundance in ahead of the battle group? That way he can contact the agencies at the refugee camp before we get there."

"Lieutenant, I'm afraid that's about all I can do for you. The Navy Department is not going to let me turn the Kitty Hawk into a refugee transport to the United States, regardless of what my personal feelings are on this matter—which happen to coincide with yours."

"Thank you, sir," said Sundance.

"Let's go make our arrangements to get you on an advance party flight," said Warpaint. "We haven't got much time."

The CAG put Sundance on the next flight to the Philippines, which delivered the pilot to Cubi Point a few hours later.

Since it was late when he arrived, Sundance took a room in the BOQ across from the Officer's Club and left an early call at the desk.

Grabbing a quick breakfast the next morning, he took a taxi into Olongapo and reached the gate of the refugee camp by 0630 hours. A high fence topped with barbwire surrounded the camp, which looked to Sundance like it held several thousand refugees. He had no trouble entering, but found all the offices of the camp closed. He had arrived too early. Having nothing else to do, he began strolling around the camp.

Even at that hour, most of the refugees were up and about, hustling from their tents for water or standing in the food lines outside larger tents. Sundance looked for other children with blue eyes, with features indicating their American parentage. He thought he saw a few. But what bothered him the most were the eyes of *all* the refugees.

As he walked along the dirt streets, many of them would stop to return his stare. Their silent eyes told him more than their tongues ever could, no matter how well they might have spoken his language. There were no tears in these eyes. Nor fear. Only a silent pleading. *Help me. Help me.*

The pilot tried to avoid these eyes, but he couldn't. And worse, he knew he couldn't help them, either.

This depressed the young pilot. The squalor and filth of the camp was obvious, but the mental suffering of its occupants also reached Sundance. He didn't have the slightest idea how he was going to keep Johnnie out of it. And after walking through the part of the camp closest to the offices of the placement agencies, he realized there were more than just a few thousand people in the camp.

Not for an instant, though, did the pilot consider walking out of the camp. The more these surroundings depressed him, the more determined he was to get Johnnie out of it—no matter what it took. There were a dozen kids he had seen in the camp that he wanted to do the same for. They hadn't spoken to him, and he hadn't spoken to them. A few of them had followed behind the pilot for a few steps. Sundance knew these kids were probably wondering if the well-dressed American was their father. He wished he was, and he wished he wasn't . . . for that morning he felt like a father to them all. And he hurt worse than he'd ever hurt before. He walked faster so they wouldn't see the twitching and dampness in his eyes—and felt like a son-of-a-bitch.

He waited at the main office of the camp for 15 minutes before it finally opened. Once inside, he had to wait another half-hour for a chance to speak to the Camp Director. She was Swedish, in her 50s, and overworked. When Sundance explained his reason for coming to the camp, she told him, "Lieutenant, I've got more than 800 children in this camp who probably have American fathers. Nobody wants them. They're our main source of trouble. They steal, fight, and do anything else that's necessary to survive. Now, you're asking me for special help for one of them?"

"Well, ma'am, if you can't help me, who can?"

"Why don't you try working through one of the church-affiliated agencies? That's why they're here. They have contacts everywhere."

Sundance walked into the agency headquarters established by the Lutheran Council first. He'd been raised a Lutheran back in Hudson, Texas. Though it was uncrowded, he still had to wait an hour before being seated opposite a Vietnamese refugee who worked for the agency. She told him that everyone wanted to go to America, and they had filled their quota for the current year seven months earlier. Sundance could put Johnnie's name on the list for next year, but there was no assurance he'd be approved. *Damn, Johnnie can't stay in this place for a year,* thought the pilot. When Sundance asked to speak to the director, he was told he'd have to make an appointment two days later. He walked out.

Across the dirt street was the building housing the offices for the Catholic Church. Sundance thought, *I should have come here first. They're the biggest. If anyone can help me, they can.* It was in a larger building and there were twice as many people working in it as in the Lutheran offices.

Sundance waited only a few minutes before having an opportunity to explain his problem. And he was interviewed by an American—a young man who seemed to know what he was doing. When Sundance explained he had only five days to get Johnnie on his way to the States, the man laughed and told the pilot the quickest his agency had ever relocated a refugee was three months...and that was with political help back in Washington. *Three months,* thought Sundance. He decided to stay the rest of the afternoon in the Catholic agency, filling out all the necessary papers to start the processing to get Johnnie out ...in three months. He didn't know what else he could do.

It was getting dark by the time Sundance returned to his BOQ room. After collapsing on his bed and resting for an hour, he forced himself to get up. Despondent, he ate sparingly at the Officer's Club and made his way back to the BOQ. To Sundance, leaving Johnnie for three months in the camp was like condemning the boy to a prison. The pilot slept fitfully.

In the morning, he returned to the camp as soon as the offices of the relief agencies opened. Wandering among the agency buildings, he saw the symbol of the Red Cross on a door of a small building already crowded at eight o'clock. The sign above the door said *International Red Cross.* Seeing the long line waiting to get inside, he walked past the building. Then it occurred to him, *hey, maybe there's some action in there.* The pilot turned around and went to the end of the line.

When Sundance reached a counter inside the building 45 minutes later, he had to wait another 20 minutes to get someone's attention. Shouting to make himself heard, he briefly explained his problem. The worker he spoke to gave him a card and pointed to an office behind the crowd, telling Sundance to wait by its door.

There were five people already waiting at the office door. Sundance waited too. It was another hour before he was ushered into the room. It appeared to be a Vietnamese refugee though, behind the desk. Sundance thought, *I've just wasted another half-day.*

"Can I help you?" the 30ish, pleasant-looking woman said, without an accent. The nameplate on her desk said, "Miss Phung Nguyen."

Encouraged by her lack of accent, Sundance sat down. He couldn't remember how many times he had explained his plight in the last 36 hours, but he did it again.

She told him, "If you can get a Stateside sponsor for Johnnie, we can get a visa processed within 72 hours."

"I don't understand," Sundance said.

She smiled. "If you can find a family in the United States who will agree to sponsor Johnnie, the International Red Cross can arrange for his visa into the United States in three days."

"But everyone else says it'll take three months to a year," insisted the pilot.

"Everyone else is *in business* around here. We are here to *help* the refugees," she explained.

The woman patiently described how most of the relief

agencies in the refugee camps were more concerned with prolonging their jobs than processing refugees. "When the refugees are gone, their jobs will be gone, too."

Sundance couldn't believe his ears.

Miss Nguyen handed him a file of papers, told him how to fill them out when he located a sponsor, and gave him her office's phone number. Sundance walked out of the IRC building feeling like the richest man in the world.

He was 50 yards from the IRC building when he heard someone calling, "Lieutenant! Lieutenant!"

Turning around, he saw it was Miss Nguyen running toward him. She held a manila envelope in her hand.

"Lieutenant, I almost forgot. When Johnnie comes into the camp, you must tell him to state the International Red Cross is handling his placement. There are more than 10,000 refugees in the camp. It would take days to locate him if he didn't know to come to our offices."

Realizing the disaster that had just been avoided, Sundance was speechless for a second. Then he said, "Miss Nguyen, how can I thank you?"

She looked up at the much taller man, and Sundance noticed her almond-colored eyes for the first time. She was not beautiful by Western standards, but she was not unattractive either. Her glasses hid part of her petite, oval face. The pilot could see she had a lovely olive complexion.

"Find a good home for Johnnie." She abruptly turned and ran back to the IRC offices. His eyes followed her. She moved gracefully like an athlete.

Looking within the envelope, he saw the name "Johnnie Thompson" written across a white card identifying the boy as an applicant at the International Red Cross.

The Kitty Hawk was due to dock in two hours. Sundance could hardly wait to show Johnnie his card. It was not until the jitney was halfway back to the Naval Base that he realized maybe he shouldn't be quite so elated. *Who's going to sponsor Johnnie?* he thought. Remembering the visa required 72 hours, he realized he had less than 24 hours to find a sponsor for Johnnie.

Transferring to a taxi inside the base, he directed its driver to drop him off at the Cubi Point Officer's Club. After considerable persuasion and promising to pay for the calls, the manager of the Club permitted Sundance to use his office telephone.

It took the international operator only 15 minutes to get through to Hudson, Sundance's hometown 45 miles southwest of Corpus Cristi.

When his mother answered the phone, he said, "Hi, Mom! It's me, Tom."

"Well, hello, Tom," said his mother. "How are you. What's wrong?"

"Nothing's wrong. I'm great. I just had to talk to you. Is Dad home?"

"Sure, wait a minute. I'll get him on the other phone."

"Hello, son," his father drawled.

"I've got something real important to ask you." Sundance explained about Johnnie and that he needed a sponsor for the boy in order to get him to the States. When he finished, his mother said, "Tommy, can you give us some time to think this over?"

"Mom, I've only got 24 hours to get everything done!"

"Well, hold on. Let me talk with your Dad."

While his parents conferred with each other, Sundance's confidence began to ebb. It was a long shot to call his parents, but he had emphasized that the boy was a Texan.

"Son?" his mother said.

"Yes," said Sundance.

"I don't know whether we're doing the right thing, but we'll try to help you."

"Fantastic! You're beautiful!" exclaimed Sundance. "I'll call you back as soon as I can give you his arrival time. I love you, Mom. You guys are great!"

Saying goodbye to his parents, Sundance immediately dialed the number Miss Nguyen had given him. She was pleased to hear Sundance had found a sponsor so quickly. She asked for his parents' address, ages, and other details and told the pilot she would have the visa application processed by the end of the day. Sundance then headed for the pier at which the Kitty Hawk would dock.

He waited impatiently on the pier for a full hour before the Kitty Hawk was tied up. It was the longest hour that he could remember. When the Officer's Brow was dropped, he rushed aboard and made his way to the ship's hospital wards. He found Johnnie dressed and ready to go ashore. He walked up to the boy and handed him the manila envelope from Miss Nguyen.

"Johnnie, you're going to the States."

The boy stood there, looking up at the pilot, not taking the envelope. "What do you mean?" he asked.

"Here, look in this envelope." Pulling out the white card, Sundance said, "The International Red Cross is going to get us a visa. My parents in Texas are going to sponsor you."

The boy took the white card and asked, "What does that say?" He was pointing at his name.

"It says 'Johnnie Thompson.' Can't you *read* your own name?" Then the pilot remembered what the doctor had told him and wished he hadn't asked.

"That's no good," said Johnnie, handing the card back to Sundance.

"What do you mean, no good?"

"It doesn't have my sister's name on it, too."

"Your sister?"

"I'm not going anywhere without my sister," said the boy, looking Sundance boldly in the eye.

"You didn't tell me you had a sister."

Sitting on the bunk behind the boy was a slight girl, darker than Johnnie. Sundance hadn't noticed her until now.

"This is Jessica," said Johnnie, half-turning toward his sister.

Jessica was a few years younger than her brother, in addition to being cute as a button. It appeared she had a different father than Johnnie. Her hair was not straight like her brother's. It cascaded in curls down below her shoulders. That, combined with a few other features, suggested to Sundance that her father had been black.

"Hi, Jessica," said Sundance, struggling for something to say or do. "How old are you?"

"I'm eight years old, sir. Thank you for helping my brother."

Sundance just stood there, looking first at Jessica, then back to Johnnie, then back to Jessica. Jessica smiled at him, and Sundance knew what to do.

"Jessica, it's nice to meet you," said Sundance, putting his hand out. When she placed her small hand inside his, Sundance said, "You're going to the States, too."

"Johnnie, how soon are you supposed to be leaving the ship?"

"They told us we'd be leaving in 30 minutes."

"Okay, I've got to get some help. I'll be right back." Sundance headed for Sweetwater's stateroom, where he found the other pilot hurriedly packing a small suitcase.

"Where you headed?" asked Sundance.

"I'm going to visit a sick friend in Manila."

"What's her problem, lovesickness?" asked Sundance.

"Something like that. She's got a friend. Want to come with me?"

"No, I've got work to do," said Sundance, "and it includes you. I need your help for about an hour."

"Sorry, friend. My flight leaves in 45 minutes."

"I'm sorry, too. You're coming with me, Romeo." The firmness in Sundance's voice made Sweetwater stop packing and look up.

"What gives?"

"Remember Johnnie?"

"You mean the Vietnamese kid?" asked Sweetwater.

A pained expression appeared on Sundance's face. "Yeah, right...the Vietnamese kid. I found an agency to get him to the States and my folks are going to sponsor him. But about five minutes ago, I learned he's got a sister, too. I've got to get out to Cubi Point to call my folks again, and you've got to escort the kids to the International Red Cross agency at the refugee camp."

"What do they need an escort for?" asked Sweetwater.

"There are more than 10,000 people in that camp. If they got lost in that mess, I'd never find them."

"They won't get lost, Sundance. You worry too much. Come on, if I don't catch my plane, I'll have to take a bus or rent a car to get to Manila."

"Hey, jerk!" Sundance said angrily. "*You* come on. Don't tell me they won't get lost. Nobody in that camp gives a damn about kids with American blood in them. For Christ's sake, they don't even have a mother! Don't you remember what happened on the junk?"

"Okay, okay." Sweetwater threw his suitcase on his bunk and followed Sundance back to the hospital ward. It took some explaining to get Sweetwater on the same bus with the refugees. Sundance told the camp representative, "No way are we going to get separated from these kids. Either they come with us in a taxi, or you let us go with them in the bus." Sweetwater went with them on the bus.

Before catching a taxi for Cubi Point, Sundance found a phone. "Miss Nguyen, this is Lt. Karnes again. I just found out Johnnie has a sister. She's eight years old and her name's Jessica."

"Are your parents going to sponsor her, too?"

"I hope so. I've got to call them. A friend of mine named Sweetwater is escorting the kids to the camp right now. He'll drop them off with you, okay?"

"I'll be expecting them. Call me as soon as you speak with your parents."

Glancing at his watch, Sundance saw it was four-fifteen. "When do you close?"

"Our offices close at five."

"Can I ask a favor? Watch those kids for me. I'll be back to you as soon as I can."

"Don't worry. I'll keep the children with me."

The manager of the Officer's Club was still cooperative. By the time Sundance reached his parents again, it was almost five.

"Mom, it's me again."

"Well, it's nice to hear from you again. What are you up to now?"

"Mom, Johnnie's got a sister."

"Are you sure you know what you're doing, son?"

"I just found out. She's eight years old and speaks English just as well as Johnnie." Before he could say more, his mother interrupted, "Tom, let me talk to your father about this again."

This time, Sundance had to wait longer. He wasn't feeling good about it when his mother came back on the line. "Son, your father and I have talked it over. This is getting too much for us to handle. I'm sorry but I don't think we can do it."

There was a long pause.

Finally she said, "Why don't you call Reverend Johnson at the Community Church. Maybe he'll know someone who can take them."

"Okay, Mom. I'll try that. Can you transfer me?"

"Good luck, son. I admire what you're doing, but it's too much for us."

"That's okay, Mom. I'm asking a lot. Thanks anyway."

"I'll transfer you."

When Reverend Johnson came on the line, Sundance again

explained his predicament. The Reverend told the pilot he would have to get permission from the deacons to undertake such a responsibility, and the deacons didn't meet until the next month. He reminded Sundance it was difficult enough finding homes for the occasional residents of Hudson who often came to the church for assistance. After the Reverend suggested he call back in a week, Sundance simply asked, "Can you switch me back to the Hudson operator?" The minister said goodbye and rang the operator.

"This is the operator. Can I help you?"

Sundance thought, *boy, can you help me!* By this time, he had been on the phone for 20 minutes.

"Operator, I'm calling from the Philippines. This is Lieutenant Tom Karnes of the U.S. Navy and..."

"Hi, Tom. This is Dori Robinson. Remember me?"

Sundance racked his brain.

"I was a sophomore when you graduated," she said. "I guess you don't. I remember you, though. You were our best basketball player. What's happening?"

"Dori, I have two children who need a place to stay. I mean some people who will take care of them. You know... sponsors."

After he fully explained what he needed, Dori suggested, "Why don't we call the Volunteer Fire Department? That's where I send all the emergency calls. Do you remember Walter Wood?"

Sundance remembered Chief Wood. He had been the police chief of Hudson during the pilot's high school days. And Walter Wood would surely remember him, too. His high school days were active ones. Chief Wood had bailed him out of mischief in neighboring towns more than once.

"Sure, I remember old *Knotty,*" said Sundance.

"Well, when he retired two years ago, he took over the phone for the Volunteer Fire Department. Let's see what he can do."

"Dori, you're a godsend," said Sundance.

"Chief Wood here."

"Chief, this is Tom Karnes. Do you remember me?"

"I'm still trying to forget you! How are you, boy?" They exchanged pleasantries for a few minutes before Sundance could get around to the reason for his call. He spelled out everything, including that the two half-American refugees had different fathers. When he finished, Chief Wood asked him one question, "Tom, are they good kids?"

Sundance didn't know the answer to this question. He remembered the words of the refugee camp director, *Nobody wants them. They're our main source of trouble. They steal, fight, and do anything else that's necessary to survive.*

"Sir, I think so," Sundance answered. *I hope so,* he thought. The pilot described how the two children had been abandoned by the other Vietnamese on the junk after their mother had died. Admitting he had known the two children for less than a week, he added, "Chief, I tell you what. If you can't handle them, then I will as soon as I get married."

"Tom, if you vouch for the children, that's good enough for me. I should call Daisy to tell her what I'm doing, but she's a good ole gal and she'll go along with whatever I say. We'll take care of the kids for you." The Chief and his wife had raised four sons and three daughters already, every one of which they were proud.

"Chief, you're one of a kind," said Sundance.

"Tom, you just get those Texans to where they belong. Hear me?"

"I hear you. Tell Daisy I still remember her apple pies."

"Hey, Tom. Did you say you were getting married?"

"Well, I'm not getting any younger." Sundance didn't elaborate.

When they had said goodbye, Sundance asked, "Dori, are you still there?"

"Yep."

"Hey, look. Can you reverse the charges of this call and send the bill to me?"

"Sure can. Just give me your address, *pardner.*"

"Dori, you just saved the lives of two beautiful children."

"Send me their picture, okay?"

"You bet." He gave her his San Diego address and hung up.

Looking at his watch, Sundance saw it was after six. He quickly dialed Miss Nguyen's number. It rang four times before she picked it up.

He quickly explained the latest details.

"It's going to take me time tonight to get the paperwork in order," she told him.

"How about the kids?" he asked.

"What do you mean?"

"Where will they stay tonight?" Before she could answer, Sundance said, "Why don't I bring some dinner for you and the kids to your office? Then I can take them back to the BOQ tonight."

Thinking for a moment, she replied, "It would be nice if you brought some food. I don't think Johnnie and Jessica have eaten since this morning. And, if you wish, I'll take the children to my place tonight."

"I'll be at your office in 30 minutes."

He stopped his taxi at one of the finer restaurants in Olongapo and ordered five servings of roasted almond chicken to go. Within minutes, he was on his way with a steaming box whose aroma he could not resist. It wasn't until his fifth piece of chicken that he realized how little he'd eaten in the last three days.

By the time Johnnie and Jessica filled themselves, there wasn't much left for Miss Nguyen. Sundance reserved a leg and thigh for her, as the two children picked the rest clean.

It was after eight when they left the IRC offices and headed for the camp's gate. Miss Nguyen was recognized by the guards and had no trouble taking the children out the gate.

When they arrived at her place, Sundance was surprised. It was the upper half of a modern duplex. The view over Olongapo at night was impressive.

"Would you like to come in, Lieutenant?"

Sundance wasn't sure he should, but he wanted to know this woman better. Including why she was being so helpful. He asked the taxi driver to come back in an hour.

Sitting in the kitchen was a teenage girl who looked startlingly like Miss Nguyen.

"Lieutenant, I'd like you to meet my daughter, Kim." Kim was the same height as her mother, but with a slimmer figure and fairer skin. Sundance thought she might be part American.

"How do you do, Kim," said Sundance. "You look just like your mother."

Kim laughed. "Everyone tells me that."

Then the children were introduced, and they immediately started to speak to Kim in their native language. When Kim spoke in Vietnamese to her mother, her mother answered in English.

Looking at Johnnie and Jessica, she told them, "Yes, you are going to America. You are not going to be sold as slaves to anyone. This man has found you a fine home in Texas."

This is the first time Sundance saw Johnnie smile. The boy came up to the pilot, again looking him boldly in the eye, and said, "You are a good man." Then he turned to Miss Nguyen and said, "My sister and I are tired. Can we sleep over there?" He pointed to a corner of bare floor.

Miss Nguyen fixed her own bed for the children. It was a warm evening and Johnnie laid down without taking his clothes off. Jessica waited until her brother was settled, then curled up in the pocket formed by her brother's body.

"They've probably been sleeping like that since she was born," said Miss Nguyen. Sundance stood at her side as she turned the light off in the bedroom.

"Would you like some tea?" she asked.

"That'd be nice."

He followed her movements as she prepared the tea and carried it to the kitchen table where he sat. When she had seated herself, he asked, "What's your first name?"

"Phung. What is yours?"

"Sundance."

"That's a strange name."

"It's not my real name. It's just what they call me in the Navy."

"What's your real name?"

"Tom."

"May I call you that?"

"Sure. I'd like you to."

"Where's Kim's father?" asked Sundance.

She looked down a moment before answering. "We don't know."

"I don't understand."

"He was reported missing in action."

"He was an American, wasn't he?"

"Yes." Phung paused. She looked up into Sundance's eyes. "He was a fighter pilot in the Marines. He was reported missing in 1974."

"Were you married?"

"Yes." She added, "But it was a Buddhist ceremony. There were no records."

Sundance didn't ask any more questions. He knew what

he wanted to say next, but not how to say it. Or when.

They heard the horn of the taxi. As he got up to leave, Phung told him, "This has all happened so fast, that I almost forgot something else. The IRC will not have funds to fly Johnnie and Jessica to Texas until approximately 60 days. If they are to leave the Philippines when you do, it will be necessary for you to pay their airfares."

"That's no problem," he told her. "What will it cost?"

"I don't know what commercial tickets are. We charter planes for our people."

"I'll take care of it tomorrow, Phung."

At the door, she caught his arm, "Tom, I think you're a good man, too."

"Phung, you know I couldn't have done this without you."

Their eyes met as he took her hand and gave it a gentle squeeze.

"I'll call you tomorrow," he said.

As he walked to the taxi, the pilot was a bit uncomfortable inside. *No one's ever called me a good man. They've sure called me alot of other things, but never that before.*

At 0900 the next morning, he called the Pan Am offices in Manila and found out one-way tickets for two people from the Philippines to Houston would cost slightly more than fifteen hundred dollars. He immediately headed for the CAG office. Warpaint wasn't there, or expected back to the ship until the next day. Sundance then headed for the Captain's Office—the Skipper's in-port cabin.

After reviewing the situation with his pilot, Captain Blackburn went to his desk and wrote out the following message:

"All hands hear this. Lt. Karnes has found homes for the two abandoned Vietnamese children we picked up in the South China Sea. Both of these children had American fathers. Their new home will be in Texas. If we can raise $1500 for their airfare, they can catch a flight home the same day we leave Subic Bay. If you wish to contribute toward their airfares, please do so at the office of the Ship's Chaplain."

Handing the message to Sundance, Blackburn asked, "How's that?"

"I think that'll do it, sir."

The Skipper then announced this message over the ship's 1-MC intercom.

When he'd finished, he handed the note to Sundance and said, "Let me know whatever else I can do."

Sundance hurried to the Chaplain's Office, but it took him quite a while. The crowd prevented him from getting closer than 20 yards to the office. When the men recognized him, they started piling money into his hands also. When it overflowed, one of the seamen took off his shirt and improvised a pouch for the bills which continued to pour in. Within 20 minutes, Sundance and the Chaplain's office had collected more than $9000. They didn't know this though for another hour—that's how long it took to sort and count it all.

Sundance called Phung to find out when to make the plane reservations and then called Pan Am. He was so elated that he almost forgot what he'd planned to do that night. He called Phung back, "This is Sundance again...I mean Tom. If you're not busy tonight, can I ask you to have dinner with me?"

"I'd love to. Why don't we ask Johnnie and Jessica to come with us, so we can all celebrate?"

That wasn't what the pilot had intended, but after thinking about it, he wished he'd suggested it himself.

"Great. Why don't I take Johnnie and Jessica over to the exchange and get them some clothes? Oh, and let's bring Kim tonight, too."

After explaining the special circumstances to the exchange manager, Sundance was permitted to bring the children into the store. Johnnie and Jessica were more interested in the milk shakes at the exchange snack bar than the two new suitcases that Sundance filled with clothes.

The pilot almost forgot to call Chief Wood to tell him the arrival times in Houston of the two children. When he did, Chief Wood wasn't at the Fire Department and there was no answer at his home.

"Don't worry," said Dori, "I'll give the Chief your message."

"Can you tell him something else, too? I'm sending a money order to him for $7000. The men of the Kitty Hawk donated it."

"Wow!"

"Yeah," said Sundance. "That's what I thought, too. Thanks again, Dori."

"You *betcha*."

When Phung arrived home that night, Sundance gave her

30 minutes to prepare for a gala dinner at the Cubi Point Officer's Club. She was ready in ten minutes. They celebrated their good fortune until no one could eat anymore. When they returned to Phung's home, she suggested they get out of the taxi and walk up the hill.

Halfway up the hill, Phung reached down to Jessica and picked up the tiring child. Within a half-minute, Jessica was fast asleep.

"Phung, let me carry her the rest of the way," asked Sundance. When the child was transferred to his shoulder, the pilot was surprised how light she was. He wondered whether her thinness was an inherited trait or due to poor nutrition.

"You know," said Sundance, "I hope these kids will be okay." What he meant was he didn't like losing them so soon after *acquiring* them. Sundance had become quite possessive of the two children, and he didn't like the idea of parting with them.

"What do you mean?" asked Phung.

"I guess they'll be alright," said the pilot. "It's just that I'd like to...you know, know them better..be with them more."

She understood then what he was getting at. "Why don't you take a trip with them, for a day or two? Have you ever been to Bagiuo?"

The only place outside of Subic Bay that Sundance had been to was Manila—on a two-day spree with Slim and Sweetwater.

"Where's Bagiuo?"

She explained it was a mountain resort half a day's drive north of Subic Bay.

"Can you go with us?" he asked. His motives were not his normal ones. This time he wasn't too sure of his abilities in the area of handling two children.

"I'll have to check with the agency tomorrow."

"We can take Kim, too," Sundance added. He didn't want Phung to get the wrong idea.

"She's in school, but I suppose she can get off for a day or two," said Phung.

The next day, after all the arrangements had been made for the visas and airline tickets, the five of them headed for Bagiuo.

Having grown up in the city, neither of the children had

ever been in the country. The countryside of Vietnam had always been too dangerous. When they stopped to watch a water buffalo working in the rice fields, the kids wouldn't ride it until Sundance had climbed onto one of the docile creatures. Pictures were taken of each person astride the buffalo. They marveled at the massive shoulders of the beast.

When the car climbed above the rice paddies, they saw the cultivated terraces which had been carved along the sides of mountains centuries earlier.

Entering Bagiuo in the late afternoon, Sundance was surprised. "This place looks like a mountain resort in the Rockies," he told them. The sloping streets were lined with solidly-built wooden and stone buildings. This was in sharp contrast with the thatched huts and flimsy houses on stilts which they had passed earlier in the day. Even the streets were smoothly-paved. The residents were well-dressed and there were no street urchins in sight.

Sundance arranged accommodations in a small hotel which catered to American servicemen. "Do you think two rooms will be enough?" he asked Phung.

"I think so."

After a light dinner, they walked the streets of Baguio, the children running ahead most of the time to stare into store windows or just running off energy.

"Phung, I'm lucky that Johnnie and Jessica were on that junk."

"Why do you say that?"

"I've seen another world the last three days. The refugee camp you work in shocked me. I still can't get over the eyes of the people."

She thought for a moment, then told him, "Tom, if you were forced to escape from the United States in order to survive, and then you were placed in a camp surrounded by barbed wire in a foreign country, not knowing where you would be permitted to go next—or even when—how would you feel?"

He couldn't give her an answer.

"What would be in your eyes then?" she added.

They continued walking in silence for a few minutes.

"How come you're permitted to live outside the camp?" he asked.

"I have a temporary visa from the government in Manila. As long as I can support myself, I'm permitted to live outside."

"Why don't you come to the United States? It should be easy for you to get a sponsor."

"I could. But what I'm doing here is important. I feel needed." Sundance didn't fully understand her reasoning.

She asked Sundance about his family. He explained he'd grown up on a farm outside of a small town in Texas. He had a brother and sister, both younger. She didn't ask why he became a pilot, or any other questions relating to his profession.

He sensed Phung still loved the father of Kim and didn't ask questions of her immediate past. He did learn that she had been a top student at the University of Saigon. Her parents had planned for Phung to become a doctor. Before she could graduate, though, the war had ended and all Vietnamese who had ties with the Americans, or even the French years earlier, deemed it wise to leave their country. Her parents had stayed in Saigon, being too old to follow their daughter to a new life in another country.

When they arrived back at the hotel, the children were tired. To Sundance's surprise, the three children automatically took one of the bedrooms for themselves. Sundance had thought he'd be sharing a room with Johnnie, while Phung stayed with the girls.

As they tucked the kids into bed, this time Jessica shared Kim's bed after debating the subject for a few moments. Johnnie was only five feet away.

"Phung, I'm not tired yet. Would you like to find a place to dance or something?" Sundance wasn't ready to share a bedroom with this woman, and he didn't exactly understand why. It was almost as if he thought she was too good for him...at least so quickly.

Phung and the pilot slowly walked the streets of the mountain village. They found no nightspots offering dancing, or any other form of entertainment.

"You know, Phung, this town is almost as quiet as the town I grew up near. There wasn't much happening at night in Hudson either. We entertained ourselves." He described the pranks he and his buddies played on neighboring towns. The most amusing incident was the time he and his friends placed a cow in the office of a high school principal the evening before a three-day holiday. He also described how he and his friends had cleaned up, under the close supervision of Chief Wood.

"I used to get blamed for almost everything that happened

around Hudson," said Sundance. "Of course, they were usually right."

"You're lucky you grew up in Texas," Phung said. Her words triggered a thought in Sundance's mind. *I'm lucky about a lot of things.* He felt awkward saying it, but he decided that he had little time left.

"Phung, may I hold your hand?" The last time he'd asked this question was many years earlier, when he finally worked up the courage to approach his first girlfriend. He felt as nervous now as he had back then.

As they strolled along the sidewalk, she answered this question by placing her hand in his.

"You must be a gentleman."

"Why do you say that?" he asked.

"You're the first man to ever ask before holding my hand."

Sundance immediately resented that any man would not ask first to hold the hand of a woman like Phung. This was before he remembered he seldom asked this question himself.

Again they walked along in silence. They were now headed in the direction of the hotel.

They quietly undressed in their darkened bedroom. Sundance kept his shorts on and Phung changed into a nightgown in the bathroom.

Having been called a gentleman, Sundance did his best to live up to his new role. The night was too warm to use a cover. They talked quietly about Johnnie and Jessica and anything else which came to their minds, neither knowing how or when to make the first move toward intimacy.

Sundance said, "You have beautiful hair," as he lightly touched its length.

Phung returned the compliment, although somewhat differently. "Your hair is almost as black as mine." She touched the side of his temple as she said this.

Slowly, their heads drew together and they kissed for the first time. They held each other closely for the rest of the night, as Sundance struggled with himself. His mind hesitated to do what his body demanded. As the room lightened with the dawn, they both released the desires their bodies had fought throughout the night. This was the most unusual encounter the pilot had ever had with a woman.

Sundance could not remember when he had shared intimacy with a woman who so obviously enjoyed it—equally as much as he did. Her pleasure significantly heightened his own. Afterwards, he couldn't get this experience out of his mind. He thought to himself, *that's the best loving I've ever had!* It was several days before he realized the reason for this. It was also the first time he had been attracted to a woman for reasons other than her physical attributes.

They spent the morning of the next day visiting a mountain tribe well-known for almost lifesize woodcarvings of Moro warriors. In the afternoon they toured an orphanage run by nuns where the finest filigree silver jewelry was handcrafted by the children. Phung accepted a silver bracelet from Sundance, but not until he had purchased jewelry for Kim and Jessica also. Then Phung purchased a mother-of-pearl pendant for Sundance, telling him to give it to his mother.

Early in the morning of the last day before the Kitty Hawk departed, Sundance drove Johnnie and Jessica to the international airport outside Manila. Phung came also. The two children were relatively unemotional at the parting. Sundance was not.

He told them, "I'm coming to see you in two weeks, after my ship arrives in San Diego. I'll show you all the places I played when I was your ages." His voice cracked slightly as they said their final goodbyes. Sundance was particularly touched when Jessica reached up to give him a tight squeeze around the neck. She didn't say anything, but the look in her eyes was enough. Sundance immediately remembered the other eyes in the refugee camp, and he wished they all could shine as brightly as Jessica's.

When he returned to Subic Bay with Phung, they had little more than two hours before he had to return to the ship. After sharing each other one last time, Sundance said, "Phung, I'm coming back to..."

She interrupted him, "Please don't say that. Don't say anything. Just hold me."

When he started to explain again what he wanted to tell her, she placed a finger on his lips.

"It's better that you not say anything I will hold in my heart," she told him.

So he promised *himself* that he would return to this demure woman.

When Sundance dropped her off at the gate of the refugee camp, they said a hard goodbye. Her last words were not what he expected. "Take care of the children, Tom. They need you."

He had expected Phung to ask him to come back. To say that she loved him. Or at least to ask that he write. This is what other women always told or asked him.

Looking into her eyes, he asked, "You know what I want to tell you, don't you?"

Slowly, she shook her head up and down.

Then they kissed—a long, even meeting of their lips and their minds.

When Sundance boarded the Kitty Hawk, another pilot who had seen the *celebration dinner* at the Cubi Point Officer's Club asked, "Hey, Sundance. How'd you like that Vietnamese stuff?"

Sundance bristled. "How'd you like a couple of race-tracks around your headlights, fat mouth?"

Fat Mouth hurried away.

11

PLANE IN THE WATER

After being gone for ten-and-a-half months, the Kitty Hawk left the PI and started for Hawaii. At this point in the cruise, everyone was burnt out and the number of launches was cut way back. Instead of seven launches a day, there were only three or four. Where before there might have been 12 to 15 aircraft on each launch, now it was only 6 to 8.

It was a *Commander's moon* the third night out. A full moon lit up the deck like daytime, and the older gents could see much better. It was going to be a great night for flying.

Sweetwater, Slim, Warbucks, and Sundance were among the pilots scheduled for the night go. Their mission was to practice night inflight-refueling and come home.

Sweetwater was the last F-14 to get his plugs. After completing his refueling, he called the ship, "Strike. Gunslinger 201 on your 159 radial at angels 12. Squawking 2501. 6.5"

"Roger, Gunslinger 201. Squawk 5254, altimeter 2989. Switch Marshall," was the response from the Kitty Hawk.

"Roger, Switching. Marshall, Gunslinger 201 on your 159 at angels 12, squawking 5254. 6.5 Altimeter 2989."

Marshall replied, "Roger 201. BRC is 270. Marshall on the 120 radial, angels 10. Expected recovery time 29. Time in 15 seconds, 2104."

Once Sweetwater was established in Marshall, he started to daydream. *I'll call Ginny as soon as we get to Hawaii. What I'd give to see her tonight. And those long sleek thighs.* He continued to think about the three days they'd spent together in Singapore.

Warbucks and his RIO, Lt. Hambone Tanner, were approaching their push time — the beginning of their descent to the ship.

"Hambone, is anyone meeting you in Hawaii for the Tiger Cruise?"

"Yep. My brother and son are flying in from Minnesota."

"My son's joining me," said Warbucks.

"How old is he?"

"Jeff was eight a few months ago," answered Warbucks.

"My son's nine. Maybe they'll play together on the way back to the Mainland. Tommy has never been aboard the Kitty Hawk, so it should be quite a thrill for him."

"Hey, if I get an OK Three Wire tonight, you want to buy the sliders and autodogs?"

"You're on, Warbucks."

They were on the last lap of their holding pattern. As they began their descent, Warbucks said over the UHF radio, "204 commencing. 2989. 5.2."

Approaching the ten-mile point, the ship's Controller told him, "Go dirty and slow to approach speed."

Warbucks lowered his landing gear, flaps, and hook. He also reduced his speed to 125 knots. They would fly by instruments until they were a quarter-mile from the ship.

When they reached the quarter-mile point, the Controller said, "204. Call the Ball."

Hambone made the call. "204, Tomcat Ball, 4.2."

Warbucks switched his attention from his instruments to the Ball a quarter of a mile away on the portside of the Flight Deck.

He saw that he had a good start as he picked up the Ball on the Fresnel lens. He could already taste the slider and autodog on Hambone's mealticket. The two men in the F-14 didn't talk anymore. Warbucks' concentration on the Ball could have "started a fire."

To Hambone, landing on a carrier was like making it through a whole school year. If you get aboard, you pass. If you fail, you must repeat. Nobody wants to do that.

"Looking good. Keep her coming," said the LSO. Normally, an LSO won't even say that much, but the cruise was winding down and everyone was getting a little salty.

From the time that Warbucks switched from instruments to visual flight, he had no more than seven seconds before his tailhook would engage the arresting wire. The short comment from the LSO took up two seconds of this time span, leaving only five more seconds before they would hit the deck.

After his F-14 caught the #3 wire, Warbucks went to *military* and retracted his speed brakes. Feeling the normal recoil of arrestment, he turned off his external lights.

Both men then felt a sudden release from deceleration. Warbucks saw the nose of the F-14 popup and thought, *what the hell?* He instinctively selected Zone 5 afterburner.

Their tailhook had parted from the aircraft, releasing the F-14 from the arresting wire.

We've only got 60 knots!'' yelled Hambone. The RIO knew this was insufficient speed and prepared to eject.

In the mind of Warbucks at this instant was another thought. First, he saw his mother's face, then his father's face, and those of his wife and son. He thought, *are my bills paid? I love you Willie Ann and Jeff . . . will the insurance cover your education?*

By this time, both the LSO and Air Boss were screaming, ''Eject! Eject!''

The F-14 was barely airborne when it reached the end of the Flight Deck. As it passed the deck's edge, the left wing stalled out and dipped. Their airspeed of 70 knots was not enough to keep the F-14 airborne.

Hambone yanked hard on the ejection handle between his legs. Both men heard the explosion as the canopy was blown off. The RIO felt a jolt as his seat went up the rails.

The windblast hit Hambone's face, blurring his vision and taking his breath away. A second later, he was 60 feet from his plane. The bladders in the back of his seat inflated, pushing his body from the seat. A half-second later, his chute began to open. After it blossomed, Hambone got one swing before his feet hit the water.

After making several turns in their holding pattern, Reilly broke Sweetwater's daydreaming by asking, ''Did you hear that?''

''Did I hear what?''

''I thought I heard a 'plane in the water' just then,'' said Reilly.

Then they both heard those sickening words over the UHF, "99 Aircraft. Extend your approach time 15 minutes. We have a plane in the water."

Sweetwater's calves ached as the blood curdled in his legs. "Listen up on the tactical frequency."

"I think it's one of our aircraft," stated Reilly.

"Holy Christ. Who is it?"

"Must be either Sundance or Warbucks," answered Reilly. "Slim refueled just before we did. He hasn't had time to land yet."

Sweetwater felt a queasiness settle in the bottom of his stomach. He thought, *why does it have to happen now? We're almost home. Goddam . . . goddam. . . goddam. . .*

Feeling the aircraft veer to port, Reilly shouted, "Water! Water! You okay?"

In a moment, he heard his pilot say, "Yeah, yeah. I'm okay."

Reilly didn't believe him though. "Hey, they may be out of the water by now. We don't know the details yet. You just concentrate on getting us aboard."

Getting no response from his pilot, Reilly added, "There's nothing we can do now. But pray. We have 21 minutes to push time. Get yourself together. Let's get an OK pass tonight."

Reilly knew how close Sweetwater was to Sundance and Warbucks. He also knew his pilot had to concentrate one-hundred percent to get them back on the Flight Deck safely.

One of the greatest fears of a pilot who ejects over water is getting tangled up in the shroud lines of his parachute and drowning before help arrives. Because the distance from the water surface is difficult to judge when falling in a parachute, pilots are instructed to release from their chute the instant their feet hit the water. In Hambone's case, there was insufficient time to do this. He had another problem too — the windblast of the ejection had dislocated his left shoulder, making it difficult for him to get out of his chute.

The Air Boss ordered over the 5-MC, "Launch another helo, ASAP!"

Warbucks didn't have to worry about problems with his parachute. His seat ejected a split second after Hambone's, and at a closer angle to the surface of the water.

Warbucks knew something was wrong when he was not out of his seat immediately. Carrier pilots are instructed that if you have to think about man/seat separation, something has failed at that point. As he impacted the water still in his seat, everything went black. The force of the impact was equivalent to 50 Gs — the same as being hit head-on by a freight train traveling 80 miles per hour.

After Hambone hit the water, he felt the shroud lines tangle around his feet. Pulling the shroud cutter from his survival vest, he hacked at the shroud lines with his one good arm. He knew once his chute submerged and filled with water, it would act like a 500-pound anchor. If he was still attached, he'd go under. Even the Rescue Swimmer from the helicopter couldn't help him. He'd be pulled under, too.

In addition to the shroud lines, Hambone was worried about being sucked under by the Kitty Hawk's propellers. He had swallowed a fair amount of sea water when he hit, and in his struggle with the shroud lines, he continued to take water.

The ship continued steaming, as another five aircraft still had to be recovered.

Willie "Scoop" Anderson was flying Plane Guard. If there was a pilot in the water, Scoop usually had him smoking a cigar in the ship's dispensary within 15 minutes.

The fluorescent tape on Hambone's helmet made the job of finding the downed pilot easier. They found him in five minutes.

"There he is, Jim," said Scoop. "He's got a problem with his chute, too."

Hambone's helmet was bobbing in and out of the water due to the weight of his half-submerged chute. There was no motion in the RIO's body.

Scoop dropped his helicopter down to 15 feet from the water surface, 45 feet to the side of Hambone.

"Okay, Jim. You ready to jump?"

Jim dropped neatly into the dark water. Swimming swiftly to the downed man, he saw that Hambone's head was face-down in the water.

Jim ignored his initial instinct to hold Hambone's head out of the water, knowing he had to release the man from his chute first. He dropped below the surface of the water and felt for the remaining shroud lines. One by one, he cut them. As the last line was cut, Hambone's body bobbed up in the water.

Jim then waved Scoop in. Scoop dropped the collar into the water and dragged it by the two men. Jim grabbed it and struggled to place the limp arms of Hambone through the collar. After wrestling with the unconscious Hambone for twenty seconds, Jim signalled Scoop to pull them out of the water.

After the second helicopter was raised from the hangar deck and airborne, the aircraft circling overhead were directed to commence landing. The LSO was aware that everyone would be tense after an aircraft goes in. He knew he'd have to play it cool to keep the remaining pilots thinking about their approach.

Reilly had been talking a blue streak until Control said, "201, call the Ball."

Reilly made the call. "201 Tomcat Ball, 4.5."

The LSO replied, "Roger, Ball. Don't climb." The Ball was all over the lens, as it would be if the deck were pitching wildly. However the sea was smooth. The erratic Ball was due to the unsteadiness of the F-14 pilot.

Sweetwater engaged the #2 wire. Then he jammed his throttles to *military* and lit off Zone 2 afterburner, too.

"Your power, Water!" yelled Reilly. "Your power!"

Sweetwater snapped out of it and reduced his power. After the yellow shirt spun their aircraft out of the wire, they were taxied up the bow and parked at a forty-five degree angle across Catapult Two.

Once they were chalked and chained, the yellow shirt gave them the *cut signal* to shut down their engines. As the engines wound down, Sweetwater popped the canopy and started to unstrap. His only thought at this moment was to get into Flight Deck Control and find out what had happened.

Rushing across the Flight Deck, Sweetwater approached the front of a turning A-7, better-known as a "man-eater" because its intake can suck a man up like a vacuum cleaner.

Sprinting to his pilot, Reilly yanked him away from the A-7. "Hey, you'd better get your head out of your butt, or you'll be hamburgered!"

When they made it into Flight Deck Control, the handler said, "You had a close one out there, H²O. You'd better start paying attention while you're on the Flight Deck. Especially at night."

Ignoring the admonition, Sweetwater asked, "Who was in the plane that went in the water?"

"Warbucks and Hambone."

The pilot's eyes hardened. "What's their status?"

"One's picked up and they're still looking for the other."

"Who'd they pick up?" asked Sweetwater.

"I don't know. The helo's inbound at this time."

Sweetwater started feeling sick to his stomach. He headed for his ready room. After removing his flight gear and quickly filling out his yellow log sheet, he told his RIO, "Debrief the Ops Officer. Okay? I'm going down to my stateroom." Reaching his stateroom, he turned on his TV set. The helo had just landed. Sweetwater saw a medical officer run out and jump into the open door of the helicopter.

Sweetwater raced out of his stateroom. By the time he reached Flight Deck Control, the downed pilot was being taken down the bomb elevator to the operating room of the dispensary. Not being able to make out who it was, Sweetwater ran to the battle dressing station next to Flight Deck Control.

"Who was that on the stretcher?" he asked the first corpsman he saw.

"We can't say at this time, sir."

"What do you mean, goddam it. Those are my running mates!"

In order to avoid mis-identifications, corpsmen are instructed not to divulge the names of injured parties. Seeing how agitated Sweetwater was, the corpsman decided he'd better make an exception to the rule. "It was Lt. Tanner, sir."

"What about the other pilot?"

"He's still missing, sir. No one saw a chute. They've called in one of the escort ships to assist the helos."

It had been more than forty minutes since he had heard

the 'plane in the water' report, and Sweetwater knew from experience that Warbucks' chances were not good. He went back to his stateroom, feeling numb all over.

Lying down on his bunk, he thought about Willie Ann and Jeff, and how they would open the door of their home to find a Chaplain and Casualty Assistance Officer standing there. All Naval aviator wives fear this moment. Sweetwater shuddered to think of it now.

There was a knock on his door. Sundance and Slim walked in.

Sundance said, "I guess you heard."

"Yeah," said Sweetwater. "How about Hambone? How's he doing?"

"They're still working on him in the OR," answered Slim.

When Hambone was pulled into the helicopter, it was apparent he had drowned. There was no discernable heartbeat or pulse, his skin color was blue, his pupils were dilated, and they could detect no breathing. The SAR swimmer immediately initiated resuscitation. There was no response to his efforts by the time the helo landed on the Flight Deck.

In the dispensary, the first doctor quickly examined the RIO and said, "I detect a faint heartbeat." He immediately took measures to fully revive Hambone's heart, while a second doctor tried to relieve the congestion in his lungs.

A corpsman announced, "Body temperature 85 degrees. The electrocardiagram registers 9 E.E.G."

"Mammalian diving response saved him," said the second doctor.

"What's that?" asked the corpsman.

"When his face was immersed in the cold water, it automatically triggered a response in his body which slowed his normal functions and permitted a minute amount of oxygen to be slowly circulated between his heart, lungs, and brain."

"Where'd you learn about that?" asked the first doctor.

"In the AMA journal three months ago. It said they've revived some people who've been submerged for as long as 38 minutes."

It was 22 hours before Hambone regained consciousness, but he survived. He couldn't remember what happened after he hit the water. It would be another three months before the Flight Surgeon permitted him to climb into a plane again.

Sweetwater and the two other pilots stayed up the balance of the night, waiting for word of Warbucks. The loss of Warbucks didn't seem real. They kept thinking that the helo would find him.

Sundance thought, *Warbucks is going to come up to that door and tell us everything's okay.* But Warbucks didn't come. He would never come.

Slim vacantly asked, "What's Willie Ann going to do now? Jeff's only eight years old."

A few minutes later, Sweetwater said, "Married life doesn't seem so hot now, does it?" He paused. "I don't know whether I'd want to leave a widow and kid like that."

"Yeah," said Slim. "You're right." The three men fell silent.

Sundance had been debating the merits of the earlier comments. He broke the silence.

"I don't know. Maybe Warbucks is lucky he had a wife and kid. He was happy with them."

Sweetwater looked up. "Sure, he was happy. But look at them *now.*"

"Before I go," said Sundance, "I'd like to know what it's like to have a wife like Willie Ann. I'd like to have some kids too."

"Yeah," said Slim. "Warbucks really enjoyed his son."

"You know, what the hell," said Sundance. "We could get it anytime, just like Warbucks. Then we'd never know what it's like to be loved by a woman. I mean, really loved." For a second, his mind drifted back to the Philippines. *Was it possible?* He added, "We'd never know what it's like to have a kid either. That'd be it for us."

This came home to the other pilots. They'd never looked at their own vulnerability as closely as they were this night. They were still in the stateroom when daybreak came.

"Goddam it," exclaimed Sweetwater. Breaking the silence like this startled the other two pilots. "Warbucks' son was supposed to come aboard in Hawaii for the Tiger Cruise!" He looked at the blank expressions on the other pilots' faces.

"Well, what are we going to do about it?" said Sweetwater angrily. "Sit on our big fat asses? Come on! We're going to see Warpaint." Slim and Sundance learned what Sweetwater had in mind on the way to the CAG's stateroom.

When the CAG opened his door, Sweetwater told him, "Sir, Warbucks' son, Jeff, was planning to meet the Kitty Hawk at Pearl Harbor for the Tiger Cruise."

The CAG looked at the excited pilot through glazed eyes. He'd also had a sleepless night.

"Why can't the three of us sponsor Jeff. . . if he still wants to make the Tiger Cruise?" asked Sweetwater.

"I can't think of any reason why not," replied Warpaint.

"Can you ask the Skipper for us?"

"Sure. Wait here. I'll be right back."

When the CAG returned, he told them, "You three can sponsor Warbucks' son, as long as his mother agrees."

The three pilots marched back to Sweetwater's stateroom. Some of the aimlessness they had felt before was gone.

Sundance and Slim sat on the bunk as Sweetwater labored with pen and paper. Each time Sweetwater wrote on a piece of paper, he wadded it up and threw it on the floor. The three somber men sat in the stateroom, saying little, not knowing how to accomplish their task.

How to compose a message to Jeff's mother stumped them. Everything they started to write came out sounding wrong. They didn't know how to write a mother who had just become a widow.

"Why don't we ask the Casualty Assistance Officer in San Diego to contact her?" suggested Slim. This would be the same officer who had delivered the message that Warbucks had been lost at sea.

No one responded to this suggestion.

Finally Slim did himself. "No, that's a dumb idea, too."

"Yeah," said Sweetwater, "we've got to do this ourselves."

Sundance suggested, "Let's just write the message to Jeff. Why can't we do that?"

No one knowing why not, they decided to try it. But being pilots instead of poets, their first efforts were still not good.

Sweetwater wrote out a short note:

Dear Jeff,
   We are friends of your father and knew him well, so
we'd like to ask you to come to Hawaii for the Tiger
Cruise with us.

   He passed this note to Slim and Sundance. They agreed it
was what they wanted to say, but it didn't sound quite right.
Sundance again offered a solution. "Let's go ask the Sky-
pilot to help us."
   The three pilots gathered outside Rabbi Freeman's stateroom. After knocking on the door, they stood there, like three
small boys, shifting from one foot to another until the Rabbi invited them in.
   "Hello, boys. What are you standing out there for? Come
on in."
   Rabbi Freeman was the only Jewish chaplain on a carrier
in the U.S. Navy. Captain Blackburn had specifically requested
him as the ship's chaplain. The Rabbi was a New Yorker, and
Blackburn felt his particular blend of religion and humor
helped take the edge off the tension that often built up among
the men of the Air Wing. On the bulkhead above his desk was a
large hand-lettered poster. It stated:

The DOGMAS of the quiet past are inadequate to the
STORMY present.

The occasion is piled high with difficulty. And we must
rise with the occasion. As our case is new, so we must
think anew, and act anew. We must disenthrall ourselves.
                                           A. LINCOLN

   When a pilot started to develop a problem, either in the air
or in his family, the Rabbi was effective in isolating it and offering workable solutions. He had a way of insulting his pilots
which made them laugh at themselves. And generally return to
their usual abnormal selves.
   This morning he did not offer his unique brand of coun-
sel. He knew of the special bond existing between the three
pilots in his stateroom. He also knew they had looked up to
Warbucks as sons would to a father. Warbucks had often
helped the younger pilots out of complications with superior officers who failed to appreciate their mischieviousness.

So Rabbi Freeman waited patiently as Sweetwater explained their problem. When Sweetwater finished, the Rabbi asked, "May I see the note you've already written?"

After reading it, he told them, "Sit down for a minute while I work on this."

In a short while, he handed a new version back to the pilots. It read:

> *Dear Jeff:*
> *We are pilots on the Kitty Hawk. Your father and we were squadron mates, so we too are part of his family. This makes us part of your family also.*
> *We want you to come to Hawaii and take the Tiger Cruise with us. We are preparing for your arrival.*

The pilots silently passed the new version among themselves. As each of them read it, he wrote his name at its bottom:

> *Lt. Matthew L. Sullivan, USN*
> *Lt. Gerald M. Steiner, USN*
> *Lt. Thomas W. Karnes, USN*
> *KITTY HAWK*

"You know, boys," the chaplain said, "if you don't put your running names on this message, Jeff's mother may not recognize who's signed it." So they placed their running names beside the others.

"Why don't you add 'love' to it, too?" Rabbi Freeman advised.

When Sweetwater reached for the pen to write this word, he took a deep breath. It wasn't enough to remove the growing lump in his throat. This was the first time his eyes watered after losing Warbucks. As he straightened up, he saw that Slim and Sundance were staring at what he had written. Their faces held stricken expressions. They weren't doing much better than Sweetwater.

Sensing the sorrow which was enveloping the three pilots, Rabbi Freeman debated whether to encourage it or to change the subject. Deciding to let the men find privacy to shed any tears, he said, "Gentlemen, would you like me to take this down to the radio room? I'll have a priority placed on it."

Sweetwater nodded in agreement. As Rabbi Freeman left his stateroom, the three pilots did likewise.

The response to the telegram came the following day, when they were two days out of Pearl Harbor. Jeff's mother had written:

> *Dear Sweetwater, Slim, and Sundance:*
> *My husband often mentioned his "squadron mates" in his letters. Yes, you were part of his family.*
> *Your offer to take Jeff on the Tiger Cruise brought tears to my eyes when I thought I could cry no more. These were different tears, though. Thank you for this gift. To both Jeff and me. Jeff's grandfather will bring him to Hawaii.*
>
> *Love, Willie Ann Warrington*

When this telegram arrived on the Kitty Hawk, Sweetwater started to read it aloud to Sundance and Slim. He only made it halfway through before his voice cracked. Finishing the rest of the telegram silently, he handed it to Slim.

Slim didn't even try to read it aloud. After reading the telegram, he offered it to Sundance. None of them could speak. Unaccustomed to coping with the emotions they were experiencing, they avoided each other's eyes. None of them had ever touched another human being with such tenderness before. And received such a response.

When he could finally speak, Sweetwater said, "Dammit, when Jeff gets here, we're going to be a bunch of crybabies!"

Sundance sat at one of the desks in the stateroom, his chin resting on the hand of his upright arm. He said, "You know, the last time I cried was when my brother gave me a black eye 27 years ago."

Slim made a suggestion. "When Jeff comes aboard, maybe there should be two of us with him at all times. That way, when one of us begins to lose his composure, he can excuse himself for a few minutes."

"Good idea," said Sundance.

"Right," repeated Sweetwater, "and we can work in two-man teams with Jeff. Every six hours or so, we'll switch one man."

For the next two days, the three pilots moved in tandem, just as they did in the air. They stuck together because they did not wish to share the preparation for Jeff with anyone else.

During a Tiger Cruise, sons of the Ship's Company and Air Wing usually stay in their father's stateroom. The three pilots debated solutions to this problem.

Sundance proposed, "Why don't we alternate? The first night, Jeff can stay with Sweetwater, the second with Slim, the third with me, and the fourth..." Sundance didn't have any idea what to do about the fourth night.

As it turned out, his concern was unnecessary.

They were eager to reach Hawaii. The idea of showing Jeff a great time on the Tiger Cruise partially lifted them out of the depression they felt over losing Warbucks.

Sweetwater had a second reason for being anxious to reach Pearl Harbor. After three days in Singapore with Ginny, he was fairly certain she would marry him. He wanted to call Ginny to set the wedding date. If she were willing, Sweetwater intended to marry her two weeks after the Kitty Hawk reached San Diego.

On a hunch, Captain Blackburn had written Betty to ask that she meet him in Honolulu during the Kitty Hawk's stop-over in Hawaii.

The last time they had been together in San Diego, he had dined with Betty on the bay at the Reuben E. Lee. Afterwards they had danced downstairs on the floating restaurant, something they had not done since their separation 12 years earlier. When they left the Reuben E. Lee in separate cars that night, Blackburn and his former wife had both felt a certain reluctance to part.

Betty's return letter briefly stated:

Ed,
 Thank you for inviting me to meet you in Honolulu. I've decided to take a full week's vacation and stay at the Kaneohe Hilton. Call me there when your ship gets in.
            Betty

As Blackburn read this letter, he knew that Betty fully understood his reason for inviting her to meet in Hawaii. Twenty years earlier, they had spent their honeymoon in Hawaii. It had been in Kaneohe.

12

TIGER CRUISE

Before Sweetwater could get off the ship at Pearl Harbor, he received his mail. Among the usual letters from family and friends, there was a small box from Ginny.

Opening the box, Sweetwater thought, *it's about time she gave me something.* Due to the size of the box, he assumed it was jewelry.

He was right. With the engagement ring, was this note:

Matt,

When you asked me to take this, you gave me little choice. I'm returning it now as I know we could never live happily together.

You've said I'm the first woman who understood you, and that we have many similar interests. You may be right on the first point, but we have few common interests.

After getting off my planes, I'm just as burnt out as you are when you come into port. But where you want to sit around and drink with your squadron friends, I want to get away from my work. I want to see the world, explore new places and ideas.

I'm not putting you down, Matt. I understand that you get all the excitement you can handle on your job. Maybe you need to relax when you're ashore. But I don't want to be married to a man like that. I want to share the excitement in my life with my husband. I had some great times in Singapore. I'll never forget them.

Ginny

Sweetwater had finished the letter when Slim popped his head in the stateroom and said,

"Come on, Water. Let's go. We're supposed to meet Jeff at the airport in 45 minutes."

Stunned, Sweetwater followed Slim down the passageway.

"Hey, man. You look like a ghost. What gives?" asked Slim.

Sweetwater looked at Slim vacantly. "Oh, nothing. Where's Sundance?"

"He's on the pier holding a cab."

Arriving at the airport with 20 minutes to spare, they decided to grab a quick drink in the airport bar. As soon as they seated themselves in the bar, Sweetwater jumped up and said,

"Be right back. I've got to make a phone call."

Sundance asked Slim, "What's eating him?"

"I don't know," replied Slim. "He must be calling a girl."

Dialing Ginny's number in Malibu, Sweetwater thought, *We did have a great time in Singapore. We're going to have a lot more, too.* He couldn't believe she was trying to jilt him. He had always been the one to end affairs. It just didn't happen this way.

There was no answer. He let it ring two full minutes before returning to the bar.

It was three hours after the Kitty Hawk docked in Pearl Harbor before its Skipper had a chance to make the call to Kaneohe. Reaching the hotel, he asked, "Please ring Betty Blackburn's room."

"Just a minute," said the desk clerk.

While he thought Betty was anxious to see him, he didn't want to make any embarrassing assumptions. He was just about as nervous making this call as he was the first time he had ever called a girl for a date.

"Hello," said Betty.

"Hi," was all he said in return. There was an awkward pause.

"Well, how are you?" Betty asked.

"Fine. Real fine," he responded. He wanted to blurt out everything that was in his mind. Instead, he asked, "Would you like to have dinner tonight with me?" When he didn't hear an immediate reply, he realized how poorly he had phrased his question. He tried again.

"I mean, I'd like to take you out to dinner. If that's okay."

"Sure," was her reply.

After dinner he suggested they go dancing, being uncertain how to approach matters which had been the cause of their parting years earlier. He was afraid her responses might not be what he wished to hear.

Betty told him, "Why don't we just go somewhere quiet where we can talk?" She knew how easily she could be swayed by soft music on a warm Hawaiian evening. She wanted that later, if there was to be a later.

They drove north to Kahana Bay and parked. He asked, "Would you like to go for a walk?"

"Yes," she answered.

After walking silently along the shoreline several minutes, he slowed his pace. "Betty, I think you know why I asked you to come to Hawaii."

Looking him in the eye as they continued strolling, she said, "Why don't you tell me why?"

"I still love you," he blurted out.

"I know that," she said.

Wanting to be sure of his ground, he asked, "Do you feel the same toward me?"

Betty stopped walking. Turning to face him, she said softly, "I'm here." She paused, then said, "Does that answer your question."

He slowly nodded his head to tell her it did. Then he asked the same question he has posed on their second date 20 years earlier.

"If I were to ask if I could kiss you, what would you say?"

Her answer was the same she had given him the first time. Smiling, she said, "Why don't you ask and find out?"

He reached out to her, and a moment later they embraced tightly. They repeated each other's names, wrapping their arms around one another, grasping each other as if it was a sad parting instead of a joyous coming together.

"I want to live with you again," he pleaded.

She looked up at him. Her eyes were filled with tears and the hurt look on her face made him think he had asked too soon. She rested her head back on his chest and said nothing.

Holding her tightly, he feared losing her again. He

thought, *We're so close. It's got to be.* He told her, "I need you."

Without raising her head, she told him, "I've needed you, too, Eddie. And you weren't there."

He thought, *oh, no. Not this again.* Their fights over his many absences had been their most bitter quarrels. He was afraid of what might follow.

He continued to hold her in his arms. Betty did not release her grip. Instead, she tightened it.

"I'll be there, babe," he tenderly spoke into her ear. "I'll be there."

Betty looked up into his eyes. There still was no joy on her face. Her silence told him she needed more. He hadn't planned what he said next.

"Betty, if you'll take me back, I'll put in for shore duty the rest of my career."

Thinking his words over for only a moment, Betty said, "You can't do that, Eddie. You'll be an Admiral soon."

He knew this too. But he didn't want to spend more years in a lonely stateroom, Admiral or not.

"I mean it," he said, "I'll put in for shore duty. And if they won't give it to me, I'll retire." He paused. "I've got 26 years in now. I can retire with plenty of money."

Betty stepped back, turning away. "If you did that, you'd regret it the rest of your life. You'd come to resent me eventually, too."

He looked at her, knowing what she said might be true. At that moment, he wanted her anyway.

"Honey, I'll stay ashore. I want to live with you again."

"Eddie, maybe we can work it out. I don't want you to refuse sea duty. But promise me one thing."

Blackburn could scarcely believe his ears when Betty told him she didn't want him to refuse sea duty. He would have promised her anything.

"What?"

"Eddie, wherever and whenever your ship comes into port, I want to be there. Waiting for you. I want you to be off your ship and into my arms within an hour whenever you come in." She spoke these words firmly, though she had not planned them either.

He knew that Admirals' wives often waited in foreign ports for their husbands' ships and thought her request to be perfectly reasonable. What he couldn't understand was that this was all she asked for. He vowed he would keep his promise, regardless of the consequences.

"Betty, I'm still putting in for shore duty. But if you'll take me back and I'm lucky enough to be selected for command at sea, you'll always be in the same port I'm in. And I'll try to be off the ship in a half-hour."

"That's a deal," Betty said, extending her hand.

He took her hand and placed his other hand gently under her chin, drawing it up to kiss her.

Betty placed her free hand on his chest and pushed him back. A quizzical expression came over his face as she said, "You haven't asked me yet."

"Asked what?" he said.

"Asked if you could kiss me."

"May I kiss the most beautiful girl in the world?" These words worked just as they had years earlier.

Unaccustomed to their new roles, the three pilots greeted Jeff and his grandfather somewhat formally. After picking up Jeff's luggage, they caught a taxi and went directly to the ship.

Having been aboard the Kitty Hawk several times before, Jeff led his grandfather on a tour of its Flight Deck and hangar deck, with the pilots trailing along behind. They were all surprised and impressed with Jeff's knowledge of both the ship and its aircraft.

Stopping in front of an A-6, Jeff asked, "Granddad, do you know how many Chevrolet Vegas this plane can carry?"

"I'd be surprised if it could carry one, Jeff."

"Come on, Granddad, guess," insisted the boy.

"Okay, two," said his grandfather.

"Seven," Jeff proudly told his grandfather.

"You're kidding me," exclaimed the grandfather, looking to Sweetwater.

"The boy's right," said Sweetwater. "That's about the equivalent of an A-6's bomb load."

Walking over to an F-14, Jeff said, "That's what my Daddy flew." After briefly describing the plane, he asked his grandfather, "Now guess how many miles away the F-14 can shoot down another airplane."

"Well," his grandfather pondered, "how about 10 miles?"

"Guess again, Granddad."

"Fifteen?"

"An F-14 can shoot down another plane more than 200 miles away."

"How in the world can it do that, Jeff?" asked the grandfather.

"With a Phoenix."

"A what?"

"A Phoenix long-range missile," said Jeff.

The three pilots exchanged knowing glances. The grandfather looked to Sweetwater again.

"That's right, sir. For an eight-year-old, your grandson knows his planes."

"Yes, I think he does," responded the grandfather. Then he added, "Jeff, I'm real proud of you. You might make a fine pilot some day."

Taking a certain pride in Jeff's knowledge of the planes they flew, the three pilots felt proud of the boy, too.

The grandfather was invited to spend the night on the Kitty Hawk with his grandson. The pilots felt Jeff might like having his grandfather with him the first night aboard ship. The Kitty Hawk would sail at 0900 hours the following day.

After his grandfather left the ship the next morning, Jeff seemed quite at home on the Kitty Hawk. When the pilots suggested visiting a particular part of the ship, it became a game to see if Jeff could take them there unassisted. The boy and his three pilots would play this game frequently during the next four days.

Most of the first day was devoted to special orientation meetings and exhibits for the *Tigers*, as Jeff and the other guests were called. Since the three pilots were assigned to displaying their aircraft, Jeff spent most of the day with other children his age.

They joined up with Jeff at dinner. The boy also surprised them with his ravenous appetite.

After dinner, the three pilots took Jeff to the hangar deck where a special movie had been set up for the Tigers. As Sweetwater led them across the hangar deck, Jeff took the hands of Sundance and Slim. While this was natural for Jeff, it caught the two pilots by surprise. Their first instinct was to shake Jeff's hands loose. Embarrassed to be seen holding hands with a boy, they both held Jeff's hands rather limply.

Sundance thought to himself, *what is this? Is anyone*

watching us? Looking around, Sundance saw that no one seemed to be paying the least attention to the two pilots holding hands with a young boy. *So this is what it's like to be a father,* Sundance pondered. When he noticed other men holding hands with their sons, even holding them on their laps, the pilot tightened his grip on Jeff's hand.

Slim had no experience as a father either and was mildly shocked when Jeff took his hand. He too looked quickly around to see if any of his friends were watching. Then he thought, *what the hell. I'm supposed to be his father, aren't I?* Slim began feeling a certain pride at that moment—due to the affection Jeff was showing him. Slim was being treated like any of the other fathers on the hangar deck, and he too held the boy's hand more firmly.

As they seated themselves, Sweetwater noticed his running mates holding Jeff's hands. His first reaction was envy. He decided to better manuever himself in the future so he could receive similar attention.

It was a long movie. Jeff became restless within 20 minutes after it began. He got up on his knees in his chair to see better and seemed more interested in the other boys around him than the movie. Sundance resisted an impulse to tell Jeff to sit down and watch the movie.

Sweetwater, seated on the other side of Sundance from Jeff, was wrapped up in thoughts of Ginny. Never one to take "No" for an answer, he considered different alternatives to charm Ginny into his plans. *Maybe a quick trip to Acapulco will bring her around... or a weekend in San Francisco.*

Meanwhile, Jeff was showing signs of the long first day on the Kitty Hawk. Placing his hand in the crook of Slim's elbow, he rested his head on the pilot's arm. Within a minute, Jeff was fast asleep. When Slim realized what had happened, he whispered to Sweetwater, "Hey, Jeff's asleep. What should I do?"

Sweetwater leaned forward and looked at Jeff, then said, "We'd better put him to bed."

Slim adjusted Jeff's head, then picked up the sleeping boy. Holding a sleeping child in his arms was another new experience for the pilot. Slim felt as if he were participating in a religious ceremony and solemnly carried Jeff to Sweetwater's stateroom. Without a word, the other two pilots followed.

After Slim had gently laid Jeff on a bunk, he said, "Sweetwater, I'm going to stay in your stateroom tonight."

Sundance added, "Yeah, why don't I stay too?"

The plan had been for Jeff to stay with Sweetwater the first night, the second night with Sundance, the third with Slim, etc. Exactly what was in the minds of the pilots that night, even they did not know. Whether it was an instinct to protect the boy from unknown dangers, or maybe just to pay their dues to Warbucks, it really didn't matter. No force on earth could have made them stay elsewhere that night.

After the lights were turned off, the thoughts of the men drifted to the boy's father. The three pilots had not envied Warbucks when they received his lectures on the advantages of having a family. Instead they had felt sorry for Warbucks, as he declined to savor the pleasures found in each port. Now they understood better what Warbucks had been telling them.

The next morning, Jeff was up and dressed before the pilots. As he opened the door to the stateroom to peer outside, Slim awoke and said, "Wait a minute, partner. I'll go with you."

That woke the two other pilots.

As they sat rubbing their eyes, Slim asked Jeff, "Have you brushed your teeth yet?"

"Nope. I don't brush my teeth until I've eaten."

"Lesson number one. Pilots always brush their teeth when they get up. Why don't you brush your teeth now, Jeff? We may be too busy later." Slim was trying to buy time while he and the two other pilots shaved and dressed. Plus, the three pilots had a surprise for Jeff this morning, and they didn't want the task of searching for a young boy in the myriad passageways of the Kitty Hawk.

Jeff stared at Slim a moment, then said, "Okay."

By the time the boy had finished brushing his teeth, the pilots were almost dressed. After Jeff had stood by the door for a minute, Sweetwater said, "Jeff, why don't you sit down on your bunk?"

Jeff obediently walked over to his bunk and sat down, wondering why the pilots were so slow getting up.

"Jeff," Sweetwater said, "we've got a little something we want to give you." Pointing below Jeff's bunk, Sweetwater suggested, "Why don't you pull out the metal drawer there?"

The boy kneeled and pulled the drawer open. Inside was a large, flat box covered with green wrapping paper. A red ribbon was coiled on its top.

"Take it out, Jeff, and open it," said Slim.

Carefully, the boy lifted the box from the drawer and then sat back on his bunk. He thought, *not another model plane.* His father had given him model kits of Navy aircraft at each birthday and Christmas. Jeff already had models of every Navy aircraft which had seen duty during the last 20 years.

He quickly tore the wrappings from the box. Lifting its lid, he peeked inside. His face remained expressionless as he removed the lid and set it aside. Then he saw the familiar words, 'LCDR Warbucks Warrington' on the nametag of the flight jacket. The boy's eyes narrowed. His expression became serious as he reached a finger out to touch the lettering of his father's name. A quivering smile crossed his face as he lifted the jacket from the box.

Holding the jacket at arm's length, he studied its patches. There were two new ones he had not seen before, one on the back of the jacket and the other on the upper right breast. Looking at the patch on the breast, he asked, "Is this for the Mirage?"

"That's right, Jeff," said Sweetwater. "Only four flight jackets in the Pacific Fleet can wear that patch.

The patch was rectangular, with three Libyan aircraft flying into the lower lefthand corner. Flying out of the upper right-hand corner on the Libyans' Six were two F-14s—their side numbers displaying the figures 201 and 202. Coming off the rails of the F-14s were two Sidewinders. Diagonally across the center were the words, "The Gunslingers."

The other new patch was on the back of the jacket. It was circular, with a standing tiger wearing a cowboy-style gunbelt. Along the upper margin of the patch was the word, "ANY-TIME," and at the bottom of the patch were the words "KHADAFY, BABY."

Jeff slowly embraced the jacket, as a child might grasp a teddy bear. Clutching the jacket to his small chest, he lowered his head to hide the tears that began streaming down his cheeks.

Slim sat down next to Jeff and put his arm around the boy's shoulder. The man's eyes began to water, too. Slim looked up to Sweetwater and Sundance, as if asking for help. But they were no help.

Sundance and Sweetwater didn't return Slim's glance. They were staring through their own wet eyes at the boy holding his father's flight jacket.

Each pilot silently said his own goodbye to Warbucks at that moment. The boy's tears helped them to release their own. No words were spoken. Each man was so wrapped up in his own grief that he neither noticed the other pilots lose their composure nor cared to disguise his own.

Jeff finally stood up, slowly. Holding the jacket in one arm, he turned first to Slim, wrapped his arms around the pilot and gave him a hug. Slim returned the hug, throwing his brawny arms around the boy.

When Slim released Jeff, the boy saw that the man's face was covered with tears. Jeff leaned over and gently kissed Slim on the cheek, as he had seen his mother often do to console him.

Then Jeff turned to Sundance, who had sat down on a bunk. The pilot looked up, and the boy saw the man's eyes were already wet. Sundance too stretched out his arms and they embraced, tightly. As they released each other, Jeff gave him a short kiss also.

Sweetwater was still standing, leaning against a locker. When he saw the boy turn to him, he dropped to one knee to return Jeff's embrace. Of course, his face was wet, too.

After giving Sweetwater a hug and kiss, the boy stepped back and looked the pilot clearly in the eye. What Jeff said then thoroughly demolished whatever remaining composure the three pilots had. They were the magic words, "I love you."

Sweetwater forced a smile across his stricken face. He tried, but couldn't speak. He wanted to say the same words back to the boy. Instead, he enveloped Jeff again in his arms. It was hard to determine who was consoling who.

When the pilot finally released the boy, Jeff turned to the other pilots and repeated his simple, pure words, "I love you, too."

Slim coughed first, in an attempt to regain his poise, which set off a round of loud coughing by all three pilots. Slim couldn't believe the tears streaming down his face. He thought, *hey, what is this? I'm a man. I'm not supposed to cry.*

When the boy's gaze met Sundance's eyes, the pilot managed to speak. "I'm sorry, Jeff."

"For what?" asked the boy.

"For crying like this."

The boy's response was natural and quick. "That's okay. My mom said it's okay to cry sometimes."

Wiping his eyes, Sundance said what sounded foolish at the time, "Thanks."

After this experience on the second morning of the Tiger Cruise, the pilots also scrapped their plan to excuse themselves when they lost their self-control in Jeff's presence. They just told themselves, *hang in there.* And they did, with a little help from Jeff.

It was Sundance who finally broke the silence.

"We had the parachute riggers in our squadron adjust the jacket so it'd fit you better, Jeff." The boy tried it on. While it was still too large for his small frame, at least it didn't fall off his shoulders.

Jeff wore the jacket from then on. When the other sons of pilots saw Jeff wearing his father's jacket, they all insisted on similar privileges. By noon that day, every pilot's son aboard the Kitty Hawk was wearing a flight jacket.

Of course, Jeff had a special jacket, as he carefully explained to the other envious boys. The other men who had been aboard the F-14s which downed the Libyan attackers were bachelors.

That night, Jeff slept in his father's jacket.

And, just as the previous night, Slim and Sundance stayed in Sweetwater's stateroom. All three pilots lay in their bunks, trying to understand what had happened to them that day. Their grief for Warbucks still remained. They were also becoming fiercely proud of the boy whom they escorted. They didn't think, *if I had a son, I'd want him to be like Jeff.* Instead, it was, *I wish Jeff were my son.*

The third day, Sweetwater asked the two other pilots, "Hey, what happened to our plan to work in two-man teams?" Throughout the first two days and nights, the three pilots had been with Jeff continuously.

"You want a break?" asked Slim of Sweetwater.

"No. Do you?" Sweetwater asked back.

When they both looked to Sundance, he said, "I'm doing fine." So they scrapped that plan, too.

As Jeff and his pilots had breakfast in Wardroom II that morning, the Flag Aide of the Admiral handed Jeff an envelope. Jeff opened it and read its message aloud,

From: Admiral Grey
To: Jeffrey Warrington
It would be my pleasure to have your company for lunch at 1300 today. Please bring your escorts, too.

"Well, you're coming up in the world, Jeff," remarked Slim.

"What's Admiral Grey like?" asked the boy.

"Do you want to know what happened the first time Sweetwater saw the Admiral on this cruise?" asked Sundance. Of course Jeff did, and he heard the entire story of Sweetwater's special greetings to the Russian Bear, plus the subsequent collision with the Bear.

Then Sweetwater told Jeff about the time Slim and Sundance "cooked" the Russian ship. While the pilots described Admiral Grey as a stern leader, they also admitted that he had been fair.

"Jeff, don't worry about meeting the Admiral," Sundance assured the boy. "He's probably got a couple of grandsons just like you."

The pilots discreetly inquired if dress whites would be appropriate. They were, so when Jeff walked into the Admiral's stateroom, his escorts looked quite impressive.

Sweetwater said, "Sir, I would like to present Jeff Warrington."

The Admiral strode over to Jeff and extended his hand, "Thank you for coming up to have lunch with me, Jeff."

Jeff was surprised how spacious the Admiral's quarters were, compared to those of the pilots.

Jeff said what he thought, "You sure have a nice place to sleep."

"Well, Jeff. I've been riding Navy vessels for more than 30 years now. When you've been aboard ships that long, you're entitled to some comfort. And as your friends can tell you, I do a lot more than sleep here. This is an office, too."

"I want to be a carrier Admiral someday," said Jeff.

"Why do you want to be a carrier Admiral?" asked Grey.

"That's what my father said he would be someday."

At a loss for words, Admiral Grey looked down at the bold young boy. He had not intended to discuss the boy's father.

Jeff asked him, "Do you think my father would have become an Admiral?"

"I don't know why not, Jeff. Carrier Admirals are selected from the finest carrier pilots. Your father was certainly one of the finest on this ship. Or on any other carrier, in my opinion.

"Are you just saying that because my daddy died?"

Taken aback by the boy's bluntness, the Admiral straightened and looked at the three pilots behind Jeff. Then he looked back to the boy.

"No, son," he said softly, "I'm not just saying that. The three men who are escorting you on this Tiger Cruise are among the most highly-skilled pilots in the entire Navy. If there was anyone on the Kitty Hawk whom the three men standing behind you tried to imitate, it was your father."

Sweetwater thought to himself, *very good, Admiral. You pulled yourself out of that one.*

"Enough of these questions. Let's sit down and enjoy lunch," ordered the Admiral. The discussion at the dinner table followed the interests of Jeff for the most part, who did not ask additional embarrassing questions. When they had finished dessert, the Admiral asked, "Jeff, have you seen the Flag Bridge yet?"

"No, sir."

"Well, I have something up there for you. Let's go up and get it."

The Admiral wanted to give Warbucks' son a gift and coming up with an appropriate one had not been easy. He had finally asked Captain Blackburn for suggestions. The Skipper had graciously offered to part with a custom-made replica of the Kitty Hawk which he had ordered in Hong Kong early in the cruise. Blackburn made a habit of having a bronze replica made of each of the ships he commanded.

When the Admiral gave the foot-long bronze of the Kitty

Hawk to Jeff, the boy was speechless. On its flight deck were miniature F-14s, A-6s, A-7s, S-3s, a helicopter, Tilly the crane, the fire-fighting truck, and numerous other items which appeared on the Flight Deck of the real Kitty Hawk.

Marveling at this gift, Jeff asked, "Is this really mine?"

"Yes, it's yours, son," said the Admiral.

"Thank you. Thank you," was all the excited boy could say.

"I've got to get back to work now, Jeff. You can stay up on the Flag Bridge as long as you like with your friends," said Admiral Grey.

The three pilots saluted the departing Admiral. Sweetwater thought he had heard Grey's voice falter slightly as he told the boy that the scale model of the ship was 'really' his.

Another thought crossed Sweetwater's mind at this moment too. *Why haven't any of us called Jeff 'son' as the Admiral does?* Not having children of his own, Sweetwater didn't know the answer to his question.

Everywhere Jeff went that day, he carried the replica of the Kitty Hawk. And, again, he was one of the centers of attention for the other sons on the Tiger Cruise.

Approaching the coast of California on the fourth day of the Tiger Cruise, the Air Wing of the ship scheduled a special air show for the sons and other guests aboard.

Thirteen aircraft were designated to participate in the demonstration of the Kitty Hawk's capabilities. Since Lt. Hambone Tanner was unable to fly, he asked CAG if he could do the announcing. Most of the pilots flying in the air show had family aboard, which made it doubly exciting for many of the Tigers.

Sweetwater, Slim and Sundance had specifically requested permission to fly this day. Sweetwater had asked Admiral Grey if he would chaperone Jeff in their absence, to which the Admiral readily agreed. As the Admiral sat on the Flight Deck that afternoon, Jeff sat on his immediate left.

The air show began when a helicopter dropped eight smoke bombs in the water paralleling the Kitty Hawk's port side, at a distance of one-half mile out. The ship was making way at six knots.

Once the helo was clear, a diamond formation of four F-14s screamed by low on the port side. Warpaint led the diamond formation, with Sweetwater in the slot position. Turning 180 degrees, the F-14s then came by in a starboard echelon, a steplike formation in which each aircraft is progressively to the right of the leader. As they passed the ship this time, they lit afterburners five seconds apart, climbed to 10,000 feet, and formed a racetrack pattern. Then each plane made a run at the smoke, firing their 20mm cannons as they did so. After the last plane completed its run, the F-14s departed to the east.

Jeff asked the Admiral, "Where will the next planes come from?"

"Look up at 12 o'clock, Jeff. I think I can see them." From a cluster high above, an A-7 dropped into their view and released several flares to show how a target could be lit up at night. Then three A-7s came in and dropped 500 to 2,000 pound bombs on the smoke.

After this bomb run was completed, an inflight refueling of an F-14 was demonstrated. An A-6 tanker approached from the rear of the ship, and a trailing F-14 plugged in as the two aircraft came alongside at 1000 feet.

The F-14s returned to demonstrate both their low speed and high speed capabilities. After making vertical afterburner climbs, among other impressive maneuvers, the F-14s again headed to the east. Then a S-3A flew by the ship and dropped several sonar buoys—listening devices for enemy submarines.

The last demonstration was the helicopter again, which dropped men into the water, showing how downed pilots were rescued. They also dipped a sonar ball in the water, displaying how they listen for enemy submarines with the S-3As.

The Grand Finale was announced by Hambone on the 5-MC.

"This flyby is dedicated to Jeff Warrington in memory of his father. The men of the Kitty Hawk are proud that Lt. Commander Charles "Warbucks" Warrington served on our deck.

A diamond formation of four F-14s led the line of aircraft which approached the stern of the Kitty Hawk.

The Admiral then took Jeff's hand in his, stood at attention, and saluted the formation.

Every man on the Flight Deck saw the Admiral stand to salute, and followed suit. The National Anthem began playing over the 5-MC. Many of the sons on the Flight Deck followed Jeff's example, too. Jeff was saluting his father with his free hand.

As the line of aircraft passed in review, the slot man in the F-14 diamond formation peeled off. Executing the *missing man formation*, Sweetwater headed away from the rest of the flight. There wasn't a dry eye on the Flight Deck.

13

SHE WORE
A YELLOW RIBBON

For a spectacular homecoming, Captain Blackburn decided to deck the ship with yellow streamers before it rounded Point Loma. Personnel on the Kitty Hawk had been encouraged to write their families and friends in San Diego and ask that they, too, wear yellow or wave yellow banners as the ship pulled into port.

Betty Blackburn stood high above the Kitty Hawk as it passed Point Loma. From the top of the peninsula, the view of the ship was a moving experience, especially for those who had a loved one aboard. During her married years, this is where Betty had stood with their children each time his ship returned from a cruise.

She wore a short, yellow silk dress. Its flared skirt permitted the wind to ruffle its folds and reveal legs which hadn't changed significantly in 20 years. Betty stood on the same spot which she and her husband had arranged many years earlier, so he would know where to look in order to spot her with binoculars. It was a private matter between them that she always wore a dress which revealed an ample portion of her legs, even in cooler weather. And when he spotted her, he would flash a signal with a small mirror. Seeing Betty standing above, the wind blowing her skirt around her thighs, never ceased to heighten his passion to see her.

As the bow of the ship passed her position, Betty did not see the mirror flash from the Bridge of the Kitty Hawk. She thought, *that's the first time he didn't find me before the ship came even.* Then it occurred to her that he had probably forgotten their private ritual...he wasn't even looking for her. She didn't know whether the tears coming to her eyes were due to her joy that Eddie was finally returning, or because he had forgotten to look for her.

She wondered whether the decision to get together again would work. How many other things would he have forgotten which were special to her?

On the Bridge of the ship, its Skipper was concerned with the large number of small craft which flocked to both sides of the Kitty Hawk as it entered San Diego Bay. Many of them were also decked out in yellow streamers. Occasionally, an inexperienced boat owner, deciding to view the Kitty Hawk from the other side, would cross its bow at the last minute. After a successful cruise with relatively few mishaps, Blackburn was anxious to get his ship tied up without further incident.

His XO said, "I've never seen so many boats on the water to greet us. There must be over 300 out there."

"If they don't keep off our front, there may be a few under the water, too," replied Blackburn.

A runner from the Comm. Room relayed this message to the XO. "Sir, the Ship's Arrival Officer reports that more than 30,000 people are waiting at the pier."

"There's probably another 5,000 up on Point Loma," said the XO.

The Skipper walked quickly to the port side of the Bridge. Staring upwards, he wondered, *would she remember?* Taking a pair of binoculars, he searched the bluff far above. In less than a minute, he found her. He felt a warm rush through his limbs as he saw her standing tall.

"Get me a mirror," he told his orderly. "Quick!"

It was two minutes before the Marine orderly delivered a mirror to the Bridge. Blackburn held it in the sun, hoping its rays would find Betty. Looking in his binoculars again as he balanced the mirror, he saw her frantically waving, almost lifting herself off her feet.

Up above, the tears were rushing down her cheeks. She was sure they would make it—now.

Jeff stood at the top of the superstructure with his pilots. They had worn their dress whites for the occasion, and Jeff was as proud of his "fathers" as they had become of him. The men had made a pact among themselves to send a letter or gift to Jeff each month.

The most profoundly affected of the three pilots was Sweetwater. While his affection for Jeff was no more than that of the other two pilots, he had decided he wanted a son of his own. And when he thought of Ginny, he wanted a daughter, too—just to see what kind of girl Ginny would bear him.

After four days with Jeff, Slim didn't think Sweetwater was so nuts after all about wanting to get married. Slim had even told Sweetwater, "If there was some way I could have a son without having to get married, it might be a lot of fun."

Sundance had said little to his shipmates about Johnnie and Jessica. Or of the woman back in the Philippines who had captured his heart. He was anxious to reach Hudson, which he had last visited four years earlier.

As the Kitty Hawk docked and the Officer's Brow was attached, a Navy band on the pier struck up, "She Wore A Yellow Ribbon." The first man down the gangplank was its Skipper. Blackburn took six seconds to shake hands with the Mayor of San Diego and accept a plaque before turning to the woman in the yellow silk dress.

Throwing both arms around her waist, he lifted Betty off her feet. She didn't touch the ground until two minutes later.

He smothered her face with kisses. He didn't give a damn who was watching.

The first contingent of men off the ship were those who had become fathers during the cruise. Then the others streamed down the ladders, rushing into the arms of wives, families, and lovers. Words of love which were spoken were barely heard. The wild cheering of more than 30,000 people almost drowned out the Navy band.

Jeff came off the ship on the shoulders of Sundance, balanced as they came down the ladder by the other two pilots. Even though it was a warm morning, the boy wore his father's flight jacket. The pilots had gently attempted to discourage this, thinking Willie Ann might break down as they had themselves upon first seeing Jeff with the flight jacket. Jeff insisted, though. After stepping onto the pier, they made their way to the VIP area. Jeff stayed on Sundance's shoulders.

Jeff's grandparents were with his mother when she reached up to kiss her son. As Jeff transferred to the shoulders of his grandfather, the only one who was without tears was the boy. The pilots tried not to, but tears were contagious that morning. And there were special reasons within the small group that surrounded Jeff. Even Jeff's grandmother gave each of the men a warm hug and kiss. The group walked arm-in-arm to the car of the grandparents.

At the car, Jeff got down from his grandfather's shoulders and gravely shook hands with each of the pilots. The three men stood there, awkwardly, not knowing what to do or say.

Tears in her eyes, Willie Ann still smiled as she brushed the cheeks of each pilot with a kiss. Sweetwater was the last to receive her short embrace; and, just for a moment, she touched her forehead to his shoulder. Then Willie Ann stepped into the backseat of the car, her son following her. As Slim started to close the door, Jeff put his hand out and said,

"Wait a minute, Mom."

Getting back out of the car, he strode over to Sundance and reached his arms up to the pilot. Sundance bent down, heard the words "I love you" again, and received a hug from the boy. This was repeated with the other pilots. When Jeff got back in the car, the three men silently watched it pull away.

Members of the crowd who noticed the three pilots with reddened eyes, wiping their tears away as they marched side-by-side, must have thought it a strange sight indeed. It was no stranger than the thoughts running through the anguished minds of Sundance, Slim and Sweetwater. One of the most bitter-sweet experiences of their lives was ending.

Twenty minutes later, they were seated at the bar of The Bail-Out Tavern, a noisy gathering spot just outside the Naval Base on Coronado Island. Even though it was still morning, the place was packed, mostly with men from the Kitty Hawk and their friends. The three pilots each ordered two beers. When they arrived, the first beers lasted less than five seconds. The second beers received more attention.

"I've got to make a phone call," said Sweetwater.

This time Ginny was home.

"Ginny, this is Sweetwater!"

"*Who* is this?"

Realizing there was too much background noise in the bar, he shouted, "It's me, Sweetwater."

"Oh. Hi, Matt," she said without emotion.

"Is that all?" he asked.

There was no answer.

"I want to see you," he said. "This time I'll do a better job of proposing."

"I don't think that's a good idea."

"Okay, how 'bout if I just come up? Can you pick me up at LAX?"

"That's not a good idea either."

Damn, Sweetwater thought, *she's playing hard to get again!* He asked, "Would it be a good idea for you to come down to San Diego?"

"No."

"Would you prefer to fly directly to Acapulco, and meet me there? I've got three weeks leave." When there was no response to this proposal either, he told her, "I've changed, Ginny."

"It sounds like you're right at home, in one of your usual haunts."

"I'm a new man," said Sweetwater.

"Then why are you calling me from a noisy bar?"

"It's a long story," he answered. Ginny didn't know that Warbucks had been lost at sea. There had been no time to write and tell her that he and his running mates were "fathers" to Jeff on the Tiger Cruise. It seemed too complicated to explain to her now.

"I love you, Ginny," he finally said, dejectedly. "Don't you care at all for me?"

"Yes, I did begin to care for you, Matt. But you're still a child. You want to play with women, not love them. You're not ready to marry me, or any other woman."

Getting nowhere, he decided to change the subject. "I tried to call you from Hawaii. Where were you?"

"On my honeymoon."

"What'd you say?"

"My honeymoon."

"How can you go on a honeymoon? We're not married yet."

"I am."

It began to sink in. He took a deep breath. *Sonofabitch, I can't believe this.* He asked, "You're not joking, are you?"

"No."

"Well, how..." He wasn't sure what to say.

"Matt, we had a lot of fun. Someday you may make a great husband for someone. But I don't want to gamble."

"Who's the lucky guy?"

"I've known him for three years. He's a pilot, too. We share many interests." She didn't want to elaborate any more.

Still not ready to give up, Sweetwater said, "Ginny, I don't care how great this guy is. I'd make you a better husband."

"Matt, he's never called me from a bar."

Sweetwater was stumped for a response.

"Good luck, Sweetwater. You're one helluva guy."

"Yeah, sure. You've got..." He heard the dial tone on the phone.

"Wait...Ginny. I want..." Holding the receiver, he stood there, looking vacantly around. After a minute, he slowly set the receiver on its hook and walked out of the bar. He didn't hear Sundance and Slim calling out to him.

Several hours later, he sat up in the bunk of his stateroom on the Kitty Hawk. The ship was quiet as a morgue. He said to himself, "I'm one helluva turkey."

NAVY JARGON

AILERONS—movable flaps attached to trailing edge of wing.

AIR BOSS—nickname for Air Department Officer on carrier.

AIR FOIL—surface of wing, aileron, rudder, or propeller blade designed to obtain reaction against the air through which it moves.

ALPHA STRIKE—a certain number of aircraft required to carry out a raid on a target.

ANGELS—altitude expressed in thousands of feet.

ANGLE OF ATTACK—the acute angle between the direction of a relative wind and the chord of an air foil.

AOC—aviation officer candidate.

ASAP—as soon as possible.

ATTITUDE—term used by Landing Signal Officer during landing of aircraft, to change the nose position of the aircraft relative to the Flight Deck.

AUTO-DOG—soft ice-cream which comes out of machines.

BAT PHONE—direct line to all critical personnel on carrier.

BATTLE GROUP—carrier with 5 to 7 escort ships.

BDS—battle dressing station, a small operating room on the Flight Deck near Flight Deck Control.

BIRD FARM—nickname for carrier.

BLUE SHIRT—person who chocks and chains aircraft on Flight Deck.

BOGEY—enemy aircraft.

BROWN SHIRTS—plane captains.

CAG—Carrier Air Group, also nickname for commander of CAG.

CAP—combat air patrol.

CAMEL STATION—name given to area where U.S. battle group sails in the Arabian Sea.

CHARLIE—message from Air Boss clearing an aircraft to commence his approach.

CINCPAC—Commander-in-Chief, U.S. Pacific Fleet.

CRUISEBOOK—photo "yearbook" of a carrier cruise.

DIEGO GARCIA—small island owned by the British in the southern Indian Ocean.

DITCH—nickname for Suez Canal.

DOWN CHIT—temporary grounding for medical reasons.

5-MC—Flight Deck loudspeaker.

FO'C'SLE—bow of ship where anchors are kept on 02 level; also used for large meetings, weddings, etc.

FRESNEL LENS—optical landing system on port side of Flight Deck which indicates aircraft's relative position to the Flight Deck.

GREEN SHIRTS—catapult and arresting gear crew.

HELO—helicopter.

HOMEPLATE—nickname for carrier.

KIMSCHE—a Korean delicacy which smells like rotten cabbage.

KNOTS—measurement of speed, slightly faster than miles per hour.

LOOSE DEUCE—two aircraft flying in a formation which provides each other support.

LSO—landing signal officer.

MILITARY—maximum power, but without afterburner.

99 AIRCRAFT—message to all airborne aircraft.

1-MC—ship's loudspeaker.

PLANE CAPTAINS—men responsible for care and maintenance of aircraft.

PLANE GUARD SHIP—escort ship which trails carrier a quarter to half a mile during night recoveries.

PLAT CHANNEL—pilot landing aid television camera, located on surface of Flight Deck, to aid in critiquing pilot landings.

POCKET ROCKET—condensed book for emergency procedures.

POGEY BAIT—candy, gum, etc.

PRIMARY FLIGHT CONTROL—where Air Boss controls aircraft within a 5-mile radius of the carrier and up to 3,000 feet during day visual flight rules.

QUARTER-DECK—officer's brow on carrier.

R&R—rest and recovery leave.

READY ROOM—briefing room for squadron pilots, also gathering spot during off-duty hours.

RED SHIRTS—fire fighters.

RIO—radar intercept officer.

ROLLER—hot dog.

SEA CABIN—skipper's quarters at sea, just off the Bridge.

SDO—squadron duty officer.

SIGNAL DELTA—message to all aircraft to hold at a certain altitude.

SLIDER—hamburger.

SPASIBO—'thank you' in Russian.

TAC CAP—tactical air cover for attacking aircraft.

TALLY HO—message meaning the object or aircraft has been spotted.

TILLY—large Flight Deck crane for lifting damaged or overturned aircraft.

TOPPING OFF—refueling.

TRANSVERSE G'S—gravitational forces applied to the front of body.

TRAP—an arrested landing.

WARDROOM—officer eating area.

YELLOW SHEET—Naval aircraft flight record.

YELLOW SHIRT—person who directs aircraft on Flight Deck.

ZONE-5—maximum power with afterburner.